THE ICE BARN

The Ice Barn

Ian Pateman

Anywhere Books

To the memory of my father, who I also should
have loved better

For Avril, for listening and offering
encouragement every time I despaired

The Ice Barn

Ian Pateman

Anywhere Books

To the memory of my father, who I also should
have loved better

For Avril, for listening and offering
encouragement every time I despaired

This book is published by
Anywhere Books, Bath UK

Paperback Edition ISBN 978-1-7391121-0-3
eBook Edition ISBN 978-1-7391121-1-0

First Printing, 2022

1

A Kobold, Summer 1899

Ahead, he could see the mouth of the mine, a dark and forbidding void incised into a moon-whitened wall of rock. Now that he was here, he found he was afraid to enter into its daunting maw, though not from concern for what creatures - fox, wolf, bear, or mountain lion - might be lurking inside. As he had climbed the narrow path from the town below he had persuaded himself that the smell of the men who had been working there that day would keep such predatory animals away. Nor was it a childish dread of the dark that halted him momentarily; of the unnameable demons darkness could conceal. During his climb, with the accompanying echo of every step, the possibility of being followed each of those echoes had contained, he had gradually come to lose the certainty of his enterprise. He still did not know if it was a good thing or bad, where it might lead.

He felt pride, certainly, that in some small way he was making a contribution, helping his family survive, and that in doing so would be taking another step along the path from dependent childhood to being a man. Alongside such pride however, he felt shame at the way this contribution, this personal transition - if that was what it was - had been attained, the covert way it had been made. That he could not proclaim it, announce to all this proof of his approaching manhood, seemed to rob the gesture of any transformative power it might otherwise have contained.

Pushing away his uncertainty he entered the mouth of the mine.

Passing from the moonlit world into darkness, he felt like a *kobold,* the secretive beings his maternal grandfather had told him about in so many night-time stories back in Germany when he was a child. Kobolds dwelled deep in the mines, the old man had told him, and were of two contrary natures. Some helped the miners in their labours, protected them from dangers, and led them to whatever they sought. Others were disruptive, malevolent. They concealed the gold, or silver or tin that was being dug for, or made tools break, caused timbers to shear, roofs to fall, poisonous gas and flooding waters to leak, or they led the miners off into dark, meandering passageways from which they would never return.

He took a match from his pocket and struck it on the rock and lit the waxed taper he had been carrying. The world span and fluttered briefly as the broken shadows of the hewn rock faces danced into life around him. As it flared, its soft roar echoing from the surrounding walls, the sound of the burning taper momentarily drowned out the other, subterranean sounds - the scurry of small creatures, the drip and sputter of falling water, the ticking of the rock, settling and breaking; of small stones, freed from their million-year-old resting places, tumbling to the ground.

Once the flame had settled and he had re-orientated himself he could make out the worked rock-face a few paces ahead. There were tools there - picks and shovels, a crowbar, oil-lamps, shoring timbers, ropes, and two pairs of yoked wooden buckets - each throwing their own fluid shadow onto the stone where the men had last worked.

At the work-face he pushed the end of the taper into a fissure in the rock, then reached into his pocket again and took out a small leather pouch tied at the neck with a leather cord. He loosened the cord and poured its contents into his opened palm. The pool of golden grains flowed gently across his skin in response to the trembling of his hand, glimmering dully in the dancing light.

Was this really what the men here had travelled so many thousands of miles to discover? Did they really believe this could be the source of their happiness - not love, not health, or honour or friendship: that this was the ultimate goal of their lives?

The grains felt heavy in his hand, though they looked so insubstantial. The first time he had held it, he had been surprised how heavy it was, this thing that men sacrificed their lives, the lives of their loved ones to attain; how its weight belied its grainy, dust-like nature. Was that its attraction: the impression of substance beyond its slight nature? Or was its value to be found only in the fact it was so scarce - like love, like happiness; that it was so hard to find?

He shook his head, his juvenile mind not yet able to grasp such adult motivations, and turned his hand slowly over. The fine grains fell from his palm, catching the inconstant light, the cascading warmth of their reflected glow lightening his thoughts as they fell. He paused to consider what he had done, the price he had paid, the probable consequences, then began to scuff around in the ground with the side of his boot until the gold was lost in the heap of loosened soil and stones - the last gleanings from the rock work-face - amongst the discarded tools on the cavern floor.

The deed was done. Whether for good or bad, or of no consequence, it was irretrievable now. A fact, not a myth or an old man's distracting fairy tale.

He hoped the traces would soon be found.

Part 1

Black Lady Blind

2

The Turn of a Card

Jack Bunney's skin was slick with sweat. The night was hot and humid, stoked by an unseasonable wind blowing in from the south, and the air in the saloon was still and heavy with smoke. The staccato waves of laughter and conversation, the dull tread of boots on the saw-dusted wooden floor, seemed to make the air in the room vibrate, its thrum punctuated by the more regular rhythms of the piano. They had been playing now for more than three hours. Bunney's eyes were sore from the smoke and alcohol, his mind dulled from concentrating on the diamond-backed rectangles being dealt out on the baize.

He could feel the stares and glances of the others in the saloon directed towards them; sensed a quietening of the general hubbub in the room. The stakes had suddenly been raised; the pot on this hand stood now at six hundred dollars. Even Brogan Sullivan's ladies had come over to watch the game, seeing in it the possibility of some percentage for themselves. One of them - Belinda was her name - was standing behind him. She was a handsome girl; he liked her. He had been with her a couple of times, when he had won and had felt the need to pay back whatever luck she might have brought him - a gambler's tentative nod in the direction of Fortune.

Tonight, though was different; he no longer had need of any such mascot, would never need such things again, neither for luck, nor for that other thing, which he had more or less learned to do without anyway. The drink, he had found, tended to keep other hungers at bay. His luck was turning though, and now he had his own lady of good fortune coming to stand permanently at his side. Her name was Rosalind. She was going to be his wife.

On the table in front of him, his cards showed two Jacks, Hearts and Diamonds - love and money Sullivan's girls called them - and a pair of fives. Sullivan, sitting opposite, was dealing. He straightened the edge of the deck on the table-top and dealt out a final blind card to each hand.

Bunney's fifth card slid across the table towards him. He left it lying where it landed, lodged against the Jacks and Fives.

The player sitting to his right - a thin, nervous prospector with a bushy red moustache and a dark carbuncle on his nose - snatched up his new card and held it cupped close to his chin. Bunney wondered what the man was doing sitting in this game. The cards he was dealt were almost mirrored in his face. The only good hand he had held they had all folded; his three Kings had won him just forty dollars. The man sighed deeply, and folded on the ace-high and nothing he had showing.

"Try dealin' me some kinda hand next time, could ya?" he grumbled as he put down the cards.

"They come as they come," Sullivan said quietly, almost as though talking to himself.

"Yeah, so it seems," the man said in a petulant tone.

"You have a problem?" Sullivan asked, his eyes lifting unhurriedly to look squarely at the man. His face was devoid of expression, but the stare showed clearly what he was thinking. The man held his gaze for barely a second, then shook his head and looked away.

Ignoring the distraction, Bunney brought his right hand slowly up from his lap to the edge of the table and took a studied sip from his whiskey, then returned the glass to the shallow brass dish set into the table by his place. A bottle, half empty, stood next to it. Opposite, Sullivan's brandy glass stood on a small silver tray, a folded, monogrammed cotton napkin beside it. Brogan Sullivan owned the saloon, and could afford such indulgences, though Bunney knew that while playing he rarely took a drink. Bunney peeled up the corner of the blind card with his thumb. The Jack of Clubs.

He took another careful drink and set the glass back in its dish. He did this with every hand, to disguise any emotions he might otherwise show, informing the other players whether his hand was bad or good. Always at the same speed, unhurried, unconcerned, whatever the hand or card, however large or small the pot. He was a good player, but lately his luck had been bad. Tonight though he had a feeling things were about to turn.

"Well?" Sullivan enquired lazily. "What's your bet?"

Brogan Sullivan was a good player too. Jack Bunney had lost a sizeable amount of money to him over the past few months, probably the best part of a thousand dollars. Sullivan still held his markers, but he was a fair-minded and patient man, at least when it came to gambling. The two pairs Sullivan had showing peeked out on either side of his blind card, threatening to surpass Bunney's own full house. Bunney separated half of his chips and threw them onto the pile in the middle of the table.

"Two hundred," he said, and took another studied drink from his glass.

The player seated to his left flipped over the cards he had already been dealt - a pair of sevens and the ten and Queen of Clubs - and shuffled them into a tidy block, face-down, on top of his blind card. Bunney liked the way the man had been playing. He was a quiet, steady player. He had won a couple of good hands early in the game, but then the cards had turned against him.

"Way too rich for me," the man said, and leaned back in his chair to watch how the game would play out.

Sullivan had both red Queens showing - also love and money - and a pair of eights. He reached out and casually turned up the edge of his blind card. There was no reaction in his face, in his hands or body as he counted out four fifty-dollar chips from his stake pile and pushed them into the pot.

"See your two," he said, then separated and pushed forward another three piles of chips. "And raise you fifteen." There were several exclamations from among the watchers, and a heightened murmur of interest added to the overall commotion in the saloon.

"Let's find out what you've got there, Jack," he said. "Let's see if you really are a gambler."

Bunney looked down at his chips. He had only two hundred and twenty dollars on the table and maybe another twenty dollars in change in his pockets. He did not want to have to fold on such a hand. With two pairs showing, he knew Sullivan might also be holding a full house, but one of the Queens he would need had already gone, and if his blind card was an eight, making the house the other way, Bunney's Jacks and fives would win.

"It's your bet," Sullivan reminded him, his cigar jammed into the corner of his mouth, its stub clamped between his teeth. Bunney pushed his remaining chips forward and immediately Sullivan's eyebrows rose and his hands flipped open, framing an unspoken question.

"How much for the store and a half-dozen claims?" Bunney asked. He owned the town's grocery store, won in a game of poker, as had been the claims. He had kept the store, though he was never a storekeeper, and had hired a clerkish Austrian named Boehme to run it. The store provided his food, and lodgings, in the lumber-room above the store, and the income it brought in added to his stakes.

"What would I want with your claims?" Sullivan said. "We both know there's no real gold here anymore."

"I don't think you'd want too many of your customers believing that," Bunney replied. Sullivan shrugged his shoulders.

"There're other towns," he said. "Other games."

"Is anyone else interested?" Bunney half turned and shouted over his shoulder.

"I'll give ya five dollars each for 'em," someone shouted close by. Bunney threw back an obscenity and turned back to Sullivan.

"And the store?"

"Including stock?" Bunney nodded slowly. Sullivan thought for a while then said, "Five hundred." Bunney laughed out loud. "*With* the stock, I said. That alone's worth two thousand! More if winter comes early. A thousand."

"Eight."

Bunney paused to consider, looked quickly across at Sullivan sitting implacably in his chair, then nodded again and called for a pen and paper. As he wrote out the note for the store, he thought about including the man Boehme as part of the inventory, but did not know whether such a thing was possible - to sign over the rights to another man without their permission. Sullivan would probably keep him on anyway, make him manager, unless there was someone else he owed a favour to. He made out the note for the store and its contents, added the agreed sum, and signed it.

"You're still four hundred and eighty dollars short," Sullivan said, his eyes fixed steadily on Bunney's, a sly smile flickering across his lips.

Silence fell in the room. Even the piano player had stopped playing and had come over to watch the outcome of the game. Nervous coughs and grunts, the scuffing of booted feet on floor-boards punctuated the stillness; the laughter of two oblivious drunks sitting at a table in a far corner. Bunney looked around slowly. In the mirrored wall behind the bar, he saw the room reflected, the eager faces of the watching crowd, the composed figure of Sullivan, his red and gold brocaded waistcoat, the black velvet lapels of his jacket presenting an image of a man fully in control of himself, his destiny; and then his own, less clear-cut and assured image opposite, looking pallid and drawn, his clothes creased and soiled; between them, the sharp green circle of table, the chips and credit note piled upon it.

He suddenly felt distanced from the whole proceedings, as though he were in that other world behind the glass of the mirror, as though his image was the real person, looking out at a reflection of himself, watching Sullivan casually straighten his cuffs, then place his cigar carefully against his glass on the edge of the silver tray. In the reflection, the gold signet ring on Sullivan's little finger flashed dully in the lamplight.

In a mirror world, that was where Bunney felt himself to be whenever he was drinking. In there, things seemed more certain, more predictable. In that stilled world where no one spoke, where people went about their business silently, never demanding anything of you, he always felt safe; much safer than he ever did out here.

"Come on now, Jack," Bunney heard the man in front of him say, the real man playing cards with him in the real world, demanding his attention. There was an arch tone to Sullivan's voice.

"There must be something else you have. Something a bit more... substantial." As he spoke, he made a sinuous movement with his hands, tracing an outline that everyone watching understood. Knowing laughter rippled around the table. Bunney had made no secret of his anticipated arrival.

"You must have something else valuable to offer."

The day she arrived, it seemed as though the whole town was out waiting. Some of the men had given up half a day's prospecting just to see her, and even their women had sacrificed time from their gossiping, though Bunney knew they would have more than enough to tattle and whisper about before the day was through. Everyone was excited; everyone wanted to see the bride who had been made a whore by the turn of a card.

Everyone except Jack Bunney. All he wanted was to see his bride-to-be, even though he knew that such a creature no longer existed. She had vanished even more quickly than she had come into being. Something less precious, less certain, had been created in her place, a product of Jack Bunney's own black conjuring. And now he was afraid of his creation, of what it would do to him in return. He was surprised too that Sullivan, for all the man's improbity, had chosen to see the process they had together set in motion through to its illogical end.

The stagecoach appeared, coming along the broken road at the upper end of the town, trailing a broiling screen of dust. Some of the men waiting on the veranda outside the saloon began to whistle and cheer. Bunney saw Sullivan signal for them to be quiet, and one by one they all ceased until, as the coach slewed to a halt in front of them, the gathered crowd had fallen silent. The driver jumped down and opened the door, and what looked to Bunney little more than a young girl stepped down.

Bunney groaned. She looked so pretty, even from up here, through the dusty window of the lumber-room. She was dressed all in black, apart from a thin slash of crimson lace trim at her throat. As though she was dressed in mourning. A black straw hat with a bowed silk ribbon sat upon her head, tied under her chin with another black ribbon, the upper part of her face partially hidden beneath the shadow of its brim. Still, she looked so pretty, so innocent. Prettier than a man like him could ever have deserved.

Her black boots and the hems of her dress were covered in dust, and in her left hand she carried a black parasol and a small black bag. My sweet Black Lady, Bunney thought, and the memory came back to him - of the Queen of Spades, Sullivan's blind card, nonchalantly flipped over and lying face-up on the baize; the four hundred and eighty dollars she had been worth to him, until he had lost her, everything she might have been.

He cupped his head in his hands, to contain his regret, his sorrow, while continuing to watch what was happening below. In her free hand she held his photograph - he recognised the silver-gilt frame he had sent the picture in, to impress her - as she searched among the faces milling round her, trying to find his one, singular countenance among them. She looked confused, and much younger than he had expected. Sullivan, standing only a few feet in front of her, coughed into his hand, to draw her attention. When she glanced towards him he bowed to her and held out his hand.

"I'm looking for a Mr Samuel Bunney," he heard her say uncertainly, as she continued looking around, ignoring Sullivan's proffered hand. Bunney flinched at the sound of his name. It sounded so unfamiliar, an echo from a discarded past. No one had called him Samuel since his mother had died. The name Jack had come later, a more acceptable abbreviation of his middle name, Jackson, and mainly of his own choosing, being preferable to the Rabbit and Jackrabbit his family name conjured up more readily in other people's mouths. The young woman's voice was soft and thin, exactly like his mother's had been, and out here in the wilderness, in this hard-hearted town, amidst its trouble-hardened people, her Boston accent sounded too refined.

He was glad to see she had spirit, though. He needed her to be strong. To survive what was about to happen. It would be his only redemption, such as it was.

"He was to meet me. I'm to be his bride," he heard the young woman say, more proudly now, directing her statements to everyone in the crowd.

"We know who you are, Miss Pearce," Sullivan said, bowing again. "My name is Brogan Sullivan. Welcome to the town of Hope."

Bunney cursed, and kicked at the wall in frustration. He knew he should be down there confronting Sullivan, claiming what had once been his. But he was afraid - of her, afraid to own up to what he had done. He had no fear of Sullivan, but had no idea where he would find the courage to face her, to offer an apology, let alone an explanation.

"I'm sorry, but Jack... Mr Bunney, is indisposed," Sullivan continued.

A faint murmur of laughter rose from the crowd, and a voice shouted "When ain't he?" provoking further laughter. As Bunney watched, he saw the German boy move out of the crowd to stand close behind Sullivan, his head cocked to one side in the odd way he had of seeming to be curious about everything. It was always easy to recognise the boy, with his thick mane of golden hair - the town's lucky mascot, some claimed. He was always hanging around Sullivan, not that Sullivan seemed to mind. He used the boy to run errands, and they were always laughing together, as though sharing some secret joke.

"Where is Mr Bunney? I really need to..." Bunney heard Rosalind start to say, as she turned to face Sullivan, then she fell in a dead faint to the ground.

3

Hope

When she had arrived, it had been the middle of summer. Hope, the place was called, though it had seemed to her a desolate place, despite the better expectations she had had of it and had tried to keep in some proportion on her long journey here from Boston. Early June, and already the streets of the town had been continually shifting fields of dust, and the bed of the river that skirted its edge but a deserted, impassable stretch of cracked boulders and stones, a damp, dark ditch crawling down its middle. What the people here called the lagoon, below the body of the town, was just a shallow, reed-filled marsh, no more than a breeding ground for frogs and flies and mosquitoes.

During the brief summer months, after the thaw of spring, the river was dammed off up-stream and the water from the mountains diverted to the mines for the prospecting. In the fall, when the rains began again, the dams would be cracked open to keep the lower workings from getting washed away. Then the river would flow around the town again, and the lagoon would be a place where kids could swim and play. That was, until it froze over again for the winter. She had heard there were even people who camped out on it; the ice was that thick and strong. She had not been looking forward to the winter. She had been warned it would be hard.

Summer was bad enough. It was hot here, hotter than she would ever have expected so far north. Then there was the endless dust to contend with, and the flies and mosquitoes; the lizards that sat and watched you, cold-eyed and motionless, from the shaded angles between the ceiling and walls. Someone ought to take a gun too, she thought, and shoot the dogs that roamed the streets and alleyways, that shat and pissed any damn place they wanted, even on the boardwalks where people were supposed to walk. She had lost count of the times she had come in trailing the stink of the stuff, the hems of her petticoats messed and browned. No matter how hard she tried, how high she stepped or lifted her skirts, she always seemed to manage to drag it in with her. Without the dogs, without their shit all over the place, the flies wouldn't be half as bad.

She had never been able to understand why these people had dogs with them here in the first place. Most of them had barely enough to keep themselves and their families alive, let alone feed some sad, mangy old mongrel that for everyone's sake would be better off dead. It seemed to her anyway that most of the dogs were left to fend for themselves; they roamed the streets in packs, their yelping and baying kept folks awake throughout the night. She supposed though that they kept down the rats and coons and other vermin you could see all the time scavenging around in the yard beneath her window. Which was worse, the dogs or the rats or the flies she could never decide.

Her room was on the top floor, in the eaves, at the back of the saloon. The single, small window looked out to one side along a bare face of rock. At the top of the rock two pine trees were growing, no more than shrubs really; their roots stuck out and hung down like a thick fringe of hair on some craggy, weather-beaten forehead. She hoped that the trees, and the rocks were staying where they were until after her time here was done.

She had been lucky with this room, luckier than some of the others, like Belinda and Lucy. Their rooms were larger, but they were in the eaves facing onto the street on the other side of the building. Their rooms were always like furnaces. At the front, where they were, the sun beat down all day on the shingles, and the dust from the street blew in through the window if it was open. Then there was the noise of the traffic, and the animals, the constant brawling and arguing, the tired rattle of the old men jawing and hawking and spitting all day and night in their rocking chairs on the veranda below. She did not know how Lucy or Belinda could stand it, though she imagined all the rooms would be equally cold in winter.

"A clear conscience and I sleep like a log. It's no worse than the other things we have to put up with," Belinda said, or some other declaration of what sounded almost like acceptance, whenever the subject came up.

"Our punishment for being born pretty and not tough

enough to do the real work of the world. Men's work, I believe they call it." She had laughed bitterly then at her own joke. "One day we'll get our turn, wait and see." Lucy had just shrugged her shoulders when they had both looked at her.

The dense, spread branches of the pine trees and the wall of rock shaded her room through the worst of the heat of the day. But still, sometimes, the heat in there too could be almost unbearable. In the small hours of the night, when they were done with working, when it was cooler, she would stand naked at the window, bathing her skin with a dampened cloth, savouring the cool breeze that slid down the rock-face and crept in through the window, winding its invisible way around her body. Only then did she feel safe, that no one, other than the gentle wind could touch her, that no one could see her.

Invisible, like the breeze, that was what she wanted to be. Not to be seen. Here, she felt like a pinned butterfly, on permanent display. The men and the women here, they all knew what she was; they knew her story, had rehearsed its telling behind her back often enough. They watched her, the men; they wanted her, their lust hanging from their tongues like spit. Sometimes, she saw their hands move furtively in their pockets - searching for the necessary, elusive dollar, the last speck of gold dust they might have missed? Or engaged in some more impoverished exchange with themselves?

They couldn't afford her, but that didn't stop the need in them, the wanting. And then there were the taut, straight-haired, iron-hard women they were married to, those cold-faced bitches who looked away from her disdainfully whenever she passed, who hated her for her softness, the possibility of desire she encompassed; her as yet unblemished youth. That, she knew, was the only reason they hated her. She reminded them too painfully of what they had lost, or had squandered, all they had sacrificed to the tarnished dreams of these sorry sons-of-bitches they had found themselves irredeemably tethered to in this living Hell on Earth.

She almost felt sorry for them - the men, not the women. She could understand the men; their dreams, and their lust. Their lust was simple, honest; it gave nothing and asked for nothing in return. Just like her own - a moment of sympathy, of counterfeit affection; the temporary gratification of an unknowable, fleeting hunger; a doubly begrudged dollar thrown onto the unmade bed.

"That's the thing gets me, the way they resent you as soon as they're done. Like you're no longer good for anything else." Belinda had said on another occasion, declaiming against an unjust world that defined her adversely whichever way it chose, and which she was powerless to change. As she spoke she had pictured her words in the air with emphatic motions that had seemed incongruous with her tiny hands.

"Some of them are okay. Some try to be nice," Lucy had added, for once joining in the debate, yet still revealing how misplaced she was here, in this town, in this occupation.

"Yeah! Like they do it to us for a favour."

"They're just lonely. They're people too, just like you and me."

"Don't you dare ever say that! They are not like me," Belinda had stated, glaring at Lucy, then she had added, "What do you think, Rosie? Are they just like you too?"

She had said nothing, though she agreed with Belinda.

She didn't like it that they all called her Rosie, not her given name, Rosalind, but it went with her situation - another reduction to something less than she was. Rosalind Pearce - that was her name; the person she knew and understood herself to be.

What she had never been able to understand though was the proud stupidity of the others, the married women - their bovine blindness to the sorry state of their existence. The giving over of themselves to the weakness, the equally blind stupidity of another. True, she was herself given, exchanged - a semi-precious object to be gambled on. To be lost or won. Her life here, like theirs, was an endless, one-sided transaction, but at least it was not a life she had determined for herself. Whatever else the sad bitches might say of her, *her* failings had not been of her own choosing.

It was not meant to be like this. She had made her way, alone, across those thousands of miles of wilderness that lay between here and Boston, in the expectation of being made respectable; to become one of those married women. Mrs Samuel Jackson Bunney, an esteemed resident of the township of Hope. When she arrived, however, it was to discover she had already been given away to somebody else in a much less holy exchange of vows.

Her body, her soul, her possessions, even the clothes she wore, belonged to another. To a man she could not even claim as husband. The life she had hoped for, the one she had been offered, she had soon enough discovered had hardly been worth losing, and as far as respectability went, that had never been at stake. A respectable man was a thing her prospective husband had never been; such creatures, she had soon come to understand, did not come often to a place like Hope.

Her heart had not been broken by this betrayal, only her pride, and with it her dreams of a respectable life. She and her intended husband had never met; she had never had the chance to love him. He had placed an advert, coldly stating the fact of his looking for a wife - a woman, young, preferably not unattractive, with a strong back and heart, and a willingness to work, the advert had asked for - in the papers back in Boston. She had written him a long, thoughtfully composed letter, and he had written back a few cramped lines itemising the briefest details of his life and supposed habits. With the note he had enclosed a photograph. In it he had looked like a bandit. He had said he was a grocer, the owner of a grocery store. His eyes had looked dark and unfocused, as though he had not been able to hold them still for even the few seconds the picture had taken to make. His hair had been dark too, and long, parted in a straight bright line down the middle of his scalp. It had looked greasy, unkempt, once it escaped the confines of the parting, and had hung in tight curls around his face, spilling down onto his shoulders. His cheekbones had been high and sharp, his face long and gaunt, and his thin lips, like the eyes, had carried no expression. A thick black moustache had split his face in two, folding in waxy fingers around the sides of his mouth.

The more she had looked at the photograph the more certain she had become that she could live with this man, even come to love him, bear his children. His apparent reluctance with words had not concerned her. He did not have to talk too much, and there had been something about the vagueness of those eyes that had drawn her. He had not looked anything like how she had expected a grocer to be. Instead, there had been an air of bravado, almost of danger about him. While she had wanted to be respectable, she had also wanted some excitement from time to time.

She saw him sometimes now, Mr Samuel Bunney, no longer a grocer, just the loser and gambler he had always been. Most times she saw him he was staggering along the street, drunk and mumbling to himself, incoherent, or sprawled asleep in some muddy alleyway with the street-dogs licking at his face, lapping up his vomit. The times she saw him like that, she still thought he looked like a bandit.

She had tried to resist the fate imposed upon her, had refused at first to accept the role assigned to her. But Sullivan, her acquired master, had offered her a choice: agree to work off the debt owed by her fiancée - as he called Bunney, blithely making his debt her responsibility - and he would ensure the men he sent to her were of the better kind; men who would treat her gently and with respect. Otherwise, he said, he could not offer her any such assurance. He gave her a week to think over her situation and offered her a room and keep on credit while she considered. She had no money, beyond a few dollars, no other means of paying for passage back to Boston. Menial work, if she were able to find any in this rapidly dying town, would pay for no more than her keep, and she would remain in thrall to Sullivan for a lifetime. No-one here would help her, that much she had quickly grasped; everyone knew what had happened, but none had challenged the claim Sullivan made on her. At the end of the week, raging against the injustice of it, but fearful for her survival if she tried to leave, and seeing no alternative if she remained, she had agreed.

Sullivan promised her she could leave, as soon as the thousand-odd dollars still owed him had been repaid. It did not seem likely that the man who had rolled up the debt would make a contribution. On her own, if she did what she was told, she calculated it would take her three years to pay off that sum. She managed to put a little something aside for herself whenever she could, if the man she had been with had liked her, had given her an extra half-dollar. If she ever did get to leave she did not want to be forced into selling herself in the next town she came to just to keep herself alive.

She had learned quickly what she had to do to make the men like her. Belinda was a good teacher. She knew the things men liked to have done to them, the things they liked to do. Lucy seemed reluctant to learn such things, or even talk about them. Sometimes, when some man less awful than the others had been especially nice to her, the buoyant child inside Lucy would rise to the surface, shaping her gestures, her spirit, enlivening them, but otherwise she was too sweet to be a whore. She did what she had to do, nothing more. She accepted docilely rather than performed; the likelihood was that she would be stuck here forever. Belinda, on the other hand, echoing her own decision, said that her reason for staying was because all other options open to her seemed far worse.

"What, I'd be better off making beds, dusting and ironing, slopping out bed-pans? Working a hundred hours a week in a factory, poisoned to death before I made thirty, for a fraction of what I make doing this? Or breaking my back trying to coax out enough just to keep alive from some man's precious, parched piece of ground, getting humped and impregnated once a year to show his gratitude?" She had nodded as Belinda spoke; recognising the options that had shaped her own reluctant acceptance of her present situation.

"Anyway, there's nothing much else I can do, leastways not better," Belinda added, brightening. "And I like men, the way they can be when they want you, and so far, most have been good to me. Not too many scars showing for a dozen years of this, inside or out. As for Brogan, he's not so bad, as whore-masters go."

"He's still not a husband. I didn't ask for this," she had countered to Belinda's apparent defence of the man who claimed ownership of her but did not dare do so in the face of God.

"He's a saint compared to some I've known," Belinda replied, and she believed her, having seen the memory of it rising like shadows in her eyes.

She knew Brogan was a reasonable man, as men in his position went, despite what he had done to her. He knew they kept back some of the money from the men, on top of the cut he allowed them, and yet he said or did nothing about it. And at least he didn't beat them, or want them all the time for himself. In fact, she had noticed he didn't seem too interested in women, other than for the money they could make for him. It still surprised her that she had never had to sleep with him.

By September it had become almost too cold for her nightly bathe at the window, but she braved it out as long as she could: her one consolation. One night she heard noises and talking down in the yard below. Leaning out she saw Brogan down there, dressed only in his boots and long johns, burning clothes in the rusted oil-drum they used as an incinerator. He was talking to someone, though she could not see who it was, or hear what he was saying; it was too dark, and he was talking too low. The crackling of the fire too interfered with her trying to hear.

Then she caught glimpses of someone moving about in the shadows in the alley that led to the yard. They looked small, or were only hunched up and shivering in the cold. Then she realised that the person was naked, the white of their back and shoulders picked up by the flames. For a moment she thought it was the German boy, the one who was always hanging around with Brogan. Then something in the figure's movements struck her as too feminine, and she was made uncertain again.

Whoever it was, their hair was shoulder-length and fair; it threw back the light of the fire, and she could not see their face because they kept it cupped in their hands. The tell tale side of their body remained turned away from her, and as she looked, whoever it was withdrew further into the shadows of the alleyway. She wondered why they did not just move up close to the flames. The fire took hold of the clothes, flared up for a few moments, and then began to die. Brogan threw in the stick he had been using to stoke the fire and turned towards the alley.

"You're a damn fool. There was no need to panic," she heard him say, his voice clear, heightened now in anger, and then he pushed the other person back against the wall. They lifted up their left arm to shield the side of their face as though they feared Brogan might hit them.

"You have to trust me, learn how to handle things. It's what I pay you for. To do as I say."

Brogan's hand was indeed raised, the hand clenched in a fist beating slowly against the air in front of the other's face, though it appeared to be more in frustration than in anger, and once he was finished talking he let it fall to his side. The other one did not answer, or if they did, she could not hear what they said, and then they were both gone, and she started to wonder if it had all been just her imagination.

She realised she was shivering. The night was colder than she had thought. She closed the window, quickly put on her nightdress, and crawled into her bed. The room smelled faintly of smoke.

That night, she dreamt she was swimming in the ocean. In the dream, she remained under the water for a very long time.

In the morning, at breakfast, Lucy was unusually quiet, even more so than she normally was. She looked pale and drawn. The soft crescents of flesh beneath her eyes looked bruised and her long blonde hair, of which she was normally so particular, had not been brushed and was tied up in a loose tail at the back of her neck. She looked like she had been crying all night, but would not say what had upset her. Belinda tried to comfort her, but Brogan came in and ushered her away, then led Lucy up to her room, the hint of a limp in her gait making her seem even more forlorn.

"This is none of your concern. She's fine. Just a little under the weather," he said to them from the foot of the stairs, but he threw them back an agitated glance as though he doubted the certainty of his own words. "You get on with your own business. She'll be all right," he told them, and continued to shepherd Lucy up the stairs.

The next few nights Lucy did not take any customers, and they saw nothing of her during the days. They knocked on her door a couple of times but she did not answer. Brogan took up her food and locked the door to her room behind him. All they could hear up there was the steady rhythm of his boots pacing on the floorboards, and the occasional distorted rumble of his voice. Then one morning Lucy came down for breakfast, smiling sheepishly, and was soon talking again, in her usual clipped, apologetic way, and it was as though nothing had happened. They asked her what the problem had been. She smiled at them, yet looking sad and distant, and shook her head and said nothing, fighting back a tear.

4

A Rich New Seam

"You'll not get out of it this time," Bunney said, the grime on the lower part of his face split by a triumphant grin.

Brogan Sullivan looked up and snorted in contempt, then shook his head slowly. He had only let Bunney in because the drunk had said he had something to tell him. What he had not expected was that Bunney would try to blackmail him again. The man looked a mess. His clothes were dirty and dishevelled, the fronts of his trousers and jacket stained and shiny with vomit, booze and sweat. His hair was matted and grey with dust. From the look of him alone it was clear there could never be any way back for him, and there was a wildness in his eye that said he was already three parts crazed.

"Not again, Bunney," Sullivan said, trying to conceal his frustration. "You've tried this before, remember?"

"That was before I knew about the boy."

Sullivan laughed. "What boy?"

"The Dortmund boy. I'm talking about the Dortmund boy. I know you. I know what you do."

"Then you have the advantage of me."

"The way you two are, always together, exchanging little confidences. I know the other things you do. I've seen you." Sullivan's eyes flicked up.

"You've seen me? Where? Doing what?"

"Two nights past, the alley behind the saloon. Him buck-naked and you burning his clothes. Had the boy put up a fight?"

Sullivan laughed again, but there was no humour in his laughter. "You're mad, Bunney," he said. "You've no idea what you saw."

"You're not denying it?"

"I'm denying what you seem to be accusing me of. Whatever you think you saw, you're mistaken."

"What were you doing then?"

"That's none of your business. You're jumping to conclusions without the facts."

"But it seems to me you're the one has to disprove it, not the other way." Sullivan had remained seated all this time, ensconced in his bosun's chair behind his desk. He nodded several times, deep in thought. The oil-lamp suspended on a brass chain from the ceiling above the desk lit up his hands as they drifted over the tooled leather desk-top and started to almost mindlessly shuffle the papers that lay scattered across it. The veins in the back of his hands were dark threads in the lamplight, and the shade of the lamp threw a deeper block of shadow across the upper half of his face and head.

"What do you want, Bunney?" he eventually asked.

"Money, the store…and my wife. You know I don't need to prove anything. The idea of it would be enough."

"Okay, Jack!" Sullivan said, suddenly standing up and stepping round from behind the desk. He came to a halt facing Bunney, a few feet from him, his thumbs hooked in his belt on either side of its silver bull's-head buckle. The lit end of his cigar glowed dully at the corner of his mouth.

"Maybe I shouldn't have pushed you so far," he said. "I could have just called, but I was curious how far you'd go. As for the rest, it was hard to see a way out once it had started. They'd all got so excited. Then, when you tried your blackmail nonsense…"

"You're saying it was my fault?"

"No! Just the way the cards came out, and being what we both are, probably neither of us could have backed down. But, we could have worked something out, told them it was a joke we had figured out together. They would have seen the fun in that. They wouldn't have felt too let down."

Bunney paused, his face turned to the floor, his body swaying slightly as he stood, his hands clasped together in front of him to still their trembling. When he looked up again some of the anger and certainty in his eyes had gone.

"Was that really what you'd intended?" he asked, almost gently.

"Yes! If I'd backed down I could never have sat at a card table again. They would all have begrudged paying if I won. I would've had to play half the time to lose, otherwise…"

Bunney nodded. He had never stopped to consider what this had meant to Sullivan. He had been so angry. What Sullivan had said made sense. The whole town had gone crazy for a while, almost like gold had been found again. The real gold was running out, everybody knew that, even though they all acted as though it wasn't. It was as though there had been a desperate need welling up inside them to find some new rich seam to mine. His anticipated bride had filled that need; at least, she had in the eyes of the prospectors - a rich virgin seam everyone had wanted to be the first to stake a claim to. If Sullivan had backed down, as he said, from then on he would have had to fight for what he won fair and square.

"The store you can have," Sullivan said. "As manager, if that's what you want. But as for the girl, she doesn't want you. Look at yourself, for Christ's sake. You never were the better option, even before what you did."

"What I did?" Bunney shouted, the anger returning along with the memory of the first time he had seen her, stepping from the coach. "You're the one turned her into a whore. You could have…"

"And what would she have been for you, Jack? Cook, cleaner, shopkeeper… And whore too? You could almost say I saved her. At least here she gets paid for it, and I think she knows she's better off here than with you."

"I want her to tell me that, and you to tell her you've not been square about how it happened."

"Do you now?" Sullivan paused. "Have you told any-one else about these things you supposedly saw?" he asked eventually.

"Not a soul," Bunney lied. He had told one person: Belinda Curtis. She was the only person he could trust. Sullivan may have been her master, but she was the most fair-minded per-son Bunney had ever met. She always said what she thought, and straight to a person's face. She would do what was right, if ever the need arose. At first, she hadn't believed any of what he told her, so he had written it down, had given it to her in a dated envelope with the instruction she should give it to the sheriff, or to someone, if anything should happen to him.

"So, are we in agreement, about the store?" Sullivan asked. Bunney thought for a moment, then nodded. Manager sounded fine. He didn't need the aggravation of running the store, but it would provide a place to sleep, money coming in. Let Sullivan take the risks, and the Austrian do the hard shift.

"Good! So what do you want to do about Rosie?" Bunney shrugged. He had no idea what he should do. Sullivan was probably right. Why should she want to speak to him, let alone reconsider the possibility of becoming his wife? He had nothing to offer. He was a gambler, without money, and the store would not really be his. And there was the drinking, which he had developed a real taste for, a bitter need for its consolation - for the other, illusory world it led to, where he at least felt safe. He still did not know if he had the courage to face her. Whenever she saw him in the street she looked away, or crossed to the other sidewalk, or hid her face behind her parasol.

"I can get her down here if you want," Sullivan said. Bunney shook his head and ran his hand slowly down over his face and along the line of his jaw, finally pinching out the loose wattle of skin at the top of his throat.

"No, not now. Maybe later, when things have settled some," he said, turning to leave.

5

An Older, Deeper Voice

With the passing weeks she got as good at her job as she could want to be. She did not want to get any better. Then it would be something else - a giving in to something darker inside that she would rather stay hidden.

"It's like a test," Belinda said. "Of yourself; of your character. You either fight it or you give in."

"And if you can't fight?"

"You have to. You have to tell yourself you're better than that. If not, the chances are you'll end up a lush, dossing with the other losers, doing the work in some back alley just to pay for the booze, or whatever else you find to provide a temporary release into oblivion."

She decided she was going to be a fighter, not a loser. It was the only good thing about this place, about her situation;

it had taught her how to fight. She knew that if she could close out all that needed closing out, one day this would all be over. This was not how she saw the rest of her life's path unwinding. Away from here, maybe back in Boston, no-one would need to know what had happened, what she had been. And then, one week, her monthly blood did not come. She waited another week, pretending to Brogan her time had come anyway, refusing to take customers in case he was counting the days since she had last bled. Another week passed, and she knew she was not mistaken.

The thought of a baby thrilled and terrified her. How would Brogan take it? Would he let her keep it, or insist she got rid of it? She remembered his raised fist that night in the alleyway. The thought of violence made her nauseous. Or was that the baby, the changes she already felt taking place in her body? And if she did keep it; what would that entail? Another mouth to feed, another vulnerable body to clothe. She would not be able to work for weeks, and would have to use what little she had saved just to pay for her keep, and for the baby, even if Brogan allowed her to stay. She could see the possibility of her ever getting away receding like the thread of a tantalising dream.

Belinda had told her of the things that could be done. But she was scared; they all sounded so primitive, so dangerous, and the thought of pain frightened her. And then there was the question of God. She hadn't talked to Him much of late. There was no church or chapel here to encourage or induce her to pray, and anyway, she was still angry with Him for what He had allowed to happen. But this was different. This, if she could find the courage to do it, would be of her own choosing. Would He ever forgive her if she took the life of a child?

Another two weeks passed. She did not tell Brogan or Lucy or Belinda of her condition; she did not know how, or what she should say. To ask Brogan for help seemed redundant, certainly if his response would be one of anger, and to begin with an apology to any of them seemed inappropriate: she had done nothing of which she should feel ashamed. Instead, she felt scared and alone, and with every day more conscious of the other life growing inside her. Already it felt like a stone, heavy and portentous, weighing her down. She knew she would have to make a decision soon.

Then one night she was down in the saloon. It was quiet, and to pass the time she was watching the men playing poker. As she watched the cards turning she experienced a flash of something like déjà-vu. Fate, a game of poker, a mere turn of a card: that was what had brought her to this state. A wave of anger and resentment washed through her. She made a decision, of sorts, again ceding responsibility to the agency of something outside of herself, beyond her control. She decided that she too could play games; if Fate wanted to use her as its plaything, then at least she could write the rules by which they played. She decided to let the turn of the cards determine what she should do. In the next hand, the first card dealt face-up on the table was the Black Lady, the Queen of Spades, the Death Card, as some of the more superstitious players called it. That felt about right to her, an appropriate enough sign. Birth at one end, death at the other. From where she was, there was nothing else, other than however many years of hard stuff you managed to endure in between.

Why make it harder than it needed to be? Why pass on that struggle to another living soul?

Dense steam rose from the bath. She lowered her body tentatively into the water. It was so hot it hurt, and she quickly pushed herself up out of it. Her feet and ankles, the backs of her thighs had already turned red from scalding. She reached for the jug and poured half of the cold water it contained into the bath then lowered herself into it again. This time it was just about tolerable, although too hot for comfort. But comfort was not what this was about. Her breathing came fast and irregular; she gritted her teeth, settled herself down in the water and picked up the needle she had decided should be adequate for the situation. The steel felt cold in her hand. It seemed such a crude and ineffectual instrument to take the life of a child. But a crude situation, she consoled herself, required no more than a crude solution.

She braced herself, and inserted the needle inside her. It felt hot inside, having quickly taken on the heat of the water. She had no idea what she was doing, where she should direct the needle, how far into herself she should allow it to invade. She felt its point, suddenly sharp, scoring across the delicate linings of her insides - those dark, unknown regions of which she had no comprehension. Trusting to intuition, she guided the needle where it felt like a man should go. The sensations she felt inside herself did not help. The needle did not feel anything like the same; it was too thin, too unresponsive. Outside, the lower half of her body had gone completely numb. Then she felt a sharp pain, deep inside, an acute ache spread out across her whole abdomen, and a few seconds later dark red, almost black blood began to ooze out of her staining the water. She pulled out the needle. It left a long, irregular trace of blood, like an inky signature testifying to a statutory fact.

She sat in the bath, not daring to move. The blood spread out around her until the water turned almost completely red. She sat, half submerged in it, staring into its ruddy depths in confusion, in disbelief. The temptation was there to just sit in the now comfortable warmth of the water and watch her life flow slowly out of her. That would not require any courage or strength, just her passive complicity, something she had learned to do only too well. Her whole life here depended on it; nothing would have changed if she were to simply give in. Just another absence, an empty space without a name that had not been there previously. An absence that – when seen from another point of view - would be an escape.

Then she began to feel cold and her body started to shake uncontrollably. Her teeth were chattering. Another flash of pain stabbed through her belly and down into the tops of her thighs. She suddenly felt scared. She climbed out of the bath, rubbed herself down as best she could with a towel, though blood was still seeping out of her, and putting on her petticoat went to look for help. It was all she could do to make her way down and then up the flights of stairs at either end of the main landing. Belinda would know what to do, she told herself, to keep herself going. Belinda would know. But, arriving at her door she could hear that Belinda was busy; there was laughter, female and male, both high-pitched and childlike behind the closed door. She hesitated, leaning on her arm against the frame of the door. She did not want Belinda to lose money on her account, so she turned and limped back along the landing and knocked feebly on Lucy's door. When Lucy saw the blood in her lap and on her hands she screamed softly and then started to rock back and forth, stepping agitatedly from one foot to the other, cupping her face in her hands.

"What have you done? How could you be...?" Lucy whispered, almost harshly at her. "Not you. I thought only I could be that..."

"Stop, Lucy! Stop! You have to help me," she sobbed, and sank to her knees on the floor. "Go get the doctor," she pleaded, kneeling on all fours now, panting and blooded like a hunted animal.

At the mention of the doctor Lucy seemed to come to her senses, as though she knew now exactly what needed to be done. She straightened herself and rubbed the heels of her hands purposefully against the top of her thighs, saying, "Get the doctor. Get the doctor," softly to herself, then she edged past the bloodied figure in the doorway. Taking her cloak down from the hook on the door she backed out onto the landing. Her eyes were wide open and her head was shaking in horror or disbelief. She turned, and the sounds of her slippered feet on the steps faded into silence down the stairwell.

On her own again she no longer knew what she should do. Even Lucy's panicked antics were better than being left alone with her fears. Another worrying thought came to her. Perhaps Lucy had not gone to fetch the doctor. Perhaps she was scared and had run away. She could still feel cooling blood running down the insides of her thighs. She knew she had to do something; she did not want to just stay here and bleed to death. She pulled herself up by the door handle, clutching her clothing to the wounded part of her body, staggered out onto the landing again and eased herself, step by step, clinging to the banister, down the stairs, following Lucy. She remembered the night with Brogan and the naked, elusive person down in the yard, the condition Lucy had been in the following day. Now she understood. If only she had realised sooner, she could have asked Lucy for help. She should have had more faith in her, for all her fragility.

At the bottom of the stairs, she became confused. She was beginning to feel light-headed, dizzy. It had been her intention to make her way to the front of the saloon, to meet the doctor halfway, or if Lucy really had run away, to make her own way to him as quickly as she could, but instead she took the corridor that led to the rear of the building, her wet hands leaving a trail of dark bruises on the walls as she shuffled along it towards the door at the end of the corridor.

She opened the door and crawled out on all fours into the yard. Outside, snow was falling. Already the ground was covered to a depth of a couple of inches, though she did not register the cold on her hands, her knees, the tops of her feet. Her body was beyond such finer sensation. Pain racked her from her rib-cage to the tops of her thighs, smothering everything beyond. It was all she could do to keep moving and breathing. Close by, a dog barked sharply at her. There was the scurry of padded feet, a short, almost stifled howl, and not long after, she heard the pad of the other street-dogs approaching through the alleyway. The pack began to gather in the yard. They milled around her, keeping an uncertain distance, testing the feral air that drifted from her, whistling quietly to each other in agitation.

She tried to stand, staggered, and fell to the ground again. She had never been down here in the yard before. She wanted to touch the wall of rock, to know, just once, what its surface felt like. She imagined it hard and cold, and rough to the touch, like frozen sand. The dogs began to whine and whimper, and to worry at the spots of blood seeping into the snow amongst her scattered footprints. They were as confused as she was by this encounter. Humans were friends and providers, not prey, they had learned, but an older, deeper voice was calling to them now, one they could not help but heed. She shouted at the dogs to go away. They retreated nervously at the sound of her voice, then edged forward again into the silence that followed, drawn by that other voice, silent but more insistent. She raised her head to them, bared her teeth and growled at them, then barked, once, twice, and then started to laugh at herself, her antics, and finally rolled over onto her back in surrender.

Above her she could see the two pine trees cresting their scalp of rock, silhouetted against the clouds. The clouds were oddly bright. They looked hot, like in a thunderstorm. They had that orange glow clouds sometimes had when there was snow about, as though the steely flakes of ice were being forged deep inside them on some gently tempered furnace. The snowflakes continued to fall. They settled on her face like ash.

"Fall on me, damn you" she whispered urgently to the trees, the wall of rock above her. "Fall on me now. Let it be over."

The last thing she felt as she slipped from consciousness was the gentle lapping of the dog's tongues at her hands, her toes, the more urgent snuffling at the hems of her blood-stained petticoats.

A Traveller's Journal:
An Adventure Begins
Hope, October 11th 1899

From a big city to a remote mining town;
from the comforts and distractions of a
respectable urban life, to a place where
almost the only consolation to be had is
in the knowledge that tomorrow will be
equally as hard and fruitless as the day
before had been. Such has been the stark
translation of circumstances that I have
personally undergone, for today I arrived at
my destination, the secluded mining township of Hope. This haphazard accumula-
tion of houses, shops, stores and saloons
lies strung out along a valley nestled in
the midst of a stark and far-flung wilderness of forest and snow-topped mountains.
Behind me lay a journey which, although
it had been long and tiring, had thankfully
passed without menace or mishap.

But, dear reader, take heed! Before you
look to discover in me some bold and reckless spirit, drawn by an insatiable hunger
for new experiences, I fear I must dis-
appoint. For, contrary to any expectations
you might hold of me, I am not some
intrepid adventurer set upon a bold and
solitary journey into strange and unknown

lands. Indeed, many thousands before me have made that same or similar journey, and that in far more adventurous spirit than I, having been drawn by the possibility of finding luxury and comfort as reward for their labours, or as the consequence of good fortune or Fate.

Five years past, rich seams of gold were discovered in this place, and a gold rush began. The town of Hope, a focal point for the mining activities, and for all of the human commerce that by nature revolves around such an enterprise, sprang up at the mouth of a sheltered gorge at the foot of the treasure-laced mountains, and its population grew rapidly, as thousands came from near and far in expectation of finding their fortune here.

My fellow travellers on the final three days of my journey - a butcher, accompanied by his wife and daughter, looking to make a better and easier livelihood for his family than the one he had grafted out in the stock-yards of Chicago; a gaunt, middle-aged man from Czechoslovakia with barely a half-dozen words of English in his possession; and a truly adventurous and jocund young Scot, named Ingram Todd, come to try his callow hand at prospecting - all maintained an optimistic if stoically informed view of what might await them. None could know what their future here might bring, how hard or rewarding life might prove to be on this rugged frontier.

As to my own purpose for making this journey, it is neither as romantic nor as bold as theirs. Nor is it driven (as theirs must surely be, given the risks and sacrifices and uncertainty entailed), by the need to find for myself a richer, more financially rewarding future. Unlike for them, the coming months will not find me engaged in the back-breaking, soul-destroying toil of prospecting; nor will I experience first-hand the daily disappointment of unrewarded searching; or (it is also true to say), the hoped-for elation that the discovery of gold must surely bring.

So, it is with far less ambitious intent that I am come here, sent to this singular place by the Chicago newspaper in whose employment I am bound, and whose pages you are currently perusing, to try to discover the riches of a more mundane treasury – to write the stories of these sundry pilgrims and their families, of their day-to-day existence here; to relate their myriad hopes and struggles and triumphs, and (for it is a sad certainty that this will also be my task), to report their failures and disasters, even too, their occasional demise.

Maybe too, and hopefully more than once, I will have occasion to tell you of the riches they have found. Thomas E. Speake

Part 2

New Year's Eve, 1899

6

Waiting for Spring

Speake had never experienced cold like this before, certainly not back in the home country, not even back east. There had been snow there, in Chicago, the occasional white-out; ponds and streams, even the great lake that had frozen over for weeks at a time, the fused platelets of ice undulating gently to the motion of the water like the scales of a giant sleeping reptile. Never though had he felt cold as bone-deep, as seemingly never-ending as this. Not a cold that could freeze the soul.

This year the winter had been so hard the ground was frozen solid to a depth of more than two feet. The ice on the river had formed so thick men and their families were camped out on it where it widened out into a lagoon below the town. These - the new emigrants arriving still from the East and from Europe even as the gold ran out - had come too late to build anything substantial on what little habitable land there was. Always though there was the frozen expanse of the lagoon.

It was the eve of the turn of the year, the last day of the last year of the century, and winter was approaching its deepest. A fine mist hung in the cold-stilled air, casting everything within a blue-grey haze. At the entrances to tents and makeshift lean-tos, wood fires burned in braziers set on the frozen lagoon, offering inadequate protection against the cold. Fir sprays strewn on the ice served as rugs and parlour carpets, even as beds for some. Sawn and hewn log ends were the prospectors' tables and chairs; more sprays of spruce and jack pine saplings their one, windowless wall, piled thick and high against the wind, tarpaulins stretched above their lee-ward sides as shelter from rain and snow. The scent of pine and juniper resins and wood smoke, of charring meat filled the air.

The prospectors and their wives and children sat huddled around their fires, swaddled in furs and blankets, coughing out languid spits of phlegm and steam. Mangy dogs stood close at their sides, shivering and whimpering, never more than three paws set down on the frozen surface, the other intermittently favoured, trembling in the chilling air. As Speake looked down on the settlement, a cart rumbled slowly across the frozen throat of the river; the horse harnessed to it snorted and shook its head in consternation at the uncer-tainty of the surface sliding from beneath its canvas-bound hooves. At intervals the silence was broken by the soft fall of snow-slips, of thin voices calling, and by the sharp reports, like distant gunshots, of frozen sap splitting the timber of the surrounding trees.

Speake blew onto his hands to warm them, on the patches of skin exposed through his worn woollen gloves, and then rubbed at the parts of his face not covered by the flap-eared cap and worn woollen shawl he had wrapped around his neck and head, like an old woman, he thought, to keep the cooling blood from coagulating beneath the skin. He surveyed the encamped village on the lagoon; wondered what had made these people choose to endure such hardship, what lives they had left behind for this to seem a better alternative.

Still trying to imagine it, and weighing whether their reasons might be worse or better than his own, he turned and continued his climb towards the barn.

He liked being out here alone, despite the cold, away from the turmoil and the fractious commerce of the mining community. Here, lost in contemplation of the alien, wilderness plants, and of the equally alien creatures that managed to eke out an existence among them, he could persuade himself the world was a good place, that everything in it was ordered as it was meant to be. Some ostensibly guiding essence, he reasoned - whatever name or form it might have - had shaped it to an ultimately benign end. He had not climbed far though before his thoughts were interrupted by a voice calling from somewhere below and to his side.

"Good morning, Herr Speake." The sound of his own name, startled him. He had not expected to encounter anyone out on the track that led up from the town to the ice barn. He looked down and saw young Dortmund - the German boy, as nearly everybody called him - standing about fifteen feet below him at the foot of the snow-covered bank of a frozen gully. The boy's mane of thick golden hair fell onto his shoulders framing his face like a cowl. It presented an anomalous, almost startling incongruity in the barren, monochrome landscape. His hair, the colour and lustre of it, had made the boy something of a mascot among the more superstitious of the prospectors.

"See, there's gold walking among us," they would say when he passed. Like drew unto like, they believed. His presence confirmed what they needed to believe - that the town was a place of good fortune. Some even touched him, his hair, for the luck of it as he passed, much to the boy's obvious consternation.

"Good morning to you too," Speake said. "How are you today?"

"I am well enough, Sir…all things considered." The boy's voice trailed audibly from certainty as he spoke. "But tell me. Do you like my angel?" he added, pointing at the spread-eagled impression of his body he had made in the bank of snow. Speake moved closer to the top of the gully and turned his shoulders and head to see the snow-angel from a better perspective.

"Yes, it's a fine angel," he said.

"It would be good if I was able to send it to Heaven, to take care of my father, and of my uncle and grandfather," the boy said. Speake perceived the tightening in the boy's face, in the set of his shoulders, as he spoke. He half turned away, trying to conceal the mirrored tensing in his own features as he tried to think of something consoling or relevant to say. The boy's father and uncle and grandfather had all been killed but a week previously in an accident at their mine. Speake thought the boy could not be much more than fourteen or fifteen years old. He was touched by the stoicism the young man was showing in the face of such a loss.

"Do people believe such a thing in your country?"

"I do not know, Sir. Maybe I heard it from my father, but maybe it was only a childish story. In Germany he worked as a printer. He had a great love of books, of the wisdom they contained." Speake was surprised by this information. He had assumed that like most of the prospectors the boy's father had been a labourer or craftsman, a man of no more than limited education and interests. Such were the men, he had learned, who gave up all they had to gamble their futures, the futures of their wives, their children, on such a foolhardy venture as prospecting.

"I think not many people here understood him," the boy continued, with sadness in his voice. "His English words were poor. It was why he desired for me to learn. So that others would not think me stupid. It pained him when he could not make himself understood."

"That would be no reason to think him stupid. He was well liked and respected, that I know; your uncle and grandfather too. But you and I have something in common. When I was a boy, a little younger than you maybe, I too used to make snow-angels. In England, in a town called Bath, at a place called Widcombe Hill."

"You did?" the boy asked, his face brightening in surprise. "They have snow in England too?

"Yes, though never anything like this. There was one year I remember it was so cold and the snow so deep, but the following day the snow, and the angels I had made were all gone. I remember I was so angry that my father hadn't arranged for it to still be there."

"No, I do not think it is possible to depend upon such things. Fathers, I am not so sure about. How is it possible to know?" the boy said, letting out a plaintive sound like a stifled laugh which came to Speake hard and thin in the frosted air. He tried to laugh in reply, to acknowledge the boy's precocious wisdom, but he had no idea what he should say. He did not think he could openly acknowledge the other thing they had in common - the personal loss he had also suffered, the anguish he had felt. It was still too raw.

"But surely snow can be trusted?" he finally managed to say, forcing an inadequate smile to his face. "Out here at least." The boy looked around at the blanket of white covering everything around them and nodded thoughtfully.

"Yes, that may be true, but I think it cannot be true of God, nor of his angels. Not here." With these last words he kicked angrily at the snow, scuffing away the edges of the impression of the angel with the side of his boot. Once the angel had been destroyed he glanced up at Speake, his face depicting something between defiance and helplessness.

"Here, whatever people may try to tell you," he said. "I do not think their God even believes in himself," and then he turned away abruptly and started to walk heavily back down the gully towards the town.

Speake had been here for almost three months now and had been counting off the days since his arrival like the beads on an endless rosary of despair. Thanksgiving had passed, as had a dark, ungracious Christmas, and as the Dortmund boy had echoed, and contrary to the dogged faith of many of the prospectors, it had quickly become clear to him that God and His saints did not hold much sway in a place like this. There had been a preacher here, of sorts, for a couple of weeks - a man in whom the presence of God had been equally hard to discover - but now he too was gone. Perhaps, he thought, it was simply not possible to displace God – the one he was familiar with - away from His churches and books and rituals and vestments and expect Him still to function adequately in such a place. The wilderness was where the Devil had tempted Jesus after all. Perhaps here it was necessary for a man to find more appropriate gods - some more natural divinity who governed the ways of the snow and woods and stones and mountains - to intercede between himself and the world he was trying to tame.

Today was New Year's Eve, the last day of the century, a notable day in a notable year. Somehow though it did not feel like the cusp of a new year, let alone of a new century beginning. Rather it was as though time had been suspended for an eternity in the endless expanse of snow and ice. Winter here was like one long, cold night spent waiting for the dawn of spring. With the coming of spring, for those who chose to stay - the bound, the stubborn and the desperate, and as always, those who knew the ways to make money no matter what the fortunes of others - prospecting could begin again in earnest.

For Speake, though, the lethargic lengthening of the days carried a deeper significance; with the coming of spring, he could leave. He could return to Chicago, to a world he believed he understood better, to confront the last of his demons there; to challenge them in a world that did not so readily acknowledge their existence and power, as this frozen wilderness repeatedly did. Only there, amongst the city's echoes and memories, painful as they were, could he test whether they had been truly laid to rest.

There was nothing more to keep him here anyway now the gold was gone. The town was slowly dying; there were no new stories to be uncovered, only repeated anecdotes of discovery and stoic survival, a sudden death or accident, an inopportune birth; the endlessly related dreams of yet to be discovered wealth. He had wired his editor in Chicago; he had agreed that when the thaw came Speake could return.

The old boys here, the ones who knew these things from experience, told him repeatedly that there were no rich seams to be mined. The rocks, the sub-strata, were not right, they said. They had not been laid down by time in the necessary way. The veins that had been found were thin and superficial; the gold they contained could never be good. A few people had struck it lucky, in the beginning, sufficient to give birth to hope, and to this town, which had taken Hope as its name. But the surface, like all surfaces, had given the lie to what might be found beneath.

There were no providential fortunes to be made here, or so the old boys told him. They too were only waiting for spring so they could move on.

The ice barn was at the top of a narrow rock-strewn track that led up past the lagoon from the end of the main street of the town. From what Speake could see it was just a barn; timber-framed and clad and painted all over in pitch, with no windows and a steep, shingled roof whose sloping wings echoed the wilder contours of the mountain peaks beyond. It was about twenty feet wide, a little over twice as long.

Icehouses had always held a fascination for Speake. He had no understanding of how they worked, and perhaps therein lay the fascination - the mystery of it, the incredulity. There was something almost magical about being able to keep ice frozen through the heat of summer. The immutable flow of the world temporarily halted. It was partly this innate curiosity that had brought him there, although it was more the other thing, in this particular barn, which drew him most strongly. It was something he had learned about the day after his arrival in Hope - the day the Swedish boy had been found dead in the river under the ice.

"Ain't nothin' more can be done for him. Must have drowned or froze in the water. Best take him on up to the ice barn," old man Allenby had said, his voice dispassionate, once they had pulled the body from under the ice and had cleaned the boy's face to identify him for certain. Everyone there, it seemed, had known what he had meant. Two or three men had stepped forward to offer their quiet condolences to the father but no one else had said a word. Speake's discreet enquiries among the watching crowd as they carried the body away had met only with lowered heads and eyes, and a barely concealed resentment at what they obviously considered his indelicate asking.

Everybody knew about this other function of the ice barn; it was a stark necessity in an isolated and winter-bound place like Hope. Heads were bowed and caps were doffed whenever the talk was of someone who had gone to the icehouse. No one wanted to go there in winter, not even of his own free will. The ice barn was definitely a place for summer. Then, or so he had been told, you could go there to escape the flies, the dust, and the heat, and for a penny old man Allenby would let you in and would shut the door close behind you. Then, for a couple of minutes you could gladly immerse yourself in the dark, and in the blessed chill of its embrace. But that was in summer. In the winter there was always the possibility the door would not re-open, that the chill and dark would become irretrievably your own.

So far, Speake had found ways to put aside his curiosity about the barn. He had known there might be a story there, possibly the most powerful story the town had to tell. Like the other residents however, he had been disinclined to renew his acquaintance with mortality, or to re-join battle with those inadmissible demons that had driven him from Chicago to this place. There, for more than four months, he had sat and watched, impotent to help or comfort him, while his father had been gradually devoured by consumption. After his father was dead, finding himself unable to come to terms with the fact of it, he had asked to be sent here, anywhere away from Chicago and the memories that city evoked.

He had needed to escape the images that had haunted him - his father's pallid, collapsing face, his shrunken limbs, the morbid rattle of his final breaths struggling through the ravaged, congested passageways of his lungs; the gradual transformation of a once proud and intelligent man into an incoherent sac of pus and bones and dust. Now, out here, where the reality of the life he had previously lived was itself little more than a dream, the bad dreams had mostly subsided. The demons had more or less retreated. He witnessed so many impersonal deaths during his sojourn in Hope that it had become almost a commonplace for him, part of an implacable order within which the singularity of his own experience had begun to wither - just like his father's physical presence - into insignificance. Now, finally, he felt strong enough to satisfy his curiosity about the barn.

As his eyes became accustomed to seeing in the gloom, he began to discern the shapes of coffins stacked upright against the walls of ice. All but one of the coffins were open; the exposed bodies within them were so real, so fresh, they almost seemed alive. It struck him as odd that the lids had been left partially open, revealing the faces of their incumbents, as though to deliberately expose their sad condition for public scrutiny. He walked along the walls, looking at each face in turn, some of them old and weather-beaten, some younger, almost formless - faces whose history could still be faintly traced in the features that floated behind their obscuring veils of ice. These people had lived and died here: the ice on their skin, for all its softening opacity, could not conceal the hardships they had endured in pursuit of their own, or of some other's unconsummated dreams. Rather, it had fixed them at a single, definitive moment; a moment of defeat or betrayal, of cold desolation. If anything, it had made the marks of their suffering more visible, had engraved them more deeply into the texture of their skin.

The five men and the boy were dressed in dark suits; the one woman in a sombre black dress trimmed at the neck and wrists with satin the colour of blood. All of them clad in their Sunday best. It seemed to Speake they all had something they wanted to tell him, something they considered important but could not find words to express. Vapour rose from the surface of the ice enshrouding them like the fog of their silent breath, but their words and voices had deserted them, striking them dumb in frozen anger.

Perhaps, he thought, this was why they looked so lost, so sad; they could no longer complain, or say the things there had not been the time to say before. Even the boy looked old.

"Was wonderin' when you'd find your way up here. Been expectin' you the past weeks. Wasn't sure you'd make it on your own two feet, mind," a thick voice said behind him. Speake jumped involuntarily at the sound. He was aware of his intrusion into a place where he probably had no right to be. The door of the barn had been ajar, and as he had not seen anyone around to ask, he had nudged the door further open and entered. He turned. The tall, wiry figure of Josh Allenby stood silhouetted in the doorway.

Allenby was the town carpenter and undertaker, the proprietor of the barn. Despite the cold he was wearing only shirtsleeves and rust-coloured under-linen. Ghosts of old sweat mapped out the contours of his labours around the collarless neck and armpits of his clothes. The shirt and his dusted, thread-bare moleskin trousers hung loosely from his angular frame, and as always he had a cold, unlit corn-pipe clenched firmly between his blackened teeth. Speake could not recall ever having seen the pipe lit and wondered how the man's teeth had got to be the way they were. Spit crackled in the hollow stem of the pipe whenever he spoke. The sound had troubled him from the first moment he had heard it, reminding him too uncomfortably of the death of his father, the sounds of his life bubbling to extinction in the mired depths of his throat. Allenby pulled the door to behind him until only a thin slab of light entered to pierce the inner gloom of the barn, and then came to stand beside Speake.

"I'm sorry. I should have asked," Speake offered.

"That's okay. I was out back. I know you didn't come set on any mischief."

"The door was..."

"I said it's okay. Curiosity can be a powerful thing, and you seem blessed with more than a share of that." There was a taint of sourness to his words, as though he did not find curiosity a blessing at all, at least not in Speake. "Kinda spooky, though, ain't they?" he added more lightly, pushing his chin in the direction of the coffins. "As though they know somethin' we don't, and want to pass it on."

"I was thinking something similar myself," Speake said, also turning back to look at the caskets.

"Almost seems a shame to disturb 'em, them looking so peaceful. Come spring and the thaw, though, holes'll get dug, and their people'll get to say their farewells. It can be a long hard winter for the women-folk, the kiddies too, knowin' they're still here." Speake nodded vaguely, and tried to imagine what it would have been like to have had his own father here during his time in Hope, his body embalmed in the ice; the contradiction of both his physical presence and spiritual absence. He found the idea too awful to consider. To have him there and not be able to converse with him would have been worse than all the troublesome memories he had been struggling to push away.

"The older boys, the bolder ones, they come up and sneak

in sometimes just to sit and talk. Don't know if it helps any, but I jus' leave 'em be."

"I saw young Dortmund on my way up. Does he...?"

"The German boy? Sure. He's been up a coupla times. Didn't have much to say, and what he did say was all in German, so didn't understand a word, other than Papa. I guess that's the same wherever you're from."

"What is there to say?" Speake said dispiritedly, considering what he would say to his father now if he were given the opportunity. Nothing came to mind. No expressions of affection or regret, no confessions, or apologies, despite his persistent feeling that one was owed; no profound questions, other than the ubiquitous, eternal need for a reason. Why?

"Mostly they just sit an' tell 'em the things they've been doin'. You know...passin' the time, kinda quiet like, man to man."

"Putting a brave face on it," Speake ventured, recalling his own fears on being left alone in the world, the ensuing days he had spent going through the motions, politely accepting condolences, shaking hands, mouthing platitudes, when all he had wanted was to hear his father's voice telling him he forgave him.

"Could be, but it seems more needy than that. Maybe it's just the realisation there're some things can't ever be undone. It's a tough lesson to learn. Some of us take years, a lifetime to learn it." Speake glanced at the old man, his interest pricked by what sounded like a veiled confession, but the old man's face was impassive. He nodded slowly in acknowledgement and turned again to the bodies embalmed in the ice.

Now he found he was able to assign names and histories

to the misted faces, could acknowledge them for the individuals they once had been. There on the left was the Swedish boy they had taken from the river the day after Speake had arrived, and next to him, the drunkard Jack Bunney, his slit throat sutured now with stitches of ice. In the single closed coffin beside him would be the remains of Emilie Henderson, the milliner's wife, who had killed herself just three days before Christmas. And at the end, their flesh less wax-like, their carapaces of ice less dense, less opaque than those of the others, were the Dortmund twins and their father, whose boy he had just seen making his angel in the snow, and who had been found wrapped in each other's arms and suffocated by rock dust at the bottom of their mine.

The other woman, the body at the beginning of the row, he did not recognise, though he knew who she must be. It was Rosalind Pearce. She had died only days before he arrived in Hope. He was surprised at how young she looked, little more than a girl, seventeen, or eighteen at most. Her painted lips - a hint of unfitting wantonness in one so young - were a gash of blood red against the blank white of her skin, echoed in the thin line of satin trim on the collar of her dress.

He realised then that the bodies had been arranged around the walls of the barn in the chronological order of their passing, like a morbid ledger of Allenby's trade - a calendar set out by mortalities, not by days and weeks and months. Their deaths had been the brutal realities punctuating the commonplace of everyday life during the weeks he had resided in the town, providing the subjects of his more substantial stories. More than that, they had marked the stages on the personal journey Speake had been making. What he had not been able to decide was whether this process had been one of victory or of loss.

Now, though, he wanted only to remember these poor souls as the living people they once had been. He recalled the times he had spent with them, as guest, or rather as the prying interloper he sometimes felt himself to be, coming to their homes in the guise of putative friend, trying to elicit from their memories the next titillating anecdote to fashion into a story for the entertainment and distraction of his anonymous readers in Chicago. Perhaps, he thought, he could have served them better while they were alive, could have offered them more than that fleeting, remote notoriety. There had been times, not so long ago, when they had been able to look back at him, when their eyes had focused sharply on his, and their quickened voices had given shape and substance to the various experiences they related. Now, though, it was too late for them to retell their stories. Their faces looked back at him sightless and silent, their histories reduced to a row of empty, suspended instants, like blank letters on a printed page.

The truth was they had nothing more to tell him. They had nothing more to say. Like Speake, like the old boys who knew better than everybody else, they too - and the grief they were carrying inside them - were just waiting for the spring.

As they emerged from the darkness of the ice barn into the dull winter air outside, Speake had to squint and turn his head towards the shadow of the barn to allow his eyes time to adjust to the change in light. Once they had become accustomed to the relative brightness he stopped and turned to face the old undertaker.

The sight of the corpses in the barn had left him feeling

uneasy. Seeing them suspended in their moments of decease had reawakened memories of the preceding months, stirring dimmed recollections of those lesser details he had previously considered insignificant or mere background to the events he had recorded and had presented to his editor in Chicago as the true-life stories of the residents of Hope. The visit to the barn, so long deferred, had made it clear to him that his understanding of Hope and of its inhabitants - the overall perception of the place he had gradually built up in the telling of his stories, both for himself and for his readers - had been far from complete. Perhaps, he thought, if he could resurrect the closer details of their lives from their imposed slumber, the bodies stored in the barn might yet provide a better perspective of the overall story of this place.

Allenby stopped too but did not turn away from Speake's questioning look. His faded, rheumy eyes held his in an unwavering and disinterested gaze. The old man had probably seen too much in his life, Speake thought, for anything to distract him from the acquired rhythm of his ways. He looked to be about sixty or a little more, the lines of those years scouring his face. Allenby continued to look at Speake while sucking steadily on the stem of his empty pipe.

"Yes?" he said eventually, in a languid, almost paternal voice. "You have somethin' you wan'ta say?"

"I was curious whether there was anything about the boy who drowned in the river, something you might have overlooked, or chose not to mention before?" Speake asked, once prompted by the sound of the old man's voice. Allenby's eyes had held him captive, like prey transfixed by the hypnotic stare of a snake. He still found the rattle of the cold spittle in the pipe disquieting. It still reminded him of watching his father die.

"An' what makes you think there'd be somethin' I'd choose not to mention?" Allenby said, a sharper edge coming to his voice. "I've nothin' to hide. Not from you, nor from anyone. I told 'em what there was to tell, that I was in any position to tell at any rate. You were here when it happened. Day after you arrived, if I recall it right. As you saw and heard, it was an accident. My guess is the poor tyke most likely slipped an' drowned."

"You have a good memory. Yes, the day after I arrived. Quite a welcome for a naive city boy like me. It was the first story I sent back to Chicago. But you must have had a closer look at the body than anyone. Was there anything unusual about it?"

Allenby shook his head slowly and pursed his lips tighter around the stem of the pipe. "Nope, can't say there was. It was all banged up, but that would've been from the rocks and stuff in the river. Water can flow mighty steady through there, even when it's froze over."

"You believe that was what it was, damage from rocks and branches?" Allenby looked at him, and then turned his head to hawk up a gob of phlegm that he spat away over his shoulder. It made a sharp sound on the frozen ground and immediately began to change colour as it started to freeze.

"I ain't no coroner," he said, turning back.

"But you've seen a significant number of bodies?"

"Twenty-seven in Hope alone," he said. Speake thought the old man sounded almost proud of this, as though such a tally had been in some way the product of his own enterprise.

It seemed a high count, a disproportionate number for a community the size of Hope. Or was that just his over-eager imagination looking for some sinister force in operation that did not exist? Hope was a mining town, marooned in the middle of a wilderness, an insignificant huddle of shacks and tents and lean-tos that could not be found on any printed map he had ever seen. Nor were the people here like any he had ever encountered. Other than the few among them who had previously made honest livings as farmers, labourers and craftsmen, they were scoundrels and chancers mostly, gamblers and drifters who moved from place to place looking for the one opportunity - the moment of their own good, or more often, of someone else's bad fortune - to redeem them from a graceless existence. But grace was rarely to be found here, and if so, only in transitory moments, and only for the fortunate few. For most, he had learned, life in Hope was defined largely by toil and hardship, and those who survived did so mainly by dint of hard work and diligence, or through the blind indulgence of God and Nature.

It had not taken Speake long to understand that they were a breed apart from him, these place-hardened people. That had been all too obvious, with his inadequate city clothes, his fancy words and his curiosity, his college education, the stories he wrote and wired back to Chicago. There had been other differences too, less tangible. It was as though they spoke another language, one which all of his 'book-learning' as they called it, could never have equipped him to speak. Their conversations, their inner thoughts, even the dreams disturbing their sleep, were about the land, the sky, the weather, about the rocks whose veins they were hoping to bleed. It was a language of pragmatism, born of necessity; an on-going prayer offered up to the untamed gods of Nature. It was not that their lives were small: they were almost too big for any man to fill - as vast and indomitable as the country upon whose flesh they scavenged - yet they were lives circumscribed by the ever-pressing need to survive.

Speake had never before had to worry about his own survival. Here he felt helpless and vulnerable, dependent on the goodwill of others, and without the words to give voice to even his smallest fears.

"And some of those had been murdered or assaulted?" he asked, fixing Allenby squarely in the eye. There was something about him, the laconic, off-hand way he spoke, that Speake did not trust.

"A good few of 'em. This can be a rough town, as I'm sure you've seen. Just what're ya drivin' at?"

"You'd know then what the marks of a violent assault look like? The bruises on the boy's body, what were they like?" Allenby started to nod before he spoke, as though counting or running through a memorised inventory. A shiver of disquiet ran through Speake as he imagined the horrors held in the old man's mind.

"A fair number of 'em, smallish, mostly. A few larger, pale," Allenby said. "All across his neck and shoulders, some on the backs of his legs and buttocks. But you know it ain't really right for us to be discussin'..."

"As though he might have been struggling with someone?" Speake interrupted. "As though someone might have been holding him down?" Allenby thought about this for a time then nodded.

"Yeah, if you think about it that way, I suppose you could persuade yourself that."

"And were there any bruises on his chest and stomach?"

"No. Not too many to speak of. But then that's the way a body would go, I reckon, under the circumstances, caught up in the flow of the river, all tucked up forwards."

"But the boy's nose was broken, and fairly badly as I recall."

Allenby snorted. "Then my guess about that," he said, his voice tightening again, "would be that a head can be a pretty vulnerable thing, particularly when you're unconscious or drownin'. Particularly when you're already dead." Speake frowned, and studied the old man's face. Such lapses into petulance did not sit comfortably with his outward show of indifference to the fate of the boy.

"Excuse me for saying this, Sir, but you seem to have a ready explanation for things that some might find unusual." Allenby turned away and hawked up another gob of phlegm, which he spat out to within a few inches of where the first had landed. His voice, when he finally spoke, sounded weary, as though bored with the discussion.

"I've no idea where you're headin' with this, young man, but let me tell you. I've seen a lot of things out here, things you wouldn't want to see, and I hope for your sake never do. But like I said, I ain't no coroner, nor no doctor, nor less a detective. I jes' bury 'em when I have to, and whenever I can. I can't tell you no more than I have, nor other than what I believe to be true. Now why don't you jes' forget it, and go look for your story someplace else? I've told you what I know, and at bottom there ain't no tellin' either way no more, is there?" At that he walked away towards the shack behind the ice barn where he lived, leaving Speake to wrestle with his newly awakened doubts.

Winter Takes its Toll;
and a Macabre Discovery is Made
Hope, October 12th 1899

Winter can come hard and fast to a remote mining community such as Hope. Some winters come harder and faster than others, bringing with them more than mere cold and hardship, or the passing inconvenience of snow and ice.

The morning of October 11th, the body of a young boy, identified as Master Stephan Anderson, eldest son of a family of prospectors but recently arrived from Uppsala in Sweden, was discovered dead. The boy had apparently drowned by accident in the river, his body trapped beneath the ice.

Most of the prospectors maintain a fragile existence here, and for this correspondent, himself also but recently removed here from the relative comforts and security of Chicago, it was a timely indication of just how fragile a human life can be.

No one knows, or can guess at the cause of the accident, or even where or exactly when it may have occurred. By a terrible coincidence, the body was found by the boy's own father, after a prolonged search, instigated when the boy had not returned home the previous day.

His body, when found, had become trapped under a thick sheet of ice, formed at the edge of the lagoon below the town, close to where the river feeding it from the mountain enters.

No one has come forward to give any information that might explain this death, other than Mr Joshua Allenby, the town's cabinet-maker and undertaker. Mr Allenby said he had seen someone earlier that day, a person small enough to have been the child, in his estimation, walking on the path which led to the gold workings.

There is much conjecture as to what the boy's purpose in the mountains might have been. The currently held consensus is that, with the excitement about gold being so palpable, the boy hearing it discussed around him every day, and this being too the reason why his parents had brought him on what must have seemed to him a great adventure, the boy may have succumbed to the urge to try his own hand at prospecting. Being unfamiliar with the local terrain and its dangers, it is assumed he slipped on ice in the course of his searching and fell into the river. The parents have said the boy had never learned to swim.

As unexpected consequence of this accident, and through the helpful offices of said Mr Allenby, in his capacity as town undertaker, a most chilling and macabre necessity in such a winter-bound place was also brought to the attention of this correspondent. Beyond his two other professions, Mr Allenby holds a further position in the town, that of proprietor of an ice barn - a much appreciated establishment here in the heat of summer.

As the winters are so cold, Mr Allenby informed me, the ground is often frozen too hard for him to dig graves in which to bury the dead. As ghoulish expedient, when such a situation arises, the bodies are kept in the ice barn, awaiting burial until after the thaw of spring.

The Swedish Boy, Mr Allenby said, is the second body he will be required to store in this way this year, there having already been one other death since the cold of winter had arrived – that of a Miss Rosalind Pearce, who died recently under the most unpleasant and unfortunate circumstances.

As no suspicious circumstances are considered to pertain to the death of the boy, and as there is no identifiable site of death to search, the sheriff has made it known that no further investigations will be carried out.

A brief, informal service of remembrance has been arranged for this coming Sunday, despite the continued absence of any clergyman in Hope to officiate. Mr Allenby – something of a general *factotum* in the town it would appear - to give the readings. Thomas E Speake

7

The Mirror World

The alley was dark, lit only by the dim, reflected lamps of the buildings in the street at its open end. The other end was closed off by a sheer wall of rock that rose above the backs of the buildings forming its sides. The man lay on his back on the ground, his head pointing in the direction of the street, his legs half-hidden beneath the wooden foundations of one of the buildings, groaning and mumbling to himself in his broken sleep. His clothes were soiled and dishevelled, and his matted black hair and beard clung in greasy knots to the skin of his face.

"Jack? Jack Bunney? Is that you down there?" he heard someone calling softly.

He pushed his head round as far as he could and caught a glimpse of someone standing, motionless, just a little way into the alley, their inverted form silhouetted against the dull wavering light of the street behind. The face and the front of their body were cloaked in darkness. Breath, exhaled into the cold night air, billowed around the person's head in almost luminous clouds.

"Jack? Is that you?" the voice said again, still only a harsh whisper. "You know you could catch your death out here."

Bunney stirred, lifting his head half up from the ground, turning it again in the direction of the voice he thought he had heard calling his name. His eyelids fluttered open and closed against the feint light, straining to see who was there. At first he thought it might be his fiancée, Rosalind, but then he remembered that she was dead. A fox, its white winter coat stark against the dark wall of rock, ran across the closed end of the alley, disturbed from its foraging by the sounds of a human voice. Its eyes flashed two watchful flecks of blooded ice at him before being extinguished within the darkness.

"Sul...? Is tha...?" Bunney said, and then his head fell back to the ground. The other person came a few steps closer, moving deeper into the shadows of the alleyway.

"As if ya coul'n't tell it was me," Bunney mumbled almost incoherently to himself, and laughed out loud, and then he started to cough uncontrollably, his breath bursting from his mouth in thick jets of vapour. The spasm soon passed, and he settled again, although his head continued to roll rhythmically from side to side. The other person came closer and gently kicked him in the shoulder with the toe of their boot.

"Jack. Wake up. We need to talk," the man said, and kicked him again.

"Wha' d'ya wan'? Carn' ya let a man sleep? Sugar 'n' spice, an' all things nice, tha's wha' good li'l boys're..." Bunney croaked softly, attempting to sing along to some broken tune inside his head until diverted by another fit of violent coughing.

"I ain't said nothin', not to nobody," he said when he had finished coughing. "Had no time, no need for talkin'."

"You're right, Jack. There's no time left for that now. No more time for deals you had no right to make."

"Is that so?" Bunney said with disinterest, and began again to hum the broken tune. After a few seconds he stopped abruptly as something cold and hard and burning ran across the protruding rim of his windpipe.

"I reckon you know it is, Jack?" he heard someone say close by.

The skin of his throat felt suddenly warm, and he dipped his chin down to brush the unexpected warmth of it away. He started to giggle again as the tickling sensation, now rapidly turning cold, began to flow down the sides and back of his neck, then his eyes flicked open, and he stared up into the face of the darkened figure kneeling beside him. As the figure pulled away slightly from his unexpected movement, Bunney caught the traces of a sweet smell that conjured up memories from his childhood - of forested slopes, of his father splitting logs for firewood, the warmth and smell of embers in the grate. From the shadows beneath the brim of the hat they were wearing, the other's eyes stared back at him, cold and impassive, and then the mouth in the shadowed face cracked in a dark smile.

"You..." Bunney said, made clearheaded by the realisation that had come to him. Surprise, then resignation came into his own eyes as he continued to look up into the face peering down at him. He tried to remember the thing he had been told about staring at the bridge of the nose, but hard as he tried his eyes could not maintain their focus.

"Who would ha' thought it?" he said, and laughed. "You! And the crazy thing is, I can't even stop you, and..." He started to giggle, then pursed his lips and tried to raise the tips of his fingers to his mouth to stop himself, but his hand got no further than his chest before falling again to his side. "I'm so damn tired I can't move a muscle to stop you. Damn you. Damn you all."

He paused and then said more quietly, "And damn that damned Black Lady."

"You should have known how that goes, Jack. Even I know that. You should have known it was a mistake to push her so far."

"A mistake...? Yeah? Well, we all make some of...." He halted; his attention caught by the gleam of light reflecting from the shard of polished steel the man held close in front of his face.

"I guess it really is time for ol' Jack to go to sleep then," he said.

"I figure it is," the other said. "Say good-night, Samuel Bunney."

Samuel Jackson Bunney smiled, despite the sudden rush of pain in his throat. No one had said that to him since his mother had died, and that had been more than twenty years ago. A harsh, metallic taste filled his mouth. He tried to speak, to say good-night back, to say the habitual "God bless!" in reply, but the words only bubbled in his throat and frothed out of his mouth in a dark red foam which spattered on his face and spread and mingled in his beard and in the long, tangled mass of hair at the back of his neck. A flood of adrenalin, or alcohol, washed through his body, numbing his feelings, his thoughts.

A huge mirror appeared to loom up in front of him. In it, he could see himself reflected. He was clean-shaven and smartly dressed; he was smiling, and looked much younger. A beautiful young woman was standing at his side. She was wearing a black satin dress trimmed with crimson lace at the throat and wrists. As he tried to get up from the ground, to step into the mirror to enter that other world, all he was aware of - the sound of it more than the physical sensation - was his right foot kicking against the wooden foundations of the building, and the dark figure, who he was now certain was his mother, kneeling at his side.

"Goodnight, Jack," a fading voice said beside him. "No doubt I'll see you in my dreams."

8

The Swedish Boy

To his surprise Speake had discovered that most of the residents of Hope, despite a widely held and innate distrust of strangers, had been more than willing to talk about the lives they had led previously, the disappointments and deprivations that had brought them to this place. Some, though, however persistent his interrogation, had proved far less forthcoming, with even the most basic facts. Like Josh Allenby; like Brogan Sullivan, proprietor of the town brothel and saloon.

From their first meeting, Speake had not liked Sullivan, or trusted him. Although he had not previously thought himself a Puritan, he had found himself judging Sullivan's manner of livelihood as immoral and parasitic. He could find no other way to describe it; Sullivan made his money from the weaknesses of others - of the men whose needs he catered for, and of the women he used to gratify those needs. Speake had heard the story of Rosalind Pearce, several versions of it from all manner of sources, all surprisingly consistent - how Jack Bunney had gambled away her rights and her freedom in a game of cards; how Sullivan had put her to work at the saloon. He still found it hard to comprehend how any man, even one as patently disreputable as Sullivan, could have acted in such a way. He was surprised too that none of the other residents of Hope had tried to prevent it. As to the other perpetrator, Jack Bunney, he was dead now, slain by an unknown hand, and had therefore reaped the rewards of his iniquity.

Putting aside his disapproval, he had tried on several occasions to discover what might have motivated Sullivan. Beyond the damning reality of his position, he had always struck Speake as an intelligent and cultured man. Which only served to make his choices harder to understand. Speake had posed direct questions, tried to lead their few brief conversations, but the harder he had pressed, the more oblique Sullivan's responses had become, further deepening Speake's suspicions. So resolute a barrier put up by so normally gregarious a man seemed to indicate he had something to hide.

With most of the other inhabitants of Hope though, almost the opposite had prevailed. They had been almost too ready to tell him things he did not really want to know, to relate details which he would not want to, or could not use. It probably had to do, he thought, with the distance he had detected between them and himself; also sensing such difference, they appeared to have little hesitation in revealing their secrets to someone they did not consider one of their kind. Like talking to a stranger; or making confession to a priest. His education, his soft city manners, his accent, and possibly his patent vulnerability helped maintain his sense of otherness. All they sought from him, it seemed, was a sympathetic ear and the possibility, however remote, of some form of absolution through the telling of their stories.

Making his way back along the main thoroughfare of the town, returning from his trip to the ice barn, Speake had met Lucy Harrigan, one of the young women who worked in Sullivan's saloon. He had not been looking forward to returning to the boarding house. His room was cold and draughty and poorly lit, so cold the water sometimes froze overnight in the jug beside the washbasin. For furnishings, it was equipped only with a single trestle bed several inches too short for him, one rickety wooden chair, and a small table, equally rickety, on which he wrote. Since leaving the barn, the image of the frozen bodies had lingered in his thoughts. He needed distraction from the memory; the images of the open coffins, the lifeless faces inside them, would continue to visit him for days to come, that much he knew. He did not want to sit contemplating such things in a cold and unwelcoming room. The opportunity to talk with Lucy had offered the possibility of distraction and, he hoped, of providing answers to some of his questions.

Lucy was among those who had been happy to talk to him during the long, idle winter evenings when there had been nothing else to do, no more words to write, and no warmer place to be than in the saloon, nursing the single beer his restricted budget permitted. When business was slow Sullivan allowed the girls to do much as they pleased, and over the months Speake had developed what he felt was a more than casual friendship with Lucy. He had found her to be surprisingly sensitive for one in her situation, and that she spoke intelligently about her experiences, harrowing and unjust as they had often been. For her part, she had seemed to want to confide in him, or at least to an impartial outsider, and over the hours they had spent together, he had gradually come to understand some of the reasons for her palpable sadness.

While making their way west to a new life in the Pacific coast state of California, her parents, her younger sister and two brothers had all died of influenza, trapped inside their wagon without the aid of a doctor on the blizzard-bound plains of Wyoming. Lucy had somehow survived, the illness, the blizzards, the journey, leaving behind her family in un-marked graves in the middle of the prairie, and had eventually found herself in the town of Ogden on the shores of the Great Salt Lake. She was homeless, alone, and without money. The wagon master had taken the seed money he had been hold-ing for her parents for safe keeping. He had also taken their wagon and horses, with all of the wagon's contents, apart from her clothing, as payment for her continued passage to Ogden, and for 'incidental expenses' as he had called them. She had been too young to know how she might fight it.

At the age of four her leg had been broken, the thighbone, the result of a kick from a fractious horse. The break had not healed properly, and as a consequence she walked with a limp, and since the accident she had never been physically strong. The few jobs that had been on offer in Ogden, she had not had the strength or stamina to do. She had ended up begging for food, sleeping in barns, under boardwalks, in the backs of wagons, in back-alleyways, until a man - charming, assured, and persuasive, not unlike Brogan Sullivan - had found her, and had offered her a way to survive. Marriage he had called it, but from how she told it, it had been closer to slavery. She had been barely sixteen years old.

The man had dragged her, sometimes literally, from place to place, first to the ocean her family had been heading for, then north along the Pacific seaboard. The various ill-conceived ventures his soured imagination concocted along the way had barely made sufficient to meet their needs until, hearing of the riches supposedly to be plucked from the ground to the North, he had opted for what he considered a shorter route to fortune, and had eventually brought her to Hope. After a few weeks in the town, having soon come to the realisation that the best of the claims had been taken and that finding gold would require effort and hardship, he had abandoned her, taking off with a woman older and less pretty than Lucy, but who had prospered during the good years in running the boarding house where they had lodged. Sensing those times were ending, the woman had persuaded him to return with her to California, leaving Lucy with nothing but a small case of clothes and the few dollars she had kept sewn into the hem of her dress.

Finding herself again with no one to support or protect her, and with her damaged leg leaving her ill-equipped to do any other of the work available in such a town, the saloon had seemed the only option. She worked there now as one of Brogan Sullivan's hostesses, as Speake preferred to call them. She had wanted to wash, or cook or clean, or any other of the chores a woman could do without having to compromise her values, her dignity, but Sullivan had seen her otherwise. His offer of employment had not been open to negotiation - a condition, she had soon discovered, that would apply to almost every facet of her life. Now, to all intents, she belonged to Sullivan, and would probably remain in his thrall until he or his paying customers decided she could no longer earn her keep. Until he too moved on without her, leaving her again to fend for herself.

They had come to a halt in the middle of the otherwise deserted street. It had turned out to be a less bitter day than usual, though the temperature had remained below freezing. The winter mist had started to clear, but although the sun was now shimmering weakly through the hazed sky, at this time of year it barely rose above the surrounding horizon, and held no warmth. Speake kept his hands thrust deep into his pockets, his elbows tucked tight against his ribs for warmth. His suit, his shirt, his overcoat had always been too thin for the cold, even back in Chicago, and there had never been much fat on his slender frame. He did not have the money here to buy something more appropriate. The allowance he received covered no more than his food and a roof over his head, and the occasional indulgence of that consolatory beer.

Before he had set off his mother had tried to give him money to make his journey and his stay in Hope more comfortable. He had declined, maintaining against her insistence some high-minded notion of authenticity, having believed such privations would help feed his understanding, and kindle his imagination to write his stories from the perspective - in circumstances, if not in temperament or spirit - of his fellow journeymen. For the past month or more, since winter had really taken hold, his belief in such a notion had been seriously challenged.

A friend, Gillam Todd, had lent him a woollen tartan

waistcoat. Todd haled from Dumfries in Scotland, and was about the same age as Speake. They had arrived together in Hope on the same stagecoach, had become friends during the three days they had travelled together. Someone else, feeling unexpected pity for him, or perhaps playing a joke, had given him an old, moth-eaten coon-skin flap-eared hat, which he kept together and in place with a woollen shawl wrapped high around his neck and chin. The waistcoat had helped, as did the old newspapers stuffed into the lining of his overcoat, but he could still feel the cold creeping across the skin of his less well protected arms. Every few seconds a shiver writhed through his body and jolted his teeth.

As they walked together he had told her how the sight of Rosalind Pearce in her coffin, the realisation of how young and vulnerable she had been, had stirred his curiosity. There had been such excitement at the death of the Swedish boy at the time of his arrival that this other demise, horrific and noteworthy though it was, had already seemed old news to Speake. The story of the drowned boy had been the only story he had wanted to write. There had been more mystery about it than Rosalind Pearce's more sordid passing. But the memory of the blood-red bloom of the dead girl's lips, so vibrant, a vivid token of the life that had once coursed through her body, had renewed his interest. Lucy and she had slept under the same roof, eaten at the same table; endured the same profession, the same master, presumably the same clients from time to time, and Speake had been curious to hear her account of what had happened.

"Pretty much the same thing happened to me," Lucy said after a brief pause. "Not what she did. I had a miscarriage."

Her admission was no more disturbing than many others Speake had heard, but it surprised him.

"You never spoke of it before."

"No. It's kind of too personal to talk about to a…, and anyway, it makes me look stupid. I hadn't even known for sure I was pregnant. Or maybe I was only pretending to myself. It was not so long before Rosie…" She stopped abruptly.

The skin of her nose and cheeks was a mottled red against the pallor of the rest of her face, nestled in its collar of fur. The various sweeps of her thick blonde hair spilled out from the hood of her cape and broadened the angle of her cheekbones. Her eyes were blue, the most brilliant blue Speake had ever seen, an almost unnatural hue in a human body. While they had been talking, he had noticed she kept pushing a seemingly invisible strand from her face and glancing nervously over her shoulder towards the saloon. He found her uncertainty difficult to understand. Their meeting, their conversation was innocent enough, no more covert than their conversations in the saloon. She had told him nothing he had not already known, other than the revelation of her miscarriage.

"You're getting cold," he said. "You should go in." She looked over her shoulder again, considering his suggestion, and shook her head.

"It's all right. I've gotten used to it. It's odd how you get used to things you can't change." A glib smile, almost a grimace, creased the corners of her mouth.

"Let's at least go somewhere a little warmer." He led her with a hand laid gently against the back of her arm towards the boardwalk and together they mounted the steps to the porch outside the bakery. There was no-one inside the lamp-lit store. The cast-iron door to one of the ovens was open. Coals glowed hotly inside it, casting a dull red glow onto the polished floor boards. The interior of the shop looked bright and welcoming. There were pine kernels and seasonal sprigs of holly, yew and pine strewn on the windowsills around samples of the baker's wares, and a single cream coloured candle burned in each window.

"I come here sometimes just to warm up, and to torture myself with the smell of freshly baked bread," Speake said, pressing his back against the window. Lucy nodded and came to stand beside him, half turned towards him.

"It reminds me of home, when I was young," she said with a hint of sadness.

"Me too. The buns from our local bakery shop, topped with hard crystals of sugar. They were so good it's almost too painful to remember. I can't recall when I last tasted anything that good. But I'm sorry that you lost a child." Her lips curled down at the corners in dismissal.

"It's not important," she said. "It's over."

"Did Sullivan make you…?" She shook her head vigorously.

"No! Not that," she said firmly. "I couldn't do that. No, it was…" Her voice faltered. "Like I said, it was a miscarriage. Brogan and… I did some things I probably shouldn't have." A tear came to the corner of her eye, and she brushed it away with the cuff of her glove. "Damn cold. Some things you never can get used to," she said through a weak smile.

"Would it help to talk?" She shook her head again, more slowly.

"No, but thank you. We girls talk to each other about that

sort of thing, not that there's much to say. It sort of goes with the territory. Anyway, it's not my place to say. Brogan certainly wouldn't want me telling. The boy neither." Speake's eyes flicked up to meet hers.

"What boy?" he asked, trying to keep eagerness from his voice.

"Please. Forget I said anything. It's nothing. Just something that happened." Her voice had tightened, and she seemed distressed, as though she regretted the few words she had let slip.

"Please. Who was the boy, Lucy? I have to know."

"No, Mr Speake. You may *want* to know, but that's something different. Anyway, as I said, it's not my place to tell. It's their business too, not only mine."

"It could be important. This could be about a murder."

She waved away his words with her hand. "Oh, don't be exaggerating. Sometimes, you city types have way too much imagination. I got pregnant. I had a miscarriage. That's all there is to it. Better that than what happened to Rosie."

"Brogan didn't pressure you…?" he said, letting the other thing pass for now. "Was the child his?"

Lucy laughed and then shook her head. "No! You see Brogan only for what he is, what he does, and keep coming to the obvious conclusion. The fact is he doesn't really care for women, not in that way at least. Believe me, I should know. Men neither, in case you're wondering. He just isn't interested, though I believe there might have been someone. Someone who really hurt him. Now, for him, it's business, nothing more." She paused for a moment, a pensive expression on her face.

"Maybe us girls are his way of getting revenge. Some revenge, eh?"

"People react in unpredictable ways. He doesn't seem to have much respect for women, that much I can see. But..."

"He's not so bad. You shouldn't be so judgemental about things you don't fully understand. For me, the other girls, it's about making the best of a bad situation. Respect doesn't come into it. We all left that behind long ago. Brogan knows what he is, and if it wasn't him it'd be someone else, someone who would probably treat us much worse than he does. How long do you think someone like me would last out here, without someone like him?"

"Well, you could find yourself a husband."

Lucy laughed again, a short, bitter laugh. Her gloved hands, balled into fists, went to her hips, and she frowned at him.

"Are you flirting with me...? Anyway, I tried one of those remember. It didn't work out too well. I suppose, come to think of it, I'm still married to him. He never did divorce me. Maybe one day they'll hang the bastard for bigamy." Speake laughed too, and looked down at his boots scuffing at the wooden boardwalk, trying to conceal his embarrassment. He noticed the parlous state the boots were in, adding to his discomfiture. They had not been polished in weeks.

"No. I'm sorry. I didn't mean... Not that you're not..."He laughed again, and then something caught his attention out of the corner of his eye. On the other side of the street the German boy was leaning on his forearms on the railing in front of one of the stores. He was staring across the street at them, apparently unconcerned as to whether they noticed. There was no question where his gaze was directed. Speake raised his hand to acknowledge him, but as he did, the boy stood up and walked away.

"Now, there's a strange one." He nodded in the direction of the boy who, as he walked away was leaping up from the boardwalk to break icicles from the eaves of the canopy in front of one of the stores.

"Who is...?" She half turned to follow where Speake was looking. "Oh, young Dortmund? Can't say I know him too well. Brogan seems to like him though," she said casually, though Speake detected a darkening, like a fleeting memory of something painful, slip momentarily across her face. He sensed a defensiveness he had never felt from her before.

"Anyway, forget about him," she said brightening, and stepping closer to him. "I believe we were talking about flirting."

"Oh, yes. Well...you know what I mean," he said. She reached out, and the tips of her gloved fingers brushed the cuff of the sleeve of his overcoat.

"I know what you mean," she said gently. "Why would a man like you want to be seen with a girl like me?"

"No. It's not.... You've always been really kind, and I do find you attractive, and I know you're a good person, despite..." He gestured vaguely with his head and shoulders in the direction of the saloon. "That's not what you are. And I would... I mean, I do. It's just the situation with the money. I wouldn't want to have to pay to... For us to be together." Lucy laughed out loud, and a broad smile split her face. Her reaction surprised and delighted him. She was normally so restrained, so small and tightly contained within herself.

"Oh, I see. It'd be all right so long as it was for free."

"No! You know I didn't mean that. I meant, I don't think you should be something to be bought and sold. If we did…you know…I would want it to be something we both wanted."

"Why, Mr Speake, I do believe you *are* flirting with me!" she cried.

"Yes, I do believe I am. And you can call me Thomas if you like," he said, and looked down at his shoes again to hide his embarrassment.

"Can I now? Well, we'll have to see about that," he heard her say. When he looked up she was smiling at him, and the extremities of her face were even more flushed than before, then her smile faded, and she glanced quickly again over her shoulder in the direction of the saloon.

"I have to go," she said, lifting her skirts and starting to back away. "Are you coming to the party tonight? It sure is something, isn't it, a whole new century beginning? It makes you just want to wipe the slate and start all over again. Will you be coming?"

Speake nodded. "Yes. I'll be there."

"And will you dance with me?"

"Of course… If it's for free!"

Lucy laughed. "We'll have to see about that too," she said. "Just think, though. To start all over, maybe get it right this time. Wouldn't it be something?" She twisted her head to one side and looked at him, appraising him, smiling warmly as she stepped backwards away from him, down the wooden steps and into the street. She waved a few times in a child's way, flapping stiff, outstretched fingers at him, before turning and running in her hobbled manner towards the saloon. Speake watched her go, feeling his own face aglow with excitement, until she had vanished into the saloon.

A Violent and Bloody Murder

Hope, November 28th 1899

Early on the morning of 19th November, the body of the former town grocer, Mr. Samuel Jackson Bunney was discovered by a group of prospectors as they made their way to work in their mines. On closer inspection it became evident that Mr. Bunney had been murdered. His throat had been cut.

One of the discoverers of the body, a Mr. Jonas Ansell, originally from near Wexford in Ireland, said that he and his companions had not thought too much of it when first they saw Mr. Bunney apparently asleep beneath the footings of one of the buildings. Of late, Mr. Bunney had fallen on hard times, having reputedly lost everything in gambling, and had taken seriously to drinking, and it had become a not unusual thing to see his prone figure displayed at some location about the town at any hour of the day.

Only when they had called out to him and received no answer, and once one of their numbers had delivered a kick to his shoulder without evincing a response, did they come to think something might be amiss.

It was at this point, Mr. Ansell said, that they noticed the quantities of Mr. Bunney's blood that had been shed from the wound to his throat. Once his true condition had been made apparent, they immediately dispatched one of their numbers to inform the town sheriff. A doctor was also summoned, but on his arrival the victim was pronounced to have been several hours dead.

Who could have perpetrated this cowardly crime is not known, nor do the authorities have any indication of what the motive for the killing might have been? Such acts of random violence are not uncommon in a wild and remote community such as this, and too often it transpires that the culprits get away, their guilt undetected.

Mr. Bunney was generally reported as having been well-liked, and to have been usually of a friendly disposition, despite the possibly contrary indication of his latterly more unruly life and habits. He therefore had no known enemies, although rumours have been voiced of a long-running feud between himself and Mr. P. Brogan Sullivan, an established and well-respected member of the community. The feud, reportedly, had been in regard to Mr Bunney's involvement with a young woman who had formerly been in the employment of Mr. Sullivan, and who had died some weeks previously under the most disagreeable circumstances.

At the moment of writing there is no official suspicion of Mr. Sullivan being involved in any way in the crime.

The main weight of suspicion has fallen instead upon an outsider, a rough and travel-hardened drifter who had arrived in the town the previous day, a conjecture first voiced by the town undertaker, Mr. Joshua Allenby when he came to collect the body for storage in the ice barn. The man had given his name only as Stone, and for the few hours he spent here had kept himself much to himself. Further suspicion was added to his name when later that morning he was found to have departed secretly without giving reason. A bill at the hostelry where he had lodged had also remained unpaid – in truth, a far from unusual circumstance.

A search party has been sent out, acting on the intimation of Mr Allenby, to try to discover and apprehend the man and bring him back to Hope to account for his actions on the night of the murder, and to pay his dues at the hostelry.   TES

9

A Memory of Fire

"And two of your best bobbins," the customer said. Her voice was tight and flat; it carried no warmth and little respect. Mrs Emilie Arthur Henderson looked up at her and smiled. It was the smile she gave to every woman who came into the store, irrespective of her demeanour; the smile she gave to everyone she met outside on the street. It came to her face automatically, without having to think. Almost without having to move a muscle in her face.

"It's getting that time of year again, and I'm going to have to make some new mats for the table for Christmas," Mrs Leonora Thaik, the customer, continued. "I don't know how they get the way they do. They get worn out so quickly. It must be something to do with the water round here, don't you think?"

"I'm sure I don't know about that, Mrs Thaik, but you may be right," Emilie replied politely.

She slid open the drawer with the word "Bobbins" written neatly on a paper card pinned to its front. Inside the drawer, the bobbins were all arrayed neatly too, laid out row upon row from left to right according to size. Her husband, Mr Arthur Henderson, was nothing if not an orderly man. The store, and everything in it, was a testament to the orderliness, to the rigidity of his mind. Everything had to be in its right place (even Emilie, she often thought), each with its accompanying paper label written out clearly in Mr Henderson's cramped yet orderly script. She sometimes wondered where her own label was, but whenever she did she would find herself fingering the plain gold band on her finger. She looked down at the array of bobbins in the drawer and thought they looked like neatly arranged rows of anaemic turds.

"Which size would you like?" she asked, again dispensing her practised smile.

"Oh, I think the two-inch ones will do." Emilie smiled again.

Emilie did not like Mrs Thaik. The woman was the mirror of everything she despised about herself. She too was someone's wife, a possession, no more than an extension of the ego of some single-minded man. There was nothing else to her, no substance of her own. She too mouthed the right words, did the right things, made the right gestures, and always at the right times and places, whenever it was required. Perhaps, Emilie thought, given such an understanding, she ought to feel sympathy for the woman, not disdain. But no, now that she thought about it, she really did not like her. She was an interfering busy-body, always opining on other people's business, though Emilie realised this was perhaps no more than an outpouring of a more boisterous spirit held corseted within her given identity as some man's wife. But whatever her reason or excuse, Mrs Thaik knew and said far too much, about everybody and everything that was really none of her concern. There had always been at least one like her wherever Emilie had lived, and Hope, though it was different in every other aspect from anywhere else she had ever been, was no exception.

"Is there anything else I can get you?" she asked, struggling to keep the words she was aching to say held inside her as she wrapped the bobbins in a sheet of brown paper. At that moment there was the sound of a sharp impact against the window as a small bird flew against it and tumbled in a confused flurry of wings onto the sill.

"Oh my," Mrs Thaik said, her hand coming up to her mouth. "You know, it fair made my heart jump. Poor little mite. Do you think it's hurt?"

"It should have flown south a long time ago. It won't live much longer either way," Emilie said coldly, giving voice to the jealousy welling up inside her on hearing the words of sympathy the plight of the bird had evoked. No one ever gave that amount of consideration to her. Mrs Thaik looked shocked, as though she couldn't believe the harsh words she had just heard on Emilie Henderson's lips.

"Come now, dear," she said. "You don't mean that. It's only a poor little creature." Emilie said nothing, offered only the semblance of a smile in reply.

She began to wonder whether her life had always been so small, so bereft of meaning. It certainly felt that way, the years that had passed, the opportunities that had gone with them, driven from her reach by the strength of her own fears, her own cloying sense of propriety. All those years of being married to a man she did not love: a good man, a man she respected mostly, though one who had not been able to give her the things she longed for, who had offered her only trust and respect in return, and his own sense of soul deadening order. There had not even been the consolation of children. Then perhaps their being together might have had some meaning. As it was, her life stretched out behind her like a barren, featureless plain. Ahead, the only future she could see was the same bleak geography of despair, now endlessly cold and dark and snow-bound.

In ten days' time the world would be heralding the start of a new century. It would be a time of great change, of transition; at least that was what everybody said. Everyone was already celebrating what they anticipated would be the broadening of the very fabric of their existence. A boundary in their lives was about to be crossed, they proclaimed, as though in unison, making Emilie feel even more alone. The future would bring a new Utopia, a new beginning. The old, useless things of the past would wither and perish, and better things would rise in their place.

The thought of yet another boundary to be crossed - of another barrier encircling her life - only filled Emilie with dread. The crossing of such thresholds, she suspected, served as a talisman only in lives that were already proceeding satisfactorily along a straight and definite path. Her own life was coiled up upon itself like an ever-tightening spring. She was coming to count herself amongst the old and useless things, the things that by right should be discarded as the new century began.

She had been young once, strong-willed and carefree as only the young and ingenuous can be. She had been able to see her life mapped out in front of her, straight and well defined. Now she could barely imagine what it would be like to be the person she had once been. She knew she had felt alive then, that the whole world had lain at her feet, waiting to be gathered up, to be tasted of and savoured. That had been in Chicago, back in '71, just before the fire. She had been married for little more than a year. Her husband was handsome, charming and successful, though in a small, uninspiring way, and it was already obvious to her, to her family and friends that he lacked any real ambition. He had been content enough, as he was still, with his store, with his perfectly balanced account books and his regular customers, his beautiful wife. She had had money of her own then, an inheritance from an aunt in Boston, which had at least given her some degree of independence. She had had friends and family close by. She had been respectable.

Everyone had said it was a perfect marriage. But all she could see back there was a naïve and innocent child - a child who had been both fascinated and dazzled by the attraction she obviously held for men other than her husband, and by the power over them it seemed to bestow. Such power had simultaneously intoxicated and frightened her. She had craved to exercise it, but had known already that such exercise would bear a price. Men would only allow themselves to be placed in its thrall for so long, then they would demand recompense for their perceived abasement. Then they would demand their pound of flesh. She had therefore elected to use that power sparingly; had deployed it always with a sense of trepidation. She had often had to force herself to ignore its strident voice, had constantly shepherded it away, until eventually it had turned back upon itself, and had become little more than a brooding shadow of discontent hovering in the wings of her life, constantly threatening disaster.

Josh Allenby had been a handsome man back then, before he had taken to smoking that old pipe, before he had lost most of his hair, and his back had stooped, and his teeth had rotted. Then he had worked only as a carpenter; a man beneath her station, she knew, prone to a coarseness of manner and voice, but a cabinet-maker of some skill and repute. His work had been much in demand; he had made beautiful cabinets, and beds, and tables and chairs, picture-frames, their surfaces deeply polished and finished with in-laid woods and mother-of-pearl. Then he had been proud to call himself a craftsman, had not yet thought of turning his hand to making cabinets for the dead.

The thought of those teeth now made her shudder. They went too well with his latterly chosen profession, like tombstones sinking into the mouldering earth of his gums. The only kiss they had ever shared (when she had thought he might be the one to save her), his breath had smelled of lavender, and his hands and hair had carried the scents of wood-resin and glue. She still did not understand why she should have even considered such a possibility – a fleeting submission to that intoxication? A desperate reaction against the stilted world she felt closing in around her?

It was Brogan Sullivan though who had turned out to

be the one she had always dreamed of, though she had not known it then, certainly not on the night she had let Josh Allenby kiss her. Josh had come close, but she had known even before their lips had met that he was not the one she dreamed of. The one she dreamed of still.

She remembered the night of the New Year's Ball in Chicago. The memory of it was deeply engraved, and re-called too often in her thoughts - the chandeliers, the marble fire-places, the amber glow of the polished wood floor in the candlelight; the music and dancers, the patent embarrass-ment of the handsome, brash young man who too publicly declared his feelings for her, an already married woman; the disapproving glances of the middle-class grandees and matrons of Chicago all around them. Had he really talked to her about the moon reflecting on the snow and water, the silent beauty of the winter nightscape, or had that been only her imagination embroidering, during all the lonely, hopeful years that followed, on the few indiscreet words he had said to her? Whatever it was he had said, she had thought him romantic.

They had fought over her back then, Brogan and Josh. She thought they would probably be fighting over her now - now that Brogan, almost thirty years on, had suddenly decided to reinsert his presence in her life - if Josh hadn't grown too old to fight. Brogan was ten years younger, at least, and he still kept in good condition. She had been surprised, as she was to this day, that Brogan hadn't killed him back in Chicago. She knew he had pulled a gun on him once, towards the end when things had been getting out of hand, before she had managed to persuade her husband they should move on and try their luck out west.

The great fire had confirmed her decision; it had been like a sign from some higher power. It had wiped them out - the store, with all the bolts of fabrics, the threads and yarns, the wooden bobbins, all those neat paper labels, had gone up in smoke in a matter of minutes. One moment they had been comfortable, almost prosperous, the next they had found themselves owning only their lives and whatever they could carry, wallowing for survival in the unruly stream of similarly disenfranchised souls who struggled northwards against the wind along Wells Street to escape the groaning maw of the fire.

They had spent that first night and the next camped out with fifty thousand others on the edge of the prairie, beyond the old cemetery, watching the red sky boil and reel above the city, as a rain of glowing ash and embers settled amongst the wooden markers of the graves. And then finally, like blessed relief, the real rain had come, extinguishing the fire, the last seared remnants of her dreams. The city they had known had perished; a desolate landscape of charred rubble, of fractured remnants of walls and arches, their windows blind and glass-less, and the proud, ironic gesture of the intact chimney of the new pumping station were all that remained.

But something else had burnt out inside her too, and it wasn't just because they had had to use her aunt's money to start again, and that with the money had gone the last vestige of her independence. Something more vital had died in her too. Now there was but a spark of her former self; a flicker-ing ember, which flared up from time to time and gave to her soul just sufficient warmth to keep her going. It was the only thing left which gave her the strength to put one foot in front of the other, and to resurrect that practised smile across the gradually falling features of her face whenever it was required.

"Are you all right, my dear? You don't look too well," she heard a voice say. When she focused her thoughts she saw Mrs Thaik looking into her face, her head tilted to one side like an inquisitive bird. The other bird huddled motionless now on the sill. She could see its sides moving fitfully as it breathed, unless that was only the movements of the wind giving it a semblance of living.

"Yes. I'm fine. I'm sorry," she said, collecting herself. "I was just thinking of something that happened a long time ago. Were you ever in Chicago?"

"No, can't say I ever was. We came up from further south. Woodsville, Carolina. My family has lived there for four generations. I hear it's amazing what they've done there though, all those wonderful new buildings they're making. Twenty storeys high I hear some of them are. I wonder where they get their ideas."

Emilie shook her head. She had no more idea than Mrs Thaik how those who had stayed had managed to resurrect themselves and their ravished city from such a disaster. She envied them their strength, their courage and imagination. Their aspiring audacity set against her debilitating despair, though not their decision to remain.

The truth was Chicago had not been big enough for her to hide in. Not from Josh, whose flame for her had still burned strongly amidst the fading embers. Not from Brogan, or from the passions which had flared up briefly between them, but which on her side at least would forever refuse to be extinguished. Not from herself. She had thought the wilderness, the untamed land she had entered for the first time that night camped out beside the cemetery, would be vast enough for her to hide in. But she had been wrong. When they had left Chicago, Josh Allenby had followed them, always at a distance, a remove of several months, a year or two, tracking them from place to place, or so it had appeared to her, though whether by accident or design - a stubborn refusal to accept that she had no feelings for him - she still did not know for certain.

"Just following my nose for business," he had offered as explanation, the one time she had challenged him, when she had first started to find his persistent presence too strong a reminder of all she had lost. He had been proved astute enough in his bland declaration; there had been deaths aplenty in the several frontier towns - Bismark, Regina, Moose Jaw - they had lived in as they had moved gradually north and west. At least her husband had always accommodated her in that, moving on, starting anew whenever she had asked, each town less civilised, less in need than the previous one of the finer goods they had formerly offered. Never had he questioned her reasons, although he must have had suspicions, and over the years he had reduced his own contact with Josh to no more than a courteous nod whenever they met. It was the only thing her husband had ever been able to satisfy her in.

Allenby, the artless undertaker he had become, had flourished in all of those places, following her, haunting her, dealing in wood and death, and had slowly grown old.

Then, the summer before last, Brogan Sullivan too had appeared in Hope, and had set up his brothel and saloon, resurrecting the old triangle of heightened emotions. Had his arrival there been deliberate, she had often debated with herself since, driven by the same hidden motivations as Josh Allenby, or no more than fortuitous? There were certainly reasons enough for him to have come to such a place, given the type of man he had become. She almost did not recognise him; the halting self-assurance of the young man she had known having been transformed into arrogance and disdain. The detached sense of entitlement he exuded in regard to everything he wanted to have. Did he harbour that same anticipation of proprietorship over her, she wondered? If so, it was something she had found herself wanting, as demeaning and disempowering as she recognised it would be. When she had confronted him, he too had offered the same bland excuse as Josh, though not, she had found herself wanting to believe, with the same conviction.

"Where there's hardship, there's always the need for physical comfort," he had said cynically, and when it came to physical comfort, it was clear Brogan Sullivan knew what other men wanted, and how much they would be willing to pay. The real reason for his being there - his own need for comfort in the alienating world he had created for himself - she believed she could still see burning strongly in his eyes. But something, she had no idea what, stopped him from either taking that comfort or offering it to her. Whenever she went out in the one street in this dead-end place where everyone could see you, could spectate upon your every movement and reaction, she always had the feeling he amongst them all was watching her the most closely; as though he too was remembering, and longing for a renewal of the feelings they had briefly shared.

Still, in the time he had been there he had done nothing. He had simply watched and waited, and the months had passed, damning her heart with every moment of his impotent presence. Now her only recourse was to wonder whether what she saw in his eyes as he watched was indeed longing, or regret at the thing he had let pass, or simply a creation of her own thwarted desire.

The long winter nights up here were depressing. They never seemed to end. She often despaired of winter ever becoming spring. It seemed to go on forever, the long, dark nights concentrating her thoughts on her feelings of isolation. It had got so bad she had tried once before, in the darkest days of the previous winter, to end it herself, to put an end once and for all to all seasons, to all time.

She had struck the match. It had spluttered and flared. She had only to let it drop; the heap of fabric at her feet would have caught in an instant. A few moments of agony - the accumulated pain and anguish of her life condensed into one searing instant - then it would have been over. She, Mrs Emilie Henderson, would have been over. The store, the neatly labelled order that wound tightly about her like thread around a bobbin, restraining her, all of it would have been over. All that would have remained would have been the ashes of a prolonged and barren life - just one more burnt-out place for Mr Arthur Graham Henderson to impose his suffocating sense of order upon. At least then there would have been one less thing for him to ensure was correctly labelled and in its proper place.

She had not been able to do it. She had not had the strength, or her soul had not yet been suffused with sufficient despair to overcome its fear. The match had sputtered out in her fingers. She had had to make up a story to explain the burns. That had been in the January past, and she had somehow survived the crisis. She had fought against and driven her demons out into the deeper recesses of the unrelenting monotony where they had lingered, calling out to her mournfully like the wolves prowling the edges of the forest, until the respite of spring had finally come. This year though, the winter was colder, darker, and longer than any she had ever known.

The bell above the door rang, rousing her from her memories, dragging her back to the ingrained familiarity of the store. She knew by heart the sequence of sounds the door made as it opened - the turn of the handle, the grate of the tenon against the door-plate, the brush of the door across the mat, the moment of silence and the chill breath of wind intruding before the spring finally clicked over and the bell began its rattle. She thanked God that her husband kept the hinges well oiled.

She hated that sequence of sounds. Of all the things in the store she hated, she hated that the most. Even more than she hated Mr Henderson. It was the signal for her to become enmeshed once more in the sterile life he had shaped for her; to become Mrs Henderson, milliner's wife, to put away her private thoughts, and assume this cheerful, considerate persona she had adopted to keep herself from going crazy, to fool the world into thinking she was not going crazy, when all she wanted was to scream.

"Good morning Mrs Henderson. How are you today? It's turned cold again, hasn't it?" the new customer said.

It was Ruth Addison. Emilie did not really like her either. She was always complaining about one thing or another. In fact, now she thought about it, there wasn't anybody in this place she liked. Not her husband. Not Josh. Not even Brogan, not any more.

The only one she had the slightest time for was Speake, the young Englishman from Chicago. He at least appeared to be interested in her as a person, in the story she might have to tell. She had considered telling him everything, the story of her and Josh and Brogan, the lives their various passions had caused them to lead. But she was too embarrassed to admit the truth of it to anyone. There was something about him though. Something in the lean cut of his body, the lines in his face when he frowned or smiled; the bright depth of his eyes, blue-grey, like sun-lit ice, that reminded her of Brogan. The distant, younger, more romantic Brogan she had loved. She wondered now how she could ever have loved him, this man who made his living from negotiating the temporary possession of women - women who, beneath their loose morals and their brash, tawdry surface were not so very different from herself, from the person she had once been.

To have been young, innocent, romantic, to have been desirable; to have desired. To have been eager to experience, to share in true passion, if only for an instant, and to then expire. Those had been her only crimes, her seditious wishes. Why had she been made to pay so dearly?

She had asked herself the same question a thousand times of late, and had arrived always at the same uncomfortable conclusion: that Brogan Sullivan was a parasite, had probably always been so. From what she had learned of him over the past months, he had spent the best part of his adult life preying on others, and his being here now was, in essence, in respect of her own self no different. Now he had become a parasite on her soul. Set against the arid certainty of knowing their passion would never be consummated, his presence had sucked her dry. The only saving grace she could assign to him was that whatever he had done in respect of her it had been for something other than for money. For what: for love of her? She doubted it. If so, she could not envisage what shape, what texture that love might have. Still, whatever his motivation had been, the nature of the feelings behind it, it had left her empty, drained of everything she had once held precious.

Mrs Addison coughed, startling Emilie from her thoughts.

"Yes, isn't it? I couldn't be better," she heard herself answer mechanically, and felt the practised smile as it twitched across her face. "And yourself, and the family?" she added flatly.

"Oh, I'm fine, but the little ones have come down with the cold, and Jack's started to complain about his back again. It always gets worse in the winter, what with the damp and cold. I don't think mining and him were really cut out for each oth…"

"I'm so sorry to hear that, Mrs Addison. Still, only three more days and it'll be Christmas. Then there's the New Year, the big one this year. It'll be exciting for the children," she offered. It wasn't enough, she knew it; everyone expected more of her than that. Her words sounded flat, insincere.

"So, what can I get for you today? I'm sorry, but we don't have any new backs in stock for your husband," she added, unable to resist the urge to sarcasm, to experience just once how it felt. She could feel herself staring at Mrs Addison, her face a blank. She knew she was being rude, but she no longer cared. Ruth Addison looked confused, and then decided the best thing she could do was laugh.

"Oh, not much today," she said nervously. "I just needed some bobbins to make some lace."

The little bird began again to flap and rattle its wings softly against the windowpane, trying to escape the cold, trying to breach the invisible boundary that prevented it from getting in. Emilie stared at it, wondering why it should be so desperate to enter. What nameless comfort did it think her neatly labelled world had to offer, other than the basic necessity of physical warmth? At that moment the blur of a figure hurried past in front of the window. It was the Dortmund boy, hunched and huddled against the cold. He crossed quickly to where the bird was sitting, and without looking into the shop, picked it up gently and turned and bore it off cupped within the warming embrace of his hands.

Emilie felt envious. To be born away. To be succoured and comforted. It was all she desired.

"I do swear that boy's going native," Emilie heard Ruth Addison say, though she was not really paying attention to what the woman was saying, only that she was rambling on in her usual judgemental way.

"Always fussing over animals and the like, going off on his

own into the forest. I hear he's building a cabin somewhere up there. And the length of his hair, pretty as it is. I wish to God my girls had hair that pretty. What must his parents be thinking, letting him behave that way?"

"I really couldn't say. You said you wanted bobbins for your lace?" Emilie heard someone else say. It sounded much like her own voice, but it sounded too tired, too old to have really been hers. She thought her own voice should have sounded more vibrant, more alive; more like the voice of a child.

Emilie opened the drawer labelled "Bobbins", and stared down at the rows of dun-coloured turds she saw there, arranged neatly, row upon row according to size. She caught her breath, and then smiled - an innocent, unselfconscious smile she had not allowed herself to use for almost thirty years. She nodded to herself, and her hand moved slowly to the counter, encircling the box of matches her husband always kept beside the till. Her fingers fluttered momentarily over the box, then she slid it from the counter and put it in her apron pocket, and without saying a word she turned and walked out to the storeroom at the rear of the shop. Behind her, she heard what some small part of her still recognised as an offended tutting, the hollow sounds of foot-steps receding across the floor-boards, the irritating jangle of the bell; the door to the store being opened and then slamming closed.

The storeroom was dark, but she did not need to light the lamps; she knew by heart precisely where everything was kept. She pulled out a bolt of the finest satin they had and threw it out across the floor, then gathered it together and began to wrap it loosely around her booted ankles, her legs, up around her waist and chest, and finally around her shoulders. When she had finished she crumpled up the last few yards of material and threw it towards where the bolts of other fabrics were kept in their regimented racks against the wall. The thread of fabric snaked across the floor, a slick iridescent fuse.

There was no urgency in what she was doing; her hands and feet were moving of their own volition. For the past few minutes, she had been largely unaware of her actions, had instead been retracing in her thoughts the long journey that had brought her to this place. Back through all the frontier towns, those temporary havens on her onward flight to this nowhere; back to the moment when Brogan had appeared again, an apparently redeeming light on the dimming horizon of her life; back through all the unrequited moments of need and desire.

Now that journey was coming to its end, both in her thoughts and in the world at large. Her century, the half of it she had known, the too weighted years that had shaped and framed her existence were drawing to an end. Her mind, her being was back in Chicago, long before Brogan, long before the fire.

She felt contented finally, as though she had regained an almost forgotten and comforting place she had never wanted to leave. She felt as though she was about to be born again, set free in some way to start over again, like the townspeople and their expectations of the approaching century. She stood, watching intently, as before her a tiny, indefinite figure emerged from the flickering amber light which seemed now to be rising all around her, turning the familiar streets and buildings of Chicago, the interior of the shop - the old shop, the one in Chicago, the well-groomed faces passing outside the window, the flattened steel of the lake beyond, the arching sky above - to the colour of gold. As the figure drew closer, she saw that it was a child; a carefree female child who she thought she recognised, who she was certain she had once known, and whose companionship she feared she had lost forever.

The child smiled. She held something cupped in her hands in front of her heart. Emilie could not make out what she was holding. The child peered down into the receptacle of her hands, then turning away, she threw them up and away from her, and from between her opened palms a small bird rose up and flew off into the golden sky. The child turned back and smiled at her again, and called out to her in a voice she could not hear. She beckoned for Emilie to join her, then started to spin and dance and play amongst the flames as they rose rapidly all around her, engulfing her in a redeeming flare of brightness as it steadily devoured Mr Arthur G. Henderson's millinery store and every precious thing it contained.

10

The Swedish Boy

With Lucy gone, Speake still did not feel like returning to his room. He still expected the ghosts from the barn to come seeking him there once he was on his own. The prospect of dancing with Lucy later that evening, the anticipation, the dream of a New Year's kiss from her had excited him; he did not want that feeling to be dispelled by morbid thoughts.

He realised he was hungry. The hike to the barn, the tantalising smells from the bakery, the fact he had not eaten since supper the previous evening were all combining to make his stomach rumble in complaint. Turning back to the bakery to buy something to assuage his hunger, he caught sight of his reflection in the window. What he saw dismayed him; a virtual stranger looked back at him, dishevelled and unkempt, like a prospector, a backwoodsman. He lifted up his arm and sniffed the sleeve of his coat. It smelled sour, like turned milk. He was aware he had let himself go over the past few weeks, though he had not realised he had slipped so far. Tonight, he wanted to make a good impression. Looking at his reflection, he found it hard to understand what Lucy might see in him. An eligible man was not what he appeared to be. A not entirely sane one either. He would have to tidy himself up, both for her and to greet the century on a more positive footing. As she had said, it was a new beginning; a chance to let go of the past and start again.

There was an argument going on inside Jack Bunney's old store. As he approached, chewing on the last of the half-loaf of bread he had purchased in the bakery, Speake could hear raised voices, could see Sullivan and Allenby squaring up to one another inside the shop.

The manager of the store, a hesitant, putty-faced Austrian named Boehme, was standing behind them, trying to distance himself from the confrontation behind the handle of his broom. Belinda Curtis, another of Sullivan's ladies from the saloon, was also hovering around the two men, attempting to distract them. They ignored her intrusions and continued to shout at each other, standing with their faces but inches apart. Speake thought they looked ridiculous, two grown men, sparring like roosters.

His face still felt flushed from his parting exchange with Lucy. He was concerned someone might notice his agitated state, and he thought for a moment about walking away. He did not want to get involved in an argument, or to have his good mood dispelled by some probably pointless squabble. Even the hovering ghosts seemed a less disheartening prospect, but the need to do something about the way he looked outweighed his concerns.

"I ain't told him nothin', leastways, not concernin' you," he heard Allenby shout as he stepped up from the street to the boardwalk in front of the store. "Not that there'd be a whole lot to tell him now, would there?"

"You lying toad. You'd make up anything just to drag me down," Sullivan retorted.

"An' maybe that don't need too much imaginin'," Allenby spat back as Speake put the last of the bread in his mouth, turned the handle, and pushed open the door. The bell clanged harshly as the door swung open, and the two men turned to face him, their mouths slightly open, like school-boys caught in mischief.

"Well, talking of the devil," Sullivan muttered almost inaudibly, backing away from Allenby, his voice weighted with disdain. Speake pushed the door closed behind him. As he turned to face them the contrast between the cold outside and the warmth of the store made him shiver and clap his hands. It was an automatic response, and like the bell, it drew attention to him more than he would have preferred.

"Good day to you, Mr Speake. It's good to see you," Belinda said, her voice overly fawning, as she shuffled rapidly towards him, the hems of her skirts hissing across the saw-dusted floor. Coming to his side, she looped her arm through his. The smallness of her hand, the insignificance of its touch, surprised him; it nestled so lightly in the crook of his arm he could barely feel it.

"We haven't seen you in the saloon the past few days."

Speake shrugged his shoulders apologetically. "What can I say? I don't have the money for..." He left the sentence unfinished. He did not know how he should describe the distractions the saloon undoubtedly had to offer, that other world which he had no idea how to fully enter. While there, he was little more than a spectator, a tentative, disoriented explorer at best. He could feel the soft warmth of Belinda's breast, far more insistent than that of her doll's hand, pressing pleasantly against his upper arm. Her sudden familiarity surprised him. Until now she had not shown much interest in him or his questioning. Whenever he had tried to talk to her she had always claimed other things to do, and he had always felt she was trying to avoid him.

"Looking for a present for someone special?"

"No. I only came in for wax and laces for my boots," he added feebly, and looked down automatically at his feet. As the others followed his gaze, he again regretted his reflexes.

His boots were covered in dried mud and dust, and the leather was starting to crack and lift. He had not had the inclination to clean them for weeks. The boot-wax he had brought with him had soon run out, and by then the effort had hardly seemed worth it. Every morning, though, when he had put them on, he had heard the echo of his father's voice declaiming: "Keep your boots clean and you're as good as any man." Was such homily, he wondered, the only wisdom or guidance he would inherit from him?

"Best give the man his wax, Oscar," Sullivan said quietly to the manager. "Looks like those boots could use some sustenance before they curl up and die of thirst," Sullivan added, with no amusement in his voice, and his face a placid board of indifference. He and Allenby had now drifted apart. Allenby was standing stiff and erect by the door, his neck and shoulders twitching occasionally in agitation, staring out of the window. He made a hawking sound, and turned his head towards Sullivan as though he was going to spit.

"Well, go on then. Ask him," he mumbled instead over his shoulder.

"Josh, please." Sullivan glanced at Allenby and then almost apologetically at Speake, and took a step towards where Speake and Belinda were standing, still locked arm in arm. "I apologise on Mr Allenby's behalf," he said.

"It's your own doin's need apologisin' for," Allenby commented sourly. Sullivan glanced at him again, and continued as though talking about someone who was not there.

"He's been out here so long, it seems he's misplaced his manners, and as I appear to be the cause of his ill humour, I'll be the one to leave. Are you finished here?" he said, turning to Belinda, a note of sarcasm in his question. Belinda shook her head and released Speake's arm.

"No. You go on. I'll be along soon," she said idly, moving over towards a crockery service set out on a trestle.

"Good day to you then, Oscar, Mr Speake," Sullivan said. "You'll be coming to our party tonight? You're not above that, are you?" he added, almost as an afterthought as he started to turn away. Speake only nodded, ignoring the taunt.

"Good," Sullivan said. "As you've no money, I could stand you a drink or two, for all the publicity you're giving us in Chicago. Thanks to your efforts, there might be a few additional customers coming here out of curiosity, once the thaw comes. Maybe Allenby can be persuaded to buy you one too, as the odds are that at least one of those newcomers will end up with him." Then he turned and left the shop without even a glance in Allenby's direction, letting the door slam shut behind him. The echo of the bell held in the air for several moments. Once it had finally died away, Speake went to the counter and paid for the wax and laces the man Boehme had hurriedly collected from the rack of drawers ranged behind the counter.

Allenby had not moved from his position by the door. Through the window behind him, Speake could see Sullivan walking away along the middle of the street. He was calling out to someone. Following the direction of his gaze, Speake saw the Dortmund boy walking distractedly along the boardwalk. On hearing his name, the boy stopped, then jumped down into the street and ran over to Sullivan. When he had drawn close, Sullivan started to talk to him, pulling him closer with an arm bent around the boy's shoulders. As he talked, he kept glancing back towards the store.

Speake thought they looked so familiar, locked together in their conspiratorial huddle. He remembered the boy watching earlier while he and Lucy had been talking Lucy, his intent observation of their conversation. The inaudible discussion taking place in the street made Speake feel uneasy, and he wondered what bond there could be between them. The boy was too young to be a customer at the saloon, and the thought of his playing the opposite role Speake did not want to consider, though he had heard of such things happening in other places like Hope, similarly hidden from the restraining influence of cities and their legal prohibitions. Furthermore, he had no idea how much of a threat Sullivan thought he might pose to him, what suspicions his stories might arouse in others, nor how far the man would go to protect himself, or rather, how far the law here - which over time Speake had come to see was tantamount to whatever Sullivan decided - would permit him to go without fear of retribution.

His gaze drifted back to Allenby's impassive, weather-worn face, but he could find no explanation there either, only a further source of mystery. The lines etched in the old man's skin were deep and angular, like hieroglyphs inscribed in stone, written in some lost ancient tongue, compelling and unfathomable in equal measure. He knew he could never decipher them, the pleasures and pains that had engraved a record of the passing years in his flesh so certainly, any more than he could guess at the thoughts that would be turning behind the placid grey eyes they encircled.

"There was one other thing I wanted to ask," Speake said quietly, recalling something that had puzzled him up at the ice barn.

"And what might that be?" Allenby said, turning from the window to face him, his voice still thick with resentment. "Some other of your hare-brained theories you need ratifyin'?"

"No. The coffins. Why do you keep them open?" Allenby continued to look at him, his face still unreadable.

"To keep an eye on them. Make sure it's cold enough in there…"

"Then why is one closed?"

"Because of the state poor Emilie…" He paused and glared at Speake. "You know damn well why," he added sharply.

Behind him Speake heard Belinda take a sharp intake of breath, then make a sound that could have been a sob or laughter, both suppressed. His satisfaction at provoking a response from Allenby was quickly dispelled by recognition of his indiscretion in having raised the subject while she was there. He was becoming too involved in the machinations of the town and its people, so involved he was in danger of losing his own sense of proportion.

"Yes. I'm sorry," he said, half turning to her. "I hadn't thought."

"There now, does that satisfy your curiosity, smart city man that you are?" Allenby said, flicking his chin in the direction of where Belinda was standing, staring at them both, her face set like an alabaster mask. He touched the rim of his hat to her and to Boehme, and then turned abruptly.

"Don't count on no drink from me," he said, as he opened the door. Outside, Sullivan was now standing outside the saloon, his hand hooked in his belt, looking back along the main thoroughfare. Dortmund had returned to whatever he had been doing previously on the boardwalk. Speake watched the three of them, trying to figure out what bound them together so closely.

"Take no notice of them," Belinda said, coming to stand behind his shoulder. "They've been at it ever since I've known 'em. Some say they were like it back in Chicago, thirty-odd years ago. Seems there's a lot of history and bad feeling between them."

"Hatred might be a better word. Listen, I'm sorry about what I said. I didn't stop to think."

"It's all right. I knew it anyway. It just caught me off-guard. Anyway, my thinking is, two men dislike each other that much it has to be about either a woman or money. But neither of them needs money, and Allenby doesn't seem to care much about it. Can't imagine any woman wanting him either, can you?" She shuddered in a theatrical way, and they laughed quietly together.

"But he's the one who seems not to want to let it rest," Speake said.

"Allenby? He's just a lonely old fool. Maybe, like Sullivan said, he's just been out here too long. The youngsters here all think he wants more from them than company…, if you get what I mean." Speake turned to look at her over his shoulder.

"Do you believe that?"

"No. Kid's talk. He's just a lonely old man. The bodies up there make them imagine he's some kind of bogeyman. You know, youngsters get to that age when everything has to be about sex. There's definitely a ghost in his closet, though, something he never had the guts to do or see through. It left some part of him broken."

"And Sullivan?"

Belinda laughed, and turned to look at Boehme. He was making an exaggerated show of sweeping the floor behind the counter while pretending not to listen. Belinda took Speake's arm again and led him towards the door.

"Good day to you, Herr Boehme. We'll be going now," she said curtly as they left, and the man's pale face turned, in what Speake found a strange variant of blushing, to a stony blue. "Brogan's man. You can never be too careful," she said once they were outside.

"Yes, I'm starting to realise that."

"So, are you excited about tonight?"

"The party?"

"Well, yes, that, and…" Belinda cocked her head to one side and smiled knowingly.

"Ah, Lucy," he said.

"Never can keep her mouth shut, bless her. Rushed in off the street blabbing about the sweet little talk you'd had. You could do worse for yourself."

"I know," he said. She stared into his eyes for a few moments, then smiled blankly, and said: "Good."

"You never got to know Jack Bunney, did you?" she continued quickly, letting the other thing pass, as though something had been agreed between them. Speake was thrown momentarily by the sudden change of tack.

"No, I suppose not," she answered before he could reply. "I guess he was always too drunk to get any sense out of by the time you arrived. He was someone who could have told you a story about Brogan."

"The secrets of the grave," Speake said ruefully. Belinda pulled him to a stop and turned to face him.

"Well, some graves get to say more than others. At first I didn't believe what Jack was telling me, so he insisted he write it down. Said I should give it to someone, even suggested in a rare sober moment I should give it to you if anything happened. He had some twisted imagination when it came to Brogan. He was so mad about Rosie, and I thought he probably wasn't thinking too straight with the drinking. Then, when he was killed, it seemed to add up, and I was scared what else Brogan might do. So, I kept it to myself. And I have my reasons for waiting."

"Are you saying Brogan killed Bunney?"

"Who else would have wanted to? It's what everyone thinks. Jack was a drunk and a loser. Brogan was the only one had a reason. Jack wasn't killed for money, and he never got into fights. The one good thing you could say about him was that he was always a peaceable drunk."

"You still have his testament?"

"Sure," she said, placing her hands on her hips and tilting her head to one side. "But you'll have to come up to my room to get it."

An Inferno:
A Sad and Unforeseen End
Hope, December 22nd 1899

The bones and ashes of a burned-out building; the faded embers of a burned-out life. The town is today mourning the loss of one its most cherished inhabitants. The manner of her death, and that it should have come at her own hand has left many here confused and at a loss as to how to express their sorrow at her passing.

In the middle of the afternoon, of yesterday, December 21st, but three days short of the Christmas celebrations, Mrs Emilie Henderson, nee Mayhew, wife of Mr Arthur G. Henderson, proprietor of the town millinery store, burned down her husband's store, its contents, together with much of the home they lived in above it, with herself still inside.

All in the town had held Mrs Henderson in great regard and affection. Her consistent good humour, her ready welcoming smile had brightened the days of many. It is this, her naturally positive disposition that has caused such consternation at the manner and indeed the timing of her demise. No one could have suspected what heavy currents of doubt and unhappiness must have swelled so threateningly beneath the calm facade.

"She always seemed so resolute," said Mr Joshua Allenby, visibly moved by the loss, a friend of Mrs Henderson going back to when they knew each other in Chicago over thirty years ago. "Like many of us she lost near everything in the fire of '71, but it never seemed to daunt her, leastways, not that she let show. She was always a beautiful woman."

Mr Henderson is suitably distraught, and has declined to make any comment on the death of his wife, other than that the store would be rebuilt and reopened as soon as possible. "It's what Emilie would have wanted, for me to have carried on." He also suggested he would endeavour to persuade his wife's sister, herself but recently widowed, to travel from Chicago to help run the store. The thoughts and good wishes of the town are with him.

Mr Brogan Sullivan, proprietor of the Broken-O saloon, and another friend of the Henderson's from their younger days in Chicago, has kindly offered him free board and accommodation until such time as the store and his home can be rebuilt.

"It's the least I can do, help the man through his time of loss," Mr Sullivan said.

"One can't just ignore those years of friendship, the things we have shared." It is notable how - in a place where empathy and compassion are not generally perceived as qualities that might serve a man (or indeed, a woman) well - that at such times of catastrophe and loss the better elements of human nature appear more readily on display.

The smell of ashes and dust lingers still in the air, and the charred skeleton of the building remains for all to see, both of these stimuli serving as a stark reminder of what transpired, and of what has been lost. Maybe too, it may serve to focus people's thoughts on what is truly important, encouraging them, as both the year and the century draw to a close, to recognise and cherish those things that are most dear to them, while they are still able.

Fortunately, due to the efforts of the brave souls who fought it, the fire was controlled before it could spread to adjacent buildings. Once the fire had been extinguished, the mortal remains of Mrs Henderson were eventually retrieved from the embers and have been delivered to the ice barn and to the safe custodianship of Mr Allenby to be kept there in readiness for burial in the spring.   TES

11

Heaven's Gold

How many weeks and months had they been digging now? Heinz-Harold Dortmund had stopped counting; he had decided long ago that it served no purpose to keep track of the lost, unproductive days. In that time, others had struck it rich, others who it seemed to him had worked far less hard than they. It was this that kept them going. The belief that one day their turn would come.

This was what he told himself every day as he rose from his bed to dress ready for the climb to the mine, and every evening when he trailed back down the mountain at the end of another fruitless day. This was what he said to his twin brother, Gert-Harold, and to his father at regular intervals, often to their exasperation: they had heard his keen exhortations so many times before as they worked side by side.

Their efforts had not gone entirely unrewarded. Occasionally they had found morsels of gold. Not nuggets; not deep, rich seams leading off among the hard strata of rock. Mere granules, no larger than grains of sand. Dust. There seemed to be no reason or pattern to these discoveries, no indication of probability they could pursue. Some days there was gold dust, others there was not. There had never been any certainty or consistency to serve as a guide as to where they should dig next.

And so they spent their days, each day barely distinguishable from the next, save for variations in degrees of cold and heat. As they worked they rarely spoke. They each knew their purpose, their aim, the things they needed to do. Talk of home, Germany, of the things they had left behind, only led to sadness. Other than to talk of the weather, or the rock face in front of them, the other, more fortunate prospectors, there was little to say. Stoic silence, they had learned, was the best negation of disappointment.

It started with the merest of sounds, like the quiet groan of the ocean, or the distant rumble of an approaching storm. A subtle disturbance in the fabric of the world, barely audible beyond the steady chatter of their picks and spades, the softer counterpoint of their laboured breathing. They had been warned of such things, the hazards of working underground. They recognised it instantly, before the ground itself began to move around them: the sound of rock starting to tear, of the earth splitting open.

There was no time to escape, even to consider its possibility. At the moment they became aware it was happening, the ground stirred and swelled, a fissure split open in the roof of rock, admitting the light, the other strata piled far above. A slab of stone tilted and crashed from the roof to the floor of the chamber they had carved, where they were working, closing off its exit. As the tremors settled, dust started to pour down through the fissure, steadily filling the closed chamber they were now in.

At the first movements, the three men stood up straight, looking at each other in consternation. Heinz-Harold saw in the wild-wide eyes of his brother, and of his father, the same fear he knew they would see in his. He reached out through the falling stream of debris and took hold of his father's, his brother's upper arms to reassure them. The fluid strength of their bodies beneath their clothing reassured him in turn. He was with his blood family. They were of strong stock; together they would survive.

He pulled his brother and father towards him. As one they huddled back against the surrounding walls of stone, moulding their bodies against each other, and against the rock they had spent the past year and a half wounding and scarring, but which had refused to yield up its gold in any quantity. Now, it seemed, the rock wanted their flesh, their blood, their breath as recompense for all it had suffered, for what little it had given.

His brother and father clung tightly to him; their bodies pressed against his. He could feel their three hearts beating their own, separate panicked rhythms, the sharpness of the rock against his scalp, the backs of his bare hands, his hips, his spine, the ridges of his shoulder blades. Their arms were wrapped tightly around each other's; three grown men, drawn together by fear, like children lost in the wilderness.

He found himself trying to remember when he had last been this physically close to his father or to his brother.

When last he had touched either of them other than in passing while they worked. He remembered how he and his brother had wrestled and tumbled together when they were boys, but that was long ago. Now they were grown men; they had become discrete entities, more remote physically and spiritually from each other than he had ever thought possible. No longer twinned, other than through birth and physical resemblance, made separate by experience and time. The mental empathy, the strange, prescient knowledge of each other's thoughts they had seemed to possess together as children; that too was gone.

Everything was gone from him. It had all slipped away without his having noticed. Even the familiar comfort of his wife's body next to his own; that too he could not remember. Only the raw caresses of the earth. The inert flesh of the world in which he had spent the last eighteen months delving and scavenging.

Such was the sum, the limit of his memory of his dealings with the realms of physicality; the earth in which they had dug and scraped, their flesh bleeding into its flesh, their bones abraded against its bones. With the passing months it had drawn him relentlessly to itself, gradually taking over his senses. Without his realising, it had filled his being, his soul. And now, it seemed, it wished to consummate their union; to embrace him in the ultimate coupling of dust and flesh. To claim him absolutely.

Even through the pressing urgency of his fear, he found himself worrying about the boy, his only son. How he would make it in this foreign country. On his own, having been suddenly made a man. He knew it would be hard for him.

The imperfection in his eye would remain always a cause for insult, for prejudice against him. Yet another indication of his foreignness, his otherness, slight and superficial though the damage was.

And he wondered too what man, which one among the sombre and unforgiving men he knew, his wife would be forced to give herself to. To love, honour and obey. But no! Not cherish! That would be too painful a betrayal of his memory, even if it would be the only way that she and their daughters would be able to survive. What man would come to know her body in the way he had known it, all of its secret, fearful places?

And he found himself thinking of his son making angels in the snow. Of how a child could take such innocent pleasure in the smallest details of the world, in making his own, small impression on the way the world was structured. Had he ever made snow-angels as a boy? He could not remember. Had he ever been a boy; gone about the world immersed totally in boyhood's stream of innocent wonder? There were memories, dim and receding that reassured him he had.

But there were many other, stronger recollections, of later, more adult and responsible times. Of his first job, as a printer, in Dortmund; he had been barely fifteen then. Setting the wooden blocks in the racks. Scouring pitch-black ink across the arrays of mirrored letters. The succulent kiss of ink on paper; the crackling sheets of paper sliding from the press, damp, heavy, aromatic; the permanent stain of the ink on his hands - another dark incursion into his being. Then there had been his courtship, his wedding. His first adult touch of a woman's skin; his own first act of possession. Followed those few months later by the birth of the boy. The pride of it; the tears of joy. The births of his two daughters, equally joyful. Equally blessed with tears.

Then he had brought them here. Following some whim, some crazed delusion that they had had no option but to follow. His family. All that he cherished. Taking them across an ocean, a continent, in search of wealth. The faces of his wife's parents, creased with sorrow, waving them goodbye. All the good and familiar and worthwhile things they had left behind. The barren, unwelcoming landscapes they had been forced to accept in their place. As home. As consolation. The other displaced souls they had encountered in this strange land with its alien ways. And finally, the eighteen months - was that how long it had been? - of hunger and hardship that his dream had forced them to endure, while he, a skilled tradesman, an educated man who could both read and write, grovelled and sweated in the soil to secure their survival.

And why had he and his brother and father elected to dig so deep, so far into the dark heart of the earth? Why had they not stayed out in the light and air, beside the river, where the others were looking? Was it intuition, perhaps, or the product of some dark, unrecognised necessity inside him? Inside all three of them? Some stubborn, subterranean need for enclosure embedded deep in their German souls?

Or was it simply because here in the mine at least they had experienced some good fortune, had found here some few grains of gold, often where they had least expected to discover them; the impoverished sprinklings of providence? Always though, it had been only a little, as though some precocious sprite - a *kobold* perhaps, unknowingly transported with them from their homeland - had been tempting them, luring them deeper into its lair. Always they had found just enough to keep them looking. Never enough to satisfy their dreams.

Such were the thoughts that came to him, surprising him with their complexity, their sheer irrelevance to his predicament, while the crumbling rock kept steadily falling. He tried to look up along the twisting crevice rising twenty feet or more above him to culminate in a shard of light flickering at the surface. Even as he started to choke in the clouds of falling dust, the light glancing off the particles as they cascaded down from above struck him as beautiful.

"See, Papa! See, Gert!" he shouted, giving in to the misplaced feeling of elation which had inexplicably taken hold in him, and struggling to extract his arm from the rising pile of debris engulfing their bodies, to draw their attention to the myriad points of refracted light descending towards them.

"Look! See the light, how beautiful it is! It's like gold dust falling from heaven. Finally, we have found gold."

He turned his head to look at his brother, saw his own face reflected there, the familiar eyes full of tears, the mirror of his own face covered with a fine layer of water-streaked dust. His brother's hair was grey with dust. He looked like a ghost. A frightened, almost saddened ghost, grown old in an instant. The tears filling his brother's eyes were not tears of elation.

"Yes. I see it," his brother called back softly, turning his eyes away from the burning motes, and without conviction.

"We all see it, how beautiful it is," his father said. "The

world is a beautiful place, more so when you believe you are leaving it. Be quiet. Save your breath. You may need it. If we are fortunate."

His father's face was ghost-like too, a white cowl of dust rising to a rounded point on top of the natural white crown of his hair. The light in his father's eyes was easier to classify than the light he had seen in those of his brother. His father's eyes were full and bright with anger.

"Papa, why are you angry?" he asked.

"What is there not to be angry about?" his father replied, and also closed his eyes to stop the tears from falling.

His father was standing with his back to the chamber, directly beneath the crevice, facing both of his sons and the enclosing wall of rock behind them. It was how they had hurried together to seek the hoped-for safety of the walls of the chamber, Heinz-Harold pulling the others towards him and the imagined protection of the rock. The flow of debris was slowing, but still it kept falling. The loosened earth still streamed down over his father's shoulders, pouring in rivulets across his chest, accumulating around his neck, beneath his chin, rising higher than he could raise his face to escape it. Heinz-Harold reached across with his arm, the one he had freed to point at the light, to brush away the dust from his father's lips. His other arm was trapped irretrievably around the chest of his brother, held captive by the rock and his brother's body pressed against it. He did not mind his arm being where it was, the helplessness, the mild discomfort of it. He gently squeezed his brother's ribs to console him.

"Don't be angry, Papa," he said, his fingers lingering on his father's lips. Their faces were close, but not close enough for him to kiss him. He wanted nothing more at that moment than to kiss him. "Our lives have been sufficiently blessed," he said instead. "We have our children. In them we will live on. They will live out our dreams for us."

"My children are here, dying here with me. What then of *my* dreams?" his father said, his voice tired and complaining.

"No, Papa. Listen. Heinz-Harold is right," his brother consoled him, tipping his forehead forward to touch gently against both their faces. "Our children are your children too. Your dreams are our dreams; they too will be lived."

They stared at each other as best and for as long as they could, their widened eyes filled with only sadness now, as the dust rose up and covered their mouths, their straining, up-turned faces. Their breathing came short and rapid as the tightening muscles of their chests struggled to draw in air against the weight of earth pressing in around them. There was nothing more that could be said.

All words, all exchange of thoughts between them was over. Any words they might have felt the need to say had been deprived of any meaning, made as light and inconsequential as dust. They themselves had become like statues, locked in this one wordless instant. Even the empathy Gert-Harold had once shared with his brother could not permeate through the dust to convey one syllable of consolation. He closed his eyes, to spare them the sight of his anguish, but neither could he bear to watch the awful sight of his father and brother dying.

"I love you both," he heard his brother say, and he tried to mouth the same words in reply, to eradicate the sense of loss, the sadness. What he could not erase was the sting of dust in his nose and throat, filling the passageways of his lungs, drowning him, the earth slowly repossessing him from within; or the sounds of his father and brother choking, their desperate coughing cries, the convulsions of their bodies forced against his own as they struggled for their final breaths, to cling to their last precious moments of existence.

12

The Swedish Boy

It was dark in her room. Although it was still daylight out-side, the shades were drawn, darkening the crimson flock of the wallpaper to the colour of congealed blood. She kept the curtains drawn, she explained, to keep in the heat from the small kerosene lamp which burned in the hearth. It was the only source of warmth she allowed herself during the day; it was easier to stay down in the saloon than keep the fire going all day. It was certainly cold in the room, almost as cold as in his. Speake could see the thin white trails of her breath issuing from her mouth then dissipating in the gloom.

As he circled the room, trying to find a place where he felt comfortable, where he felt he belonged, the feeble flame of the lamp flickered in the wake of his movements, smearing vague shadows of his progress across the walls. The shift-ing surfaces, the sanguine light unnerved him, adding to the general disquiet he felt in just being there. Everything in the room - the curtains, the embroidered cushions and pillows, the soft, furred skin of the wallpaper, the unfamiliar items of feminine toiletry, the lingering smells of scents and makeup, the robes and frilled undergarments strewn haphazardly on the furniture – all spoke to him of sensuality, the conjugal bed; of sex. He felt naïve and incompetent. Out of his depth.

Belinda smiled at him and shook her head, and went over to her bureau, and pulled a key at the end of a silver chain from inside her dress and coat. "Settle down there, will you?" she said over her shoulder as she unlocked the top drawer of the bureau. "You're like a cat sprung up in a strange place. I'm not going to bite."

Speake came to a halt in front of the window, at the furthest point he could place himself from the pink satin plateau of her unmade bed. On a dresser beside the window, amongst the brushes and bottles of perfume and porcelain pots of creams lay a small tortoiseshell framed hand-mirror. He leaned across to inspect his face in the glass. It surprised him how drawn and pale he looked, how much he had physically altered, and how the detailed changes in his face matched the overall conversion he had seen more loosely reflected in the window of the bakery.

He had not shaved in several weeks; had not seen the reflection of his face close up in that time. His skin had turned sallow, and a scrawny lap of flesh hung loosely at his throat below the straggle of his beard which, he noticed with amusement, was tinged with ginger. He had not grown a beard before. His eyes looked wearied and unfocused, almost disinterested. He thought again what a wild man he had become, how much older he looked, and how much more like his father, the aging man he had watched wasting away. Even his own mother would have had difficulty recognising him if she saw him now.

"If you like, I'll give that hair and beard a trim when you've finished reading this. Smarten you up for Lucy," Belinda said, as he stood up from contemplation of the changes in his face. She had crossed the room, and was now standing close to him, holding three folded sheets of paper clutched close to her breast.

"It ain't no work of literary genius. Nothing like as impressive as how you write."

"You flatter me. I don't suppose you've read…"

"I have too. I *can* read. We get Chicago papers sometimes, as you well know. By the sound of you, I believe you're wearing some now." She laughed and prodded at his chest, and at first he was embarrassed that the impoverished state to which he had been reduced had been discovered, but as his own amusement started to creep onto his face, he too became aware of the almost inaudible rustling of the paper stuffed inside the lining of his coat as he moved. After the first few days he had come to rarely notice it.

"Just reaping the benefits of my labours," he offered sheepishly.

"It's okay. You're not the only one does it, and it's way smarter than freezing to death. I'd imagine some folk here think it's what newspapers are for." Speake smiled weakly, acknowledging the ridiculousness of his situation, recalling too the arguments with his mother before he left, the lofty justifications offered for his enforced poverty. What arrogance and pretension had led him to believe he might have something worthwhile to say about the people in this place, whose motivations and steadfastness he would never fully understand? He, who was unable to correctly order his own responses to the death of a parent; what had been his own motivations for choosing this? Surely not simply to escape from unpleasant memories, or in pursuit of some writerly ambition.

"And so, what is *your* story?" he asked, reverting to this last excuse, the one he offered to himself most often as justification for being there, hoping too to take advantage of Belinda's unexpected openness to try again to elicit some details of her life.

"Mine?" she said flatly, as though the subject bored her. "Simple. It's what I am. This is the life I was born to live, at this moment in time, at least. If it wasn't, then I'd be doing something else, wouldn't I? Who knows, maybe even be someone else? Different thoughts, different needs. Like I said, I have my reasons for holding on to Jack's story. All I ask is to be respected for the person I am. People's pity I don't need. Nor their judgement. And in the meantime, there doesn't seem any point in complaining."

"You make it sound simple, straightforward."

"It is, isn't it? If that's how you can manage to see it. The more complicated you make it in your head, the more complicated it becomes out there." She gestured in the direction of the curtained window. "Isn't that so?"

Yes, Speake thought, admiring the simplicity of her reasoning. It probably was that straightforward. The trick lay in learning to see things in such a way. Was that a failing of his, of the masculine mind in general, he wondered? The women he had met here, not only those at the saloon, seemed to have a more grounded, more accepting understanding of how things were. True, they complained, but they did not constantly seek outside reasons, explanations, or try to re-mould the world to their own fashion, or to suit their needs, as men almost invariably did. He envied the women their stoicism, self-defeating as it often was. But how to halt that striving for explanation; how to approach the world without question or judgement?

"Anyway," Belinda's soft tones interjected into his thoughts. "The only thing of yours I've read is the piece about the Swedish boy. It made me want to cry, the way you told it. The papers are old by the time they get here, but it helps, you know, to keep in touch with what others think and feel."

"Something to gauge your own oddities against?" Speake queried quickly, and immediately felt he had again shown too much judgement in his response.

"Yeah, you could say that." She nodded and smiled at him, and Speake could see the small lines of sorrow and regret creasing the corner of her eyes, betraying the sincerity of her smile. "You really must find us all very odd," she added, with some sadness.

"No, not odd. Different, and fascinating, and confusing certainly, and perhaps a little perverse. Some of you I do worry about, though."

"Like Lucy?" He grinned and nodded. "And me?" she inquired playfully. He hunched his shoulders slightly, and rocked his head from side to side. She laughed quietly again.

"It's okay. I know what I am, how people see me. Everyone

knows Belinda Curtis is a tough old bird. So how come you're suddenly so interested in this?" she asked fanning the pages of Jack Bunney's missive in front of her. "You didn't seem overly worried about how the boy died back when it happened. What changed your mind?"

"Maybe I've finally started to do what I claim to be here for. Maybe I've started to actually look and listen. To be concerned about the truth of things, not just how it might suit my own ends," he replied, expressing a fact about himself he had only just realised. In all the time he had been in Hope there had been a constant supply of interesting things to write about, new events occurring almost daily to distract him from his inner thoughts. At the time those stories had seemed important, demanding his attention. At heart, though, he knew that the writing of them had been little more than a distraction. The other, more personal questions had still been exercising him at some deeper, if unregistered level.

Even the death of the Swedish boy had been but part of the long process of discovery and forgetting he had been indulging in since he had left Chicago. Somewhere, the bare facts of it - the manner of the boy's death, the place, the boy himself, the possible explanations – all had become lost in the search to uncover some more personal truth. It suddenly struck him how sometimes there were things you went looking for never really expecting to find them. It was the search itself, the temporary sense of purpose it imbued that was important. That was where the justification lay, not in the almost inevitable discovery of yet more instances of the manifold inadequacies inherent in the human soul.

And sometimes, he realised with a sense of shame, that

fixed sense of purpose, the fear of its disappointment, could make you blind to everything else.

"Here," Belinda said, gently flapping the sheets of paper against his chest, breaking the chain of his thoughts. Her eyes were set intently on him, examining his face. He felt self-conscious, aware now of the physical changes the climate and this town had wrought in him, and that he now looked no different from any of the other broken and displaced people who had washed up in Hope. In the subdued light he noticed her eyes were a deep green flecked with amber - yet one more detail he had not previously noticed. Her gaze was so intense he felt she was searching for his soul.

"You're a good man. I can see that," she said. "And Brogan Sullivan can be a mean son of a bitch when he wants. I hope you're strong enough for this. If you're certain about it, you'd be giving Lucy hope, something she's not known for a long time. Try not to let her down."

"I'll try," he said solemnly, and took the proffered sheets of paper. Her tiny, doll-like hands were shaking visibly, and he reached out and tried to encompass them within his own, to still them, to give them some warmth. They were as cold as ice, but she quickly pulled them away.

"No. It would be nice, but it seems to me you're here as Lucy's saviour, not mine," she said, backing away.

"That wasn't what..." he began to say, then stopped himself and nodded, and turning to the window and opening a narrow crack of light between the heavy curtains, he unfolded Bunney's letter and started to read.

A Terrible and Unseasonal Accident

Hope, December 25th 1899

It is Christmas Day. Many among you will have sat down this day with your loved ones to enjoy a festive meal together, yet for one family in Hope, Christmas this year will be a dark and joyless time, devoid of celebration. In this place accidents happen as and when they will, and Death can strike at anyone, cutting them low in an instant. It is rare though that such a hard and broad-sweeping blow should be dealt against a single family such as has been delivered here.

Yesterday morning, at around half-past ten, twin brothers, Heinz-Harold and Gert-Harold Dortmund, and their father Harold Dortmund, all from the city of Dortmund in Germany, were working in their mine when a cave-in occurred. Rescuers were unable to reach the men before all three had succumbed.

Other prospectors who had been working in the area hurried to help once the sounds of the cave-in had brought the accident to their attention. By the time they arrived, however, it was too late to implement a rescue, the entrance to the mine having been blocked entirely by fallen rocks and debris.

"We did all we could," reported a Mr. Anthony Waller, from Lancashire in England, one of those who took part in the failed attempt at rescue. "As soon as we pulled the stuff away, more fell down. The rocks kept on falling."

After more than six hours of digging, the three bodies were finally recovered. As none of them showed any injuries that could be assigned to the accident, other than scratches and skin abrasions, their deaths were attributed to the unusual cause of suffocation, by clouds of falling dust.

"Such an awful way to go," said Mr. Joshua Allenby, who as town undertaker has now taken charge of the bodies.

"It was the damndest thing, them standing there still like that, their bodies together and stiffening and all covered in dust. It reminded me of one of them Grecian statues." The men had been found huddled together at the rear of the mine, as if they had clung to each other in their final moments for mutual succour and protection. All who saw it were touched deeply by the sight.

The tragic irony of this accident is that the Dortmunds had elected to drive a horizontal shaft into the body of the mountain, rather than to work at sluices or an open seam excavation, as is the usual practice here. No-one could offer a reason for the exceptional choice they had made, other than that it may have been for them a more accustomed way of working, their coming from a different country.

If not for such a choice the three men would probably still be alive today, celebrating the season with their family.

Later, Mr. Allenby supervised the removal of the bodies to the ice barn, where they will be kept until they can be buried next year. TES

13

An Unspoken Truth

"Look, Thomas! Look!" Speake heard a voice call out as he wandered back to his lodging. He was planning to clean himself up, and if his uneasy thoughts would allow, to sleep for a few hours before the evening's celebrations.

He had just left Belinda in her room. Bunney's affidavit had shocked him; he needed time to consider its implications, the reliability of the accusations it contained. Even if it was the truth, he doubted the letter in itself would be proof enough. When all was said and done it was just the word, the probably embittered speculations of a drunkard. It felt about as useful to his purpose - discovering the truth of how the Swedish boy had died - as the newspaper stuffed inside the lining of his coat.

At the sound of the voice, he turned to see Gillam Todd running towards him along the main thoroughfare. He was shaking his fist in the air, and his topcoat was undone, and his scarf flapped out behind him like a pennant as he ran. His face was flushed bright crimson, and as he drew close Speake could see thick, dust-streaked tracks of tears marking his cheeks.

"Look, Thomas. Look! It's gold! I've found gold," Todd said excitedly as he came to a breathless halt and extended his hand to reveal about a dozen bean-sized nuggets nestled in its palm. The tips of his fingers were grazed and bloodied beneath a coating of dirt. Speake looked up at his friend's face to congratulate him, saw an agitated light in his eyes, like some form of possession.

"It looks so ordinary. Are you certain it's gold?" he asked. He had not seen gold this close before, not in its raw state, not in nuggets of this size. All he had ever seen had been but grains and dust.

"Damn right it's gold!" Todd exclaimed. "Like a bloody miracle, it was. I'd wandered over to take a pee where I'd been at least a hundred times before, and there it was, literally lying on the ground. At first I thought I must be hallucinating. I dug around with my bare hands, trying to find more," he opened his hands in front of him, palms up, displaying the evidence of the gold, the dirt encrusted skin, the still bright wounds to his fingers.

"This was all I could find in the time I had. I knew I needed to get down before it got too dark if I was going to make it to the celebrations. I'm going back tomorrow though, at first light. There has to be more, maybe a whole seam of it. Will you help, Thomas? Half of whatever you find'd be yours. Can you believe it?" He raised his head and shouted into the air. "I found gold!"

"Congratulations, man," Speake finally had the chance to say, taking hold of both of Todd's upper arms and shaking him in excitement once his ecstatic description of the discovery had run its course.

"Of course I'll help. But I don't want any of it. It's yours, all of it. God knows you've worked for it. You're the one who found it, even if a little serendipitously. I trust you're not going to tell anyone else about that?"

"And why should I not? Is peeing not a perfectly natural thing, and having a designated toilet, does that not show what a civilised man I am? But no, fair's fair. If you help, you'd be entitled to your share. We'll call it wages, if you prefer. All I need is enough to get me back to Scotland, to buy some land to set myself up. Imagine how much we might find."

Speake was pleased for Todd. He could return now to where he belonged, not as a foolish, headstrong youth defeated by his travels, but as the prodigal son returned, a young man who had succeeded in finding what he had set out to discover. At least now one person in Hope had proper cause to celebrate the changing year. For him, not just a new century, but a new life beckoned. The town too would benefit from his find, his good fortune washing over onto the other prospectors, generating fresh hope in them too. It would lend them a renewed sense of purpose, at least until the arrival of spring. It was these small discoveries by others - although simultaneously viewed with envy – that kept the prospectors believing their own turn would eventually come. The celebrations tonight would be given added impetus by this new discovery. Speake could already hear the cracked, off-key voices singing too raucously, could picture the wizened faces, bright-eyed with expectation, the gnarled, rock-grazed hands knotted around celebratory glasses, their wiry sinews aching and twitching to be digging again. Some, he knew, would even forsake the celebrations to be packing their gear ready for the first light of dawn.

"So, tell me, Mister Todd. What does it feel like to be a wealthy man?" he asked, expecting to be overwhelmed by a breathless exposition of all the headstrong dreams that had fuelled Todd's searching. Instead, he saw a darkness slip into his friend's eyes, and the elation drain from his face to be replaced by a look of puzzlement. The tips of his fingers were still seeping blood; they had to be causing pain, yet he looked at them as though seeing them for the first time. His fingers closed loosely around the nuggets, and his shoulders slumped, and he turned away and stumbled over to the boardwalk and sat down heavily.

"You know, Thomas," he said after a few moments, his head hung down against his clenched hands. "I've no idea. This..." He shook his fist almost angrily in front of his face. "This was everything I dreamed of, and have worked for the past months. But now, all I feel is emptiness. Here," he said, touching his chest above his heart.

Speake went over and stood beside him, placing a hand on his shoulder. "Come on. It can't be that bad," he said.

"No...? Maybe not. But tell me, what exactly have I found? Happiness? Peace? Love? Anything significant? No! None of those things. It's only money. That's all it is, isn't it?" Todd said, looking up at Speake for confirmation, and holding out the nuggets again. Speake shrugged, not knowing what to say.

"It's not even actual money," Todd continued, his voice thick with resentment. "Just lumps of pretty metal some other fool will give me money for. You know, it wasn't the possibility of striking it rich that brought me here. I was hoping that here I would feel I belonged, some form of brotherhood. What I discovered was that no-one cares, or belongs. Everyone is just passing through, trying to get what they can, trying to get to some place they're not even sure exists." He looked up at Speake again.

"Even you, Thomas. I think of you as a friend, but you're not much different. You came here looking to find something for yourself, your own redemption. But I don't think you'll ever be able to see it…, because you have no idea what you are looking for. There may be answers here, Thomas, but how many will ever see it? They've brought their impoverished lives, their sad histories with them, all the values and personal truths they cling to as something precious, but which only serve to blind them to other possibilities. There's no love here, no connection. Not to man, nor God, not even to Nature. Only to themselves." He fell silent, a sad, defeated expression on his face.

"Come on, Gillam. Don't be so disheartened," Speake tried to console him, although he agreed with most of what Todd had said. He understood too how his friend's words had accurately described his own predicament.

Todd knew something of the personal truth of his life; he had been the only one Speake had felt able to confide in, having needed to share it with someone, to try to diffuse some of its debilitating power. Todd was not, however, in possession of the full details, the singular thing that Speake perceived –

that he felt now to be an integral, possibly ineradicable part of his being - as his ultimate failing. Speake had struggled to put that failing into words, had not been able to admit openly to Todd, to the world, that he had come here to escape, not simply the awful memories of his father's final days, but the harsh reality of his having been unable to help his father die.

On several occasions, his voice broken and feeble, his eyes filled with tears of both pain and despair, his father had asked, had pleaded with him to find someone or something to help him escape his suffering. His father had known he was dying, and beyond the anger at the physical betrayal, had been fearful and shamed by the changes the disease was wreaking in his body. Speake had been powerless either to prevent it or to help him endure it in a painless and dignified way, let alone to terminate it.

He had, in fact, made a few discrete enquiries. He had even found a name, an address, but had not followed it through. He had known he would not be able to commit the final act, to administer the potion, the pill, the lethal injection. To smother him, if it came to that, if no one could provide him a less crude means. An act of such intimacy between a father and son - a man he had never touched, other than handshakes at anniversaries and departures, as far as he could recall. He had not been able to do it.

This was the real, unspoken, paralysing history he had brought with him; the vision of his father summoning up the last vestiges of his strength, not to bless him, or to express his love for him, but to curse and rail with his last feeble breaths at a son who did not possess the courage or compassion - "Do you not love me enough to spare me this?" his father had cried on one occasion - to help him die while still in possession of some vestige of human dignity.

Why had he been so weak and unable to serve his father in that way? Had he really believed a human life was so sacrosanct, when its limits and dimensions were entirely prescribed by pain, humiliation and fear? He had failed his father, and he did not know if he would ever be able to forgive himself. What he did know, with a certainty, and could never forget, was that his father had died bitter and broken, unable to forgive his own son.

"Come on," he said, pushing away his own feelings of despair, and trying to console Todd again, as his friend continued to sit with his head hung down against his knees. "There are good people here too. Many know exactly what they want; not all are stupid or blind. Most are simply unlucky, through no fault of their own. It's probably just the shock of it, making you feel this way. You'll feel different in the morning." Todd still did not seem convinced. He continued to sit with his head held down contemplating his clenched hands.

"It's New Year's Eve, Gillam. The last day of the century, and there's a strong possibility you'll be a wealthy man in the next. What better start could you wish for? And, like it or not, you'll be a hero in the saloon tonight. The least you can do is stand me a drink to celebrate." Todd looked up again, his face immediately brightening.

"Aye, you're right about that at least. What's the point of finding gold if we can't celebrate it? You're looking very spruce, by the way. Would we be trying to impress someone?" Speake ran his hands across his newly trimmed beard and tugged on the now naked wattle beneath his chin. He felt slightly naked and more exposed to the elements with his scrubbed face and cropped beard and hair, but Belinda had refused to let him leave without submitting to her attentions.

"No! Not particularly. It was Belinda," he stumbled in explanation. "She insisted. What could I do?"

"Belinda, eh? And I was thinking you had a soft spot for our Lucy." Todd stood up and nudged Speake playfully to one side with his shoulder, and then slowly opened his out-stretched hand to reveal the nuggets of gold in its palm.

"Look, Thomas. It's gold. It's bloody, fantastic, unbeliev-able gold," he said, and then he hooted into the air as the initial elation of his discovery took hold again, and wrapping his arm firmly around Speake's shoulders, started to steer him in the direction of the saloon.

14

The Swedish Boy

As Speake and Todd were making their way to the saloon, Todd talking again about his discovery with renewed animation, Dortmund suddenly darted into their path from a narrow alleyway between two buildings.

"Hey! Careful!" Speake exclaimed, holding his hands out to protect himself. The boy nodded briefly in apology, then tried to dodge out of their way, but as he passed Todd caught him by both shoulders and brought him to a halt between them.

"What's the hurry, sonny?" he asked. "You really should pay more attention when you're running round like a mad fool."

"Yes, Sir, I'm sorry," the young man replied. "I apologise if I startled you."

"We'll survive, and you'll find Mr Todd is also a little overly excited just now," Speake said, glancing across at his friend, seeing still the manic light of discovery in his eyes.

"Actually, I'm glad I found you. There was something I wanted to ask."

The young man's head flicked up, and his demeanour changed, no longer apologetic, but defiant, his eyes darting between the two older men. "So, you have found me," he said. Speake turned to Todd.

"Could you give us a few minutes?"

"Sure. I'll wait over there," Todd said, indicating with his head in the direction of the bakery. Speake nodded in agreement then turned back to Dortmund.

"I thought it might be easier if we talked alone," he said quietly once Todd had left. "I have no real reason to think this, but…has Mr. Sullivan asked you to keep an eye on me? I saw the two of you talking, after you were watching Miss Harrigan and myself. You *were* watching us, weren't you?" Again, the boy remained silent, his face turned down and half concealed by his golden crown of hair, his hands pushed deep into his coat pockets.

"You and he are friends, aren't you?" Speake tried again, a slightly more insistent tone to his voice. He liked the young man, what he knew of him; he did not want to antagonise him. He seemed to have a good heart and possess wisdom beyond his years. Speake felt too that he could empathise with his situation - alone in an alien place, his father dead and gone.

"Why would he ask me to do such a thing?" the young man eventually said, looking up, still defiant.

"A feeling I have, that he does not like or trust me. The way you were behaving earlier - why *were* you watching us?"

"I was curious. You know, a man and a woman…together? Are you and Miss Harrigan in love?" Speake laughed, at the idea, the possibility of the emotion being reciprocated; at the audacity of the question from someone so young.

"It was only that," Dortmund continued, shrugging his shoulders. "I have curiosity about such things."

Despite his apparent indifference, Speake noticed a look of doubt flicker across Dortmund's face, as though some part of him wanted to divest itself of whatever secrets it held. A pang of recognition shot through him; how unbearable the knowledge of uncomfortable things could be.

"You will make trouble for me if I tell?" Dortmund asked, apparently having come to some decision.

"No. I promise," Speake reassured him. He saw the doubt still lingering in the young man's eyes.

"I won't tell Sullivan," he added, appreciating that this would be the young man's greatest concern.

Dortmund thought about this for a moment, still looking at him warily, his head cocked slightly to one side, and then he grinned.

"Like the snow?" he said. Speake nodded, and smiled back, recalling their encounter earlier that day.

"Yes. Like the snow. Does Mr Sullivan often ask you to do things for him?"

"Sometimes he does."

"What manner of things?"

"You know…small things. Errands, you call them, yes?"

"Yes. But aren't you a little young to be spending…?" Before Speake could finish, the young man's demeanour had changed again; his shoulders set, his chin jutting out.

"I'm old enough, as good as a man now. I can do whatever he asks," he said defiantly.

"I'm sure you can," Speake said, reaching out a placating hand towards the young man's shoulder. Dortmund shrugged it away. "I was concerned more that a man like him might not be a good influence on someone your age."

"I am old enough," the boy repeated. "Neither of them ever complained."

"I'm sure you are, whatever he asked you to do. Whoever it may have been with," he added after a pause, having picked up on the inference of some other having been involved. The young man's body relaxed as he allowed the weight of his body to settle back onto the soles of his feet.

"No. I cannot tell about that," he said. "It must be a secret."

"A secret?"

"Yes. I too made a promise."

Speake recalled Lucy's reticence earlier, the oblique reference she had made to something that had happened between her and Sullivan. If he had understood it right, it had led to her miscarriage in some way. There had been a third party involved, she had said, a boy, who she had not cared to name. Could it have been Dortmund? Was the boy trying to protect her in turn? Then the more troubling thought came to him: what had the they been doing together that they would wish to keep it hidden?

"And this happened between yourself and Sullivan, and a woman?" he asked tentatively. "A woman who lives...?"

"No! I did not say that. I told you, I cannot tell. Anyway, why would you want to know?"

"It *is* the reason I came here, to find out about the lives of the people here and write their stories for my newspaper. And I'd like to understand." Dortmund glared at him and shook his head, his shoulders tensing again.

"That is not your reason. You adults are all alike. You only want to use it against him."

"Well, I would suggest that if a man does something wrong, and encourages someone like you to be part of it, then it ought to be made known. You understand that, don't you? It's a question of right and wrong."

"I understand. But the question is, Mister Speake, do you? What do *you* really know of right and wrong?"

Before Speake could offer a response to the young man's impertinence, he was distracted by the sounds of horse-hooves behind them, the wet, irregular snorts of an animal's hard-drawn breath drawing near. He turned to see Brogan Sullivan approaching, leading his horse back to the stables at the end of his customary afternoon ride.

He was glad of the interruption. The young man's question had disarmed him, touching him where the deepest of his uncertainties lay. He had changed so much over the past weeks, he no longer recognised himself in many of the things he thought and felt. The boy had been justified in questioning his values. What *was* his true justification for being here, for dissecting the lives of others, ostensibly for the entertainment of a privileged readership who would never otherwise be exposed to the depravations experienced daily by the subjects of his stories? What *did* he really know about right and wrong? As for Dortmund, as soon as he saw Sullivan, he edged away to the side of the street. Speake became aware too that Todd had moved from the bakery and was standing, swaying in an agitated way from one foot to the other, only a few paces behind him.

It was now late in the short northern mid-winter day, and the watery sun was turning the sky fire-red where it settled behind the dark rim of the mountains. In the opposite direction the purple-blue shadow of night was rearing up steadily to engulf them. An owl hooted mournfully in the distance. Although the days up here lasted for only a few hours at this time of the year, for Speake, this day had felt unusually long, holding too many surprises, raising far too many unanswered questions. He was tired and disorientated, and was nervous about what would happen later that night with Lucy, how Sullivan would react to their growing friendship. There was also the evidence, if evidence it was, of Jack Bunney's statement. For the first time in his life, he felt as though he needed a drink.

The horse, a grey-dappled stallion, was sweating heavily, despite the cold. Steam rose from the trembling muscles of its neck and shoulders, and blood from the points of Sullivan's spurs marbled the white foam of sweat smeared along its flanks. The animal was still jittery from the exertions of the ride; it snorted and tossed its head in agitation as it caught the unfamiliar scents of Speake and Todd. Sullivan pulled hard several times on its bridle, calming it with a few sibilant sounds whispered close to its ear, and by brushing his bare hand gently across its muzzle.

"Mr Speake. Could I have a word?" he called out once the horse had settled. Speake turned to Todd.

"You go on, Todd. Make mine a whiskey while you're waiting."

Todd continued to eye Sullivan with suspicion. "I can wait if you like," he said softly.

"No, you go on. I won't be long." Speake had noted the quiet agitation in his friend's offer; it mirrored his own sense of apprehension. In truth, he would have preferred Todd to stay but did not want Sullivan thinking he was afraid to face him alone. At some point, a confrontation between them was unavoidable, regarding Lucy, and his growing suspicions about the death of the Swedish boy. Now was as good a time as any. He nodded gently to Todd, and the young man shrugged and started to wander off.

"How can I help you?" Speake said, turning back to Sullivan, trying not to let his anxiety show.

"Firstly, you seem to be spending a lot of time with my girls lately, one in particular," Sullivan said, a sour tone to his voice. "And I'm concerned about what I hear you've been asking, not only her, but damn near everyone in town." Speake was surprised to discover that being challenged in this way was exactly what he needed. It made him feel braver, the resentments he held against the man and his self-entitled demeanour simmering up in his veins.

"Is there any law saying I shouldn't talk to her?" he said, taking a few steps closer.

"Probably not, but most pay me for the service."

"I wasn't aware I was partaking of any service. We were talking."

"That may be, but from what I've seen, you've been getting a lot closer to her than simple sociability might require."

"And if I am? Of what concern is it of yours?" Speake spat out, still emboldened by his dislike of the man. Sullivan was too egregious, too self-assured. Then there was Bunney's affidavit. The contents of it had shocked him, had offended that inner reserve in him, or it would have if he could have been certain of the truth of what Bunney had claimed. If it was true, if it could be proved, there were things Sullivan should be held accountable for which were far worse than running a whore-house - depraved things, physical acts, the mere contemplation of which would make any civilised man shudder.

He recalled the earlier, familiar embrace around Dortmund's shoulders. He wondered if this was what Lucy had intimated. Had she tried to deflect Sullivan's attentions from the boy, and had his reaction to her intervention, possibly violent, caused her to lose the baby? It would explain her unwillingness to reveal the boy's identity. If the truth of such a scenario had been made known, even as the victim, the boy would have received little sympathy. He glanced across at Dortmund. Perhaps, he thought, Dortmund had not been the only one. Had the Swedish boy also been the object of Sullivan's perverted interest? Had Sullivan killed him when the boy had threatened to tell?

"It's very much my concern, as you know," Sullivan said. "You may not be happy with the situation, but Lucy belongs to me. Her business is entirely my business. Now, if you were looking to make some..."

"Damn you, Sullivan. She's a person too. She belongs to no one," Speake shouted, his anger pricked further by the unwelcome acknowledgement he was being forced to make of the man's claimed proprietorship over Lucy.

"Yes, indeed. A sweet girl," Sullivan said.

"Is that all you can say about her?"

"What more is there to say? She's pretty, and competent enough in bed, from what I hear, if lacking in imagination, and she has a pleasant voice when she sings."

"Is that the only way you see her, as a commodity? Don't you think people deserve to be treated as people?"

"By people you mean Lucy and the other girls? And Rosalind Pearce, I assume." Speake was surprised that Sullivan had raised the subject of this earlier instance of his casual appropriation of another's rights.

"Yes…, and the boy. Or should that be boys?" He glanced again to where Dortmund was standing. He still had his hands thrust into his pockets, feigning indifference, though he had to be aware of his own role in their confrontation. Both their voices were raised.

"How many have there been?" he demanded, finding renewed justification in the presence of someone he was becoming increasingly certain had been, and possibly was still the subject of Sullivan's perverse predilections.

"What boys? What on earth are you talking about?" Sullivan cried, throwing out his hands in dismay. The horse jerked its head away and snorted angrily in reaction to the unexpected movement, and tried to back away, its shod hooves shuffling noisily on the frozen ground. Sullivan pulled its head back down with a sharp pull on the reins and began again to whisper to it and to stroke its muzzle.

"Tell me, is there some conspiracy going on here?" Sullivan

asked once he had quieted the animal again. "You'll have me believing in ghosts soon, you sounding just like Jack Bunney." He cocked his head to one side, and peered across at Speake, his brow furrowed.

"You been drinking too?" he asked, and his face broke into a wry smile. "You going the same way old Jack went? It's the cold and the loneliness. It can get to you after a while. Look at yourself, man. You're a mess, even with the trim and haircut, courtesy of Belinda, I presume. She's always had a liking for strays and misfits. But you still look like a loser. You've even fallen in love with a whore."

"You bastard," Speake cried, and raised his hand to punch Sullivan, but before he had pulled his fist back to the level of his shoulder, Sullivan had reached out and gripped his wrist in a vice-like grip. The bones in Speake's hand and arm started to ache from the pressure of the grip.

"I don't think you want to even contemplate that," Sullivan said. Speake tried to hold his stare for a few seconds, until he started to lose courage within the cold depths of Sullivan's eyes. He nodded, and allowed his body to relax. Sullivan released his hold on his wrist.

"Now would you care to explain what you are implying?"

"I simply heard that selling women wasn't your only prurient interest," Speake said flatly. Sullivan let out a short, dry laugh.

"What on earth are you talking about?"

"I've seen Jack Bunney's affidavit."

Sullivan was silent for a moment, then he snorted and slapped the side of his boot with his crop. This time his grip on the reins was tighter, and the horse could only peck its head at the sound. It was a spirited animal, Speake thought: a fitting beast for its master. Its nostrils were flared in agitation, and its eyes were dark, empty pools ringed with blooded white. The pungent smell of it - sweat salt and lightly rotting vegetation - wafted from its hot body, tainting the air.

"Will that drunk never leave me in peace?" Sullivan said. "I'd thought that cut-throat had shut him up for good."

"That you'd shut him up, you mean?" Speake goaded. Sullivan glared back at him, and held out his free hand between them, fingers outspread, palm down, turned towards Speake.

"We are not going into that, no matter what you might think," he said, pushing the hand closer to Speake's face.

"So, the fool did write down his fool ideas?" Sullivan said when he had composed himself. "He had these crazy ideas. Imagined he saw me doing things he thought I shouldn't be."

"With the Swedish boy?" Speake probed, feeling suddenly calm.

"What...? The boy they found in the river? No! Not with him!" He glanced quickly across at Dortmund. "Not with any boy! What exactly are you asking? You always seemed a reasonable man to me, a principled man even, one I had some respect for, but your groundless innuendoes are becoming insulting. We were talking about what some spiteful drunk thought he saw me doing once in a dark alley, and which he had got all wrong, and then suddenly you're trying to accuse me of... Just what are you accusing me of?"

"Nothing. I was only asking. What were you doing?"

"That's none of your business. Bunney got it all wrong, that's all you need to know. There are others who could verify it, though I'm not saying who. Bunney was desperate to get even with me. You know the story. Anyway, I don't need to explain myself to you."

"No, that's true. But I thought you might want to give your side of the story before I submit it to the paper."

Sullivan laughed again in exasperation. "What story? God damn it, man, there is no story, other than in Bunney's liquor-addled head. And Bunney is dead."

"Yes. You made sure of that."

"No! Bunney had already damn near killed himself! Having his throat cut only spared him a few days of his miserable existence," Sullivan paused and composed himself again. "Tell me, do you really think I'd be that stupid?," he continued after a few moments. "Everyone knew what happened between us. I've told you already..." He broke off abruptly. "All right, answer me this," he said after a few seconds, moving a step closer. "Do you have a single shred of proof?"

Speake bit his lip, and lowered his eyes from Sullivan's gaze, then shook his head again. "Only Bunney's statement," he said quietly.

"Ah! Our poor, sad drunkard's statement. We both know the value of that. In which case I suggest you forget your story, Mr Speake. If you're really looking to find something interesting, why not you ask Allenby? I'm sure he has a story to tell."

"Allenby? That doesn't sound very likely," Speake said, dismissing the suspicion he had himself intermittently entertained. Coming from Sullivan though, who had known the man for so long, the idea did not sound unreasonable.

He almost felt inclined to believe what he had said about Bunney too. He seemed sincere enough, and genuinely offended by what Bunney's note implied. There were other pointers too towards Allenby being suspect, if the death of the Swedish boy really had been a crime. The boys in the town had created their own morbid mythology around him, but as Belinda had said, that was predictable given Allenby's looks and his age and occupation, and the way such things could get distorted by the baroque propensities of the juvenile mind. He had therefore come to the same conclusion as Belinda - that Allenby was nothing more invidious than a sad and lonely old man.

Sullivan stared at Speake, their faces no more than a few feet apart, his eyes locked on his as though challenging him to provide proof, or failing that, to dare to mete out his own retribution. Behind him the horse was still trying to back away, pulling on the reins at the end of Sullivan's outstretched arm. Dortmund was watching alertly, as though getting ready to give chase should the horse escape. Whatever his relationship with Sullivan, the young man did not seem to bear either scars or ill-will towards him. His loyalty was obvious, both in his demeanour, and in what he had said. Who was Speake to pass judgement then on what might have occurred between them? What right did he have, a man who could not even defend the honour of a woman he had started to develop feelings for? He bit his lip again, then shook his head and turned away.

There was nothing more he could say, nothing he could prove or substantiate. He was not even certain himself. Perhaps he was simply trying too hard to find that final story, to justify his intrusions into the lives of these people, and thereby give some sense or meaning to his sojourn in Hope.

He glanced back over his shoulder. Sullivan's eyes met his. They were blank, almost lifeless, like those of the horse, all human feeling and reason frozen from them.

Perhaps, Speake thought as he turned again from Sullivan's frigid stare, he really did not have the right to judge any of these people, to question the moral codes by which they governed their lives. Perhaps young Dortmund had seen it correctly. For all his youth, he seemed to understand this wilderness and its ways much better than Speake ever would. While his experiences here had wrought in him a number of changes, none had felt like positive transformations. They had constituted rather of a profound sense of loss, of all he had once held to be the redeeming patina of civilisation, of what he had valued most.

Exactly as Dortmund had questioned, he no longer had a clear perception of what was right and what wrong. The people here inhabited a world where the rules of justice and order he was accustomed to were difficult, if not impossible to maintain. Here things were different. Nothing was certain; nothing could be carved in stone. Here, his morals, his philosophy, his intellect, all the things that underpinned his sense of rectitude and worth, were made redundant by the absence of any absolute certainties or truths. Death was the only thing that could be relied upon, and even that, he had discovered, could be delivered in endlessly unpredictable ways.

Such knowledge had proved worthless to his needs. Even now, after all he had seen and had learned about the harsh realities of a human life, the almost predictable awfulness of its ending, he still found it hard to live with the knowledge of having been unable to help his father die. He feared the cold fact of such a failure would stay with him for all his days. Was that to be the sum of what his life would amount to? What could possibly displace that failure? Love for another? He doubted it. Love would only shrivel and die in the face of its bitter questioning. Its shadow would always be there, casting a pall over any other finer feeling he might try to hold.

As he walked away, he saw Todd still waiting for him, a short distance further along the street. He lifted his head to him briefly in acknowledgement.

"There was no need to wait," he called out, pushing his darker thoughts aside.

"You never can be sure," Todd said once Speake had drawn level, looping a reassuring arm around his shoulders. "Is everything alright?"

"I think so. The man always sounds so convincing, so reasonable. It might be interesting tonight though."

"How's that?"

"Lucy," Speake said, believing this was the only explanation needed.

"Oh, that little matter," Todd said, laughing, and jostled his friend roughly a few times with his encompassing arm.

As they walked on towards the saloon, Todd's arm still around his shoulders, Speake heard a sharp report behind him, like the crack of a whip, the sound of leather on leather, followed by the clatter of panicked hooves. They stopped and tried to turn together, to see what had happened. Closely linked as they were, one of Speake's feet caught against Todd's ankle as he turned. He stumbled and fell, pulling them both to the ground.

Looking up, Speake saw Sullivan's horse coming to a halt a

few feet in front of them. It reared up, its front legs flailing at the air. Close by he could hear screaming, though the sound seemed to him too long and slow to have been made by any human voice. In his dazed state he thought it must have been the agitated cries of the horse.

He noticed its eyes, rounded and bloodshot, its nostrils flared back wide in panic. Its pink and black lips and muzzle were curled back around its bit, exposing yellowed oblong teeth. He could see, in sharpest detail, the flat iron hoops of the shoes, the bright-worn heads of the nails securing them, the dried mud, the threads of grass and straw and moss embedded amongst the individual hairs of the hooves as they flashed above him. The sight made him think momentarily of the state of his own shoes, the wax and laces still in his coat pocket, the anticipated evening ahead, a life with Lucy possibly just within his grasp.

He turned away from the flailing hooves, and saw the German boy running towards him, heard him cry out: "Nein!"

As the hooves came down, he tried to roll away.

Sullivan coughed into his hand and moved towards the body. It lay on the ground, convulsions jerking sporadically through it. Blood pulsed rhythmically from the back of its head. The skull had been kicked in, a raw, visible indentation, near the top of the spine. A foam of dark blood bubbled out of the mouth and nostrils. The eyelids flickered wildly, and the legs scrabbled feebly against the ground, trying to make purchase in the dust, as though the young man was still trying to crawl away. Sullivan bent down and pinned them to the ground.

"Looks to me like his neck's been broke," a voice thick

with phlegm said from among the small group of people who were starting to gather.

"I guess someone should call the doctor, though I doubt there's anythin' can be done for him," the voice added. Allenby pushed his way through to where the body was lying, indicating the path he intended to follow with the stem of his pipe. He came to a halt and nudged one shoulder of the body with the toe of his boot.

"Best bring him on up to the ice barn when he's done with kickin'," he said. A last, strenuous convulsion passed through the body, and then it was still. Sullivan stood up, and turned to face the crowd.

"Anyone here manage to catch that damn horse of mine?" he said calmly. "He's sure been in a cantankerous mood today. Getting excited about the party tonight, maybe." One or two of the gathered men laughed uneasily, followed by a murmur of confusion.

"I saw the Dortmund boy go after it," a man's voice said.

"Well, that's alright then. He's the only other one the beast will let near it," Sullivan said, the last of the failing sunlight flashing dull yellow on the single block of gold set among the neat rows of white his smiling lips revealed.

"Tell him there's a dollar in it for him when he brings it back safe."

A White Christmas

Hope, December 26th 1899

For the past three months there has been snow aplenty here, almost a commonplace, and often bringing with it great inconvenience. A fresh fall of snow yesterday, on Christmas Day, however, served only to add to the festive spirit, and to dispel for many the shadow of the most recent accident.

A snowball fight raged in the main street for more than an hour, with at least a hundred taking part, both men and women, both child and adult.

A polished ribbon of ice-packed snow runs now down the middle of the main street - a joyous slide for the children, a fraught hazard for those of less agile frame. At either end of the street, a life-size snowman, each replete with broom-handle rifle, and with charcoal eyes to watch over us, now stands sentinel.

A Merry and a peace-filled Christmas to one and all.   TES

Part 3

The Ice Barn

15

A Change of Heart

Allenby had stayed on at the party in the saloon only until midnight had passed. He had wanted to see the new century in with others around him, not alone, brooding on the past, as most of his nights had been spent since the day he left Chicago. Despite the heady anticipation in the air, nothing had changed for him with the transition to another year. The past had still lingered in his thoughts, and the great event everyone had been talking about for weeks, getting agitated about what changes it would bring to their lives, had been for him simply one more day, yet one more year turning into another.

At the stroke of midnight most of the men in the saloon had rushed out into the street, firing their guns gleefully into the air, the white bursts of their breath mingling with the smoke coughing from the barrels of their pistols, shouting and screaming at nothing more than their own imaginings.

He had remained at the bar toasting himself with the last of his drink, watching them make fools of themselves, wondering whether it was the jubilation of the moment prompting them to act in such a way, or a reaction to a more primordial drive - a sensed need to chase away malign spirits from the moment of birth of the new year. From the depths of the forest the desolate howls of the wolves had echoed back their bellowing. He had not been persuaded by the men's ritual, if that was what it was. Some dangers could not be kept so easily at bay.

Moving unsteadily from the effects of the unaccustomed excess of whiskey he had consumed, on his way out of the saloon he had stumbled past the table where Sullivan was sitting in his own amused contemplation of the celebrations. Sullivan's booted feet had been up on the table, his hands hooked behind his head. Allenby had thought about saying something but had decided against it. Already he was tired of the new century, of everything he knew it would bring, and was impatient for the refuge of his bed.

"You know it was Speake I was trying to get, not the other one," Sullivan had said to him as he was walking away. Allenby had stopped, against his better judgement, had turned to face him. Perhaps it had been the fact that Sullivan had not even bothered to give a name to the young man he had killed. His customary arrogant detachment from what he had done, making everything impersonal, both good and bad. It had always been an added source of aggravation about him.

"Anyone with more than half a brain around here knows it. It still doesn't explain the why." He had suddenly felt reckless, pressed by that accumulated sense of aggravation, free of any concerns about consequences.

"Because it felt like it had to be done, I guess," Sullivan had offered, as though that was explanation enough. "Just like it was with Bunney and Rosie. I had no choice but to go through with it."

"You're admittin' you killed Bunney, then?"

"Oh, come on, Josh! You know well enough what I mean." Sullivan's hands had come down from his head and had nestled in his lap. Despite his protestation and the subject of their discussion he had seemed to find the exchange amusing.

"If anyone knows the truth of that, I'd stake my money on you. Anyway, what do you take me for, a fool?" Allenby had considered the possibilities before giving an answer.

"No! Just a killer, I suppose," he had finally said.

"Well, if that's what you believe," Sullivan had replied, his face and eyes hardening, "maybe you'd do best to remember it."

He had pulled a gun on Sullivan then, the tiny pistol - a two-barrelled Remington derringer - that he carried always with him. It had been a reaction, foolhardy and pointless, to the sense of impotence that had stirred in him. He had known there was nothing he could do to alter what Sullivan was, or to recall the wasted years he had spent yearning for a woman who preferred the attentions of a whoremonger to what he had to offer. He had pointed the pistol in the direction of Sullivan's chest. Sullivan had thrown his head back and laughed.

"Put the gun away, Josh. You know you're not going to use it."

"And what d'you think they'd say if I did?" No one in the room had seemed to notice what was going on. Sullivan had been sitting in an alcove, Allenby standing at its mouth; they had both been concealed from view to much of the room. Most of the men had still been outside, laughing and singing, or fighting now that the moment for celebration was past, or had gone upstairs with one of the women to anoint the arrival of the new century in a more pragmatic way. The few who remained in the saloon had been too drunk to move to join in the celebration, let alone notice.

"That I deserved it, probably, though I doubt that thing has the poke to kill anything."

Allenby had looked at the gun; it had looked small and ineffectual in his rough workman's hands. It was said the bullet travelled so slow you could see it moving through the air, half the speed of a normal bullet, although it would kill a man when used at close range. It was the reason gamblers favoured it; it could be kept easily concealed yet could kill, or at least seriously incapacitate a man seated on the other side of a table. He had never fired it to see if it was true about the speed of the bullet, had known he would not find the courage or conviction that night to test the veracity of the other claim.

He had smiled weakly and had put the pistol back into his pocket. Buttoning up his overcoat, and pulling the collar tight around his neck, he had turned away and resumed his unsteady progress towards the door. He remembered how the crystal pendants on the chandelier had chimed against each other as he had opened the door, admitting fluxes of cold night air.

"Happy New Year, Sullivan," he had called out without looking back. "Guess I'll be seein' you around."

The photograph was faded now, the paper dulled and yellowed with age, the image it bore reduced to vague planes and shadings of grey. It had been cut from a newspaper, back in late '70, early '71. The original picture had shown her, looking out of place, embarrassed almost, standing at the edge of a group of seated Chicago matrons - doyennes of some society gathered to sponsor good causes - Allenby could not remember which. He had removed as much as he could of the dowagers from the picture, had pasted the waste strips of paper to seal off the back of the frame.

She had been a beautiful young woman then - a vision in her long fashionably cut pale gown set against the dowdy widow's weeds of the matrons beside her - and already married. The fact of her marital state had offered him no protection. He had lost his heart to her the moment he first saw her, had not looked at any other woman since with what amounted to serious interest, even though, in the early years at least, while he could still have been considered a passably handsome man, there had been opportunity enough.

The photograph had kept him company, had offered him some small solace for nigh on thirty years. He and the picture had faded together over that time. Only the frame, burnished bright from years of handling, had stopped the picture from becoming as worn and frayed as he had become. He had made the frame himself, had in-laid the tiny facets of different woods and mother-of-pearl to make a geometric pattern running around its face - an illusion of tilted cubes alternately receding and advancing around its rim. In the bottom right-hand corner, he had fashioned a tiny mouse from the leftover shavings, its sinuous tail meandering across the bottom of the frame. Why a mouse? He could no longer recall. A symbol of industry perhaps; of secrecy and guile? Timidity, more likely, he decided.

The skills he had once had in his now work-wracked hands; where had they gone? How had he allowed them all to slip away?

He held out his hands in front of him, the glassine skin of their palms turned towards him, fingers spread apart. How had he ended up using the talents they had once possessed? In making pine boxes for folk who would never see them; occasionally knocking together a rough-hewn table and chair for some newly arrived prospector; cutting blocks of ice. Burying, storing the dead. He had tried to be a good man, to make her notice. Somehow, he had lost his way and ended up ashamed of what he had become, with only an ice barn and a wooden shack in the middle of nowhere to show for his efforts.

Whatever confidence or authority he now conveyed to others was a fabrication, carefully crafted. A surface. A thin veneer. Sufficient to persuade the simple folk out here, yet offering him little protection against the vagaries of fortune. He had been considered eligible once, witty even, handsome enough to have had women make advances to him. The only one he had wanted though was Emily Henderson. His schemes to impress her had all failed; so he had followed her, hoping that one day her perception of him would change. In that forlorn pursuit, his skills had withered and perished, along with the dreams, his looks, and whatever wit he had once possessed. The other women had come, for a while, in the good years before the fire, had allowed themselves to be seduced momentarily by the surface, the impression of eligibility, had then withdrawn as soon as they realised that was all there was; no depth, just a veneer. A crude performance, put on, not for them, but for himself, even though he had lost all notion of what he hoped to achieve.

As for his rival, Sullivan, the knowledge that he too had done nothing of worth, other than cater to the baser needs of others, offered no consolation. Without trying too hard he had ended up with everything. Even her, if he had wanted her; if he had noticed or cared.

Going over to his chair and sitting down, he picked up the wooden frame, considered for the ten thousandth time the indistinct face of the woman in the picture. What had she ever seen in Sullivan, he wondered? What saving grace? She must have had doubts, suspicions about the sort of man he was; must have smothered them for all those years beneath the blanket of her desire. In the past, he had always made allowances for such wilful blindness, knowing too well the distorting effect such unrequited passion could have. But then Sullivan had arrived in Hope, rising like a spectre from the thirty-odd years since he had seen him last, and it had become clear just how strong her feelings for him still were. Since then, even more so since she took her own life - her self-destructive statement, that only he had truly understood - he had been finding it increasingly difficult to make any such concession.

There was nothing, either, that would permit him to make any allowances for himself. The things he had tried to do, the decisions he had made over those thirty-odd years since Chicago, had been dictated, not by love, as he had always persuaded himself, but by hatred for the man he believed had denied him. Was that the hard truth of it? Had Emilie arrived at her indifference towards him without ever having been prompted by Sullivan's presence? Had it been simply an aversion to him - a man beneath her class, little more than a skilled labourer – or of what he, Josh Allenby, erstwhile cabinet maker and craftsman had become. Together, those decisions, the things they had led to, had steadily turned him into someone he was no longer proud to be. And worse, they had gradually undermined the passion he had cherished for so long, despite his having known, ever since they had left Chicago, that his feelings for her would never be matched. The only excuse he could offer for himself was that in the end he had been driven by a misguided notion that it would somehow help her: if Sullivan were dead, she would be free of him, released from the possibilities she had apparently believed the man still offered, and which had obviously caused her unbearable pain. He had had little else to give her, at least nothing she would have wanted.

He looked at the picture frame, examining its handiwork as though it were unfamiliar to him, running his fingertips gently over the image of the mouse. The surface of the wood was as smooth as glass; he had cut and sanded the veneers so perfectly. He found it hard to believe he had ever possessed the skills and patience, the courage to try to make such an object. The frame, the history it enshrined, was the only evidence that remained. Such things, much as he might wish it, could not be denied, even though he was no longer able to summon up an image of what sort of man that craftsman had once been.

He turned the frame several times through his hands to examine it more closely, and wondered whether it was too late for him to try again to make such a thing - to regain such integrity of thought and belief and action. To bring something of value, or at least of beauty into a world that seemed to him now bereft of both. To try to recover some small part of all that had been lost.

The face of the woman in the picture was barely visible now. It could have been the image of any woman, the picture taken at any place or time. Only the fashion of the clothing would have given anyone who knew about such things a clue as to where and when it had been taken. Probably, he thought, he was the only one now who would recognise her. He turned the frame over, started to pick away with a cracked and thickened fingernail at the faded strips of paper, the ghosted, self-righteous faces holding the backboard in place. When it was free, he eased out the board, then the photograph, and finally the thin pane of glass.

Setting the frame and glass down on the table beside him, he stood up and went over to the cast-iron stove. He looked at the image one last time - the fragile, insubstantial thing that had shaped the course of much of his adult life. His hand trembling, he raised the paper to brush his lips, immediately felt the sting of loss and regret in his eyes, all the years and hours and minutes of it, held back until now, crammed into this one instant.

Lifting the lid of the stove with the iron key, he let the picture drop onto the fire inside. As the flames consumed it, the photograph floated momentarily into the air - a skein of weightless dust, devoid of substance - before it settled back onto the embers and immediately shrivelled and fragmented into blackened flakes of ash.

Fate: One Man's Death,
Another Man's Good Fortune
Hope, January 1ˢᵗ 1900

Events happen, circumstances can arise, things that may cause a man to realize with a jolt of certainty just how tenuous and vulnerable a human life can be. Such an unforeseen and salutary happenstance befell this correspondent but hours past.

A few hours short of the expiry of the old century, while the world was preparing for the celebration of its passing, my own life also almost came to an end.

I have to report, however – no doubt in contradiction to the sense of relief a man might properly be expected to express at the fact of his own survival - that my own deliverance offers me scant consolation, coming as it has at the cost of the life of another. The life of someone I had come to know as a friend.

Mr. Gillam Standard Todd, a hale and always cheerful and resolute young man from Dumfries in Scotland, had given up his all, had sailed an ocean and crossed a hostile and alien continent, like many before him had done, in the hope of finding gold. What he found instead was a cold and senseless death in the frozen dirt of a place where barely another soul knew his name or cared about him, his skull crushed by the flailing hooves of a somehow malignly directed horse.

The identity of the owner of the horse, Mr. Brogan P. Sullivan, is not in question. Of the nature of the hand that steered its wild and homicidal careening, the facts are less than clear. The question remains unanswered, neither by the perpetrator, nor by the Law by which every good man trusts his life will be governed: was it the work of a human hand, or merely that of blind and uncaring Fate?

Also, what remains to be discovered still is the intention inherent in the actions of such a hand, be it human or otherwise. Gillam Todd had no enemies; there was no-one here with reason to wish him dead. He had just that day discovered the gold he had come to seek, and given his nature, there is no doubt that had he lived, a good portion of those new-found riches would have been dispensed in the service of the evening's celebration, and that such largesse would have been handed out to all with his habitual good humour and grace. With his death, the town has lost a part of its living, breathing soul.

And what of contrition, or remorse, or

recompense for what had happened, even if accident it was? "Has anyone gone after my horse?" was the only expressed concern of the horse's owner, Mr. Brogan Sullivan, while the young man lay still dying at his feet.

Now, it would seem - for I am unable to draw any other conclusion from the circumstances, and from my own embroilment in the events that led to Mr. Todd's untimely death - my own continued tenure in this place is fraught with uncertainty.

Have I an enemy here, one who wishes me dead? Was I the intended target, not the innocent Ingram Todd? Or did Fate - as Fate, in its blind indifference can often choose to do - simply and malignly elect to take from the young man that which it had apparently just as freely given to him but hours before?   TES

16

Talking's Free

"So, you're not going to do anything about it? You're going to let it pass?" Two days had passed since Gillam Todd's death and Speake was still struggling to make sense of it - that his friend had died, in his own stead most likely. He could see no reason or justice in it, no way to free himself of the guilt he felt, nor any legitimacy in Sullivan still being free and showing no remorse for what had taken place.

"What'd I arrest him for? It was an accident, like Brogan said. That horse's a spirited animal. Everyone knows that. The damn thing's even thrown Brogan at least half a dozen times. You're the only one as doubts it, and no jury here would find him guilty on your word alone."

"What about Dortmund? Have you spoken to him?" The sheriff nodded, and walked back towards his desk. He sat down heavily in the gate-backed chair behind it and hoisted his feet onto the top of the desk. He looked bored and unconcerned, more interested in the condition of his boots than in what Speake had to say. In all probability, Speake thought, for him it was just one more death in a place where death was nothing out of the ordinary. All the man wanted was an easy life. If nothing was to be gained in pursuing it, then best to let it pass as what everyone else seemed content to - an unfortunate accident. A random incident in which nothing, or no-one of significance had been lost, just another prospector who could have forfeited his life that day in a dozen other ways. Better that - dumb luck - than to cross a man like Brogan Sullivan.

"Says he thought your discussion with Sullivan was done," the sheriff said once he had settled. "That you had come to some agreement, and he was wandering off, and only turned when he heard the commotion. He claims the first thing he saw was the horse rearing up and then coming down on your friend." Speake nodded in resignation. It was predictable, given Dortmund's situation, that the young man would be reluctant to say anything that might jeopardise his relationship with Sullivan.

"Still, don't you find it odd that he didn't know there was a real argument going on? I tried to hit Sullivan. Did he not see that?" A muffled snort of amusement jerked through the sheriff's body.

"Not a wise move...! What can I say? That's what the boy told me. What can I do? Beat a different story out of him to satisfy you?" He glanced up, momentarily abandoning the contemplation of his boots. "I'm sorry about your friend, the scare you must have had, but there's nothing I can do if you can't show me any different."

Anger and frustration twisted Speake's features. He felt patronised, that his opinion was being dismissed as of no account. He wasn't even being accused of lying - the sheriff knew he was telling the truth. He was simply being ignored. "He has this town in his pocket, hasn't he?" he said bitterly.

The sheriff shrugged and readjusted his feet. "You could put it that way. There's many here as owe him. Maybe it's not that way in Chicago, or back in England, but here loyalty's counted as a virtue, whatever else happens. Brogan's a good man, in his own way. Like I said, a lot of people here owe him something."

"And what about Todd, doesn't someone owe him something?" He paused and looked around the sheriff's office, and then at the man sitting at his desk, luxuriating in the indifference his ill-deserved position afforded him. "But then I suppose you must owe him something too. Gratitude must be a powerful motivator; more powerful than conscience."

"Are you insinuating something?" The sheriff had swung his feet down and was now leaning forward across the top of the desk. Speake shook his head and turned away. Could he blame the man - for his weakness, for his sense of self-preservation? What else would he have been if he had not done whatever he had to keep himself in Sullivan's pay? Scrabbling out there among the rocks and dirt with the other prospectors most probably. A store clerk or livery man at best.

"No. I'm just disappointed," he said, without looking back, as he came to a halt at the door. "I expected better, fool that I am."

Outside, through the bars on the door, he saw Lucy on

the other side of the street, sweeping the veranda outside the saloon. Even from this distance he could discern the small hitch in her step as she moved. She seemed to be singing to herself, her head and lips moving to some unheard melody. He recalled the first time he had seen her, almost the moment he had arrived in Hope. She had been on the opposite side of the street, leaning against the newel post at the top of the few steps that led up from the dusty thoroughfare to the veranda at the front of the saloon. She had been wearing a two-tone grey striped dress, trimmed with a froth of some white fabric nestled across the swell of her breasts. At the hem, the dress had been cut high at the front, almost to the knees. She had been wearing black, calf-length, lace-up boots beneath a fringe of exposed petticoats. Speake had thought her pretty, through the too dark make-up round her eyes, the blushes of rouge on her cheeks. He had thought she could not have been more than twenty years old. She had seen him, and had given a tentative wave. Speake had pulled away from the coach window, had busied himself inside the carriage, gathering his belongings, pretending not to have noticed.

Later that evening, as he had explored the town, quickly discovering it to consist of little more than the one main street and a dozen or so side alleyways leading off mostly to nowhere, often only to blank walls of bare rock, he had seen her again, sitting on a rocking-chair, her legs stretched out at an angle across the veranda. Her petticoats had frothed out from under the hem of her skirt and spilled across the top of her boots. There had been no time to cross to the other side or turn back the way he had come. She had already noticed him, and was leaning forward in the chair, a half-smile playing on her face.

"Hello there, young stranger" she had said as he drew near. Hearing the harsh admonishments of his mother, Speake had been unable to do more than nod in acknowledgment and had carried on walking.

"You are allowed to stop and talk, you know," she called out after him. "Talking's free. There's no obligation." There had been no resentment or aggression in her voice, only a hint of resignation, or disappointment, or so he had found himself imagining. He had stopped and turned. She had gestured to him with her hands, opening out her palms at the level of her hips, tilting her head to one side. Speake had not known how to respond to the unspoken question.

"I'm sorry. I'm new here," was all he had offered.

"I wish I could say the same," she had said. She had told him her name, and some of the gossip of the town, and he had explained his reason, the professional one, for having come to Hope. She had been the first to tell him the gold was running out, that he had timed his arrival to witness the slow death of the town. Then she had teased him, saying she would not want to keep a man from his bed when he said he was hungry and tired from his travels and needed to eat and sleep.

His real reason for having fled that night had been the agitation he had felt - an inner conflict paralysing thought and word - at how strongly he had been attracted to her. Before he had left Chicago his mother had warned him to avoid such women. Wanton was the adjective she had used. Now he had been here for nearly three months, he had discovered there was far more to Lucy than the narrow, prejudiced label his mother would have assigned to her. He still found himself discomfited by the strength of his attraction to her, and remained as ignorant of what to do with such thoughts and sensations, as during that first encounter.

Despite the hours they had spent together, the signals he must have given, either intentionally or inadvertently, he still had no idea whether she held any such feelings for him. At times, the way she looked at him, the tone of her voice, led him to believe she might. He recalled their conversation, what he had taken as their mutual flirting in the street on New Year's Eve, but Todd's death had curtailed any possibility of future escalation. And too, the rational side of him countered, discounting the positive things he had learned about her: she was a prostitute. It was her trade to be adept at telling men what they wanted to hear.

Pushing away thoughts of his naive and optimistic arrival, Speake looked back at the sheriff. The man was still sitting at his desk, staring back at him, his thick-jawed face set, his grey eyes devoid of expression. Speake shook his head gently in a gesture of mild disdain. He felt empty and powerless, trapped in a set of emotions he had never previously experienced, and which his sheltered life in Chicago had left him ill-equipped to understand. It was not only the feelings Lucy had aroused in him, the self-doubt they had induced. The weeks of discomfort and hardship, his sense of isolation, the good lives he had seen being wasted and lost, had provided him with a deeper, more uncomfortable understanding of Hope and its inhabitants, undermining the better expectations he had once held.

He had anticipated that life here would be uncompromising; that was what it had certainly proved to be. What he had not expected was that those who had come here would be as indifferent to each other's wellbeing - as Todd had declaimed but a few minutes before he was killed - and as regardless of the law and its strictures as he had found them to be. Here, he could pay a woman he did not know to engage in sex with him and no-one would notice or care, and would more likely think the better of him for it. A woman could be bound to a position of humiliation and servitude and have no say or choice. A man could be robbed of his possessions, and the law would do nothing to protect or recompense him. A man could kill another - or commit other, equally contemptible crimes - and continue to go about his own life without question or blame.

17

Prospecting

As they emerged from a thick stand of pine trees Dortmund halted and motioned with his head towards where the ground started to level off several yards further along the path. Before they had set off, he had said he knew more or less the paths they should take to find Ingram Todd's claim. The path they were on was no more than a meandering, lightly-worn ribbon of trampled earth and exposed stones rising gradually beside a broken stream across the forested lower slopes of the mountains. Trees rose all around, distorting perspective and direction. The spot they had arrived at was desolate and uninviting - an unlikely place, Speake immediately thought, for anyone to have thought they might find gold. He would not have found this place on his own. A closing haze of mist drifted around them, and above, low clouds veiled the faces of the rock, tumbling down like hanging trails of lace along their folds and crevices.

"Are you certain this is the place?" he asked.

"Yes. Look!" Dortmund said, pointing. "That is where he made his fire." Towards the back of a broad levelled area, close to the foot of a looming wall of rock, Speake could vaguely make out a darkened patch of ground, a lighter mound of ash at its centre, a waif-like shadow of soot curling up the face of the rock behind.

As they drew closer, he began to make out within the shrouding mist, the outlines of a roughly assembled shelter. It consisted of no more than cut branches driven into the ground and tied together at the top to form two triangles about eight feet apart, a longer branch laid across their cross-points as ridgepole. The whole construction was draped with a stained and heavily patched sheet of canvas, its lower edges held on the ground by small boulders. At the front, Todd had threaded a cord between the hems of the hanging flaps to tie off the entrance.

"Dear God! He could have frozen to death up here and no-one would have known," Speake said, anguish for the hardships his friend had endured welling up inside him at the sight of his makeshift camp. An image came to him of Todd's face; the playful energy in his eyes, the animation of his features; he could almost hear his voice, the softly curling flow of his accent. He felt moved and saddened by the young Scot's deprived circumstances, by the depth of his commitment to the search for gold.

"How would he have survived the winter in a place like this?"

"He probably would not have," Dortmund replied flatly. Speake could take no consolation from such a bleak opinion, credible as it was. In whatever way he chose to define it – accident, murder - the fact remained that Todd had lost his life as a consequence of Speake's confrontation with Sullivan. That his own choices might have led him to lose it here anyway did nothing to ease Speake's sense of culpability. It had been the reason he had wanted to find the claim, to locate the gold Todd had discovered. Not for his own gain, but if he could put it to good use elsewhere then his friend's life would not have been forfeited entirely in vain.

Much as he had wanted to find it, Speake had doubted the wisdom of trying to locate the claim while winter still lingered. The weather here was so unpredictable; it could change in minutes from cold, brilliant calm to a sudden ferocity he would not have imagined possible had he not experienced it himself. He had been reluctant too to set out alone on the unfamiliar pathways threading and criss-crossing the outlying wilderness, and had had no idea anyway where he should look.

Since the death of his father and uncle and grandfather, Dortmund had spent much of his time in the mountains. His mother and sisters had left Hope within days of the accident, fully aware of the dangers of travelling, yet eager to escape the place that had made them a widow, orphans, before winter truly set in. Dortmund had elected to stay, having no inclination to live in the city the women were heading to. He had discovered a sense of purpose in the wilderness that suited his nature, a way of living according to the laws of the earth, and the plants and animals it nurtured. That was how he had explained it to Speake - he had no need of fancy clothes, a fine home, money; everything he needed would be provided by the land, and he in turn would give back whatever he could. His family had been unable to dissuade him, had finally accepted his decision. Left on his own, for the past months he had been building a shack on a flattened outcrop of rock that looked out across the valley, cutting and splitting trees, hauling tools and ironware from the abandoned mine in two buckets hung from a yoke across his shoulders. As a consequence, he knew the trails that wound through the mountains, both the good and those that led off to nowhere. Eventually Speake had asked if he would help find Todd's abandoned claim.

The gold did not prove difficult to find. A small stream ran to one side of the flattened area where Todd had pitched his shelter, its edges fringed with ice. Its source, a still-frozen cascade, hung down from a ledge of rock about twenty feet from the ground. Thin plumes of melt water spiralled from the lower extremities of the ice, the delicate chatter of water on water echoing from the stone. On the far side of the stream, a bank of scree and sand had built up over time. Todd had laid two tree trunks roped together to form a bridge across the water. A shovel stood stabbed into the sandbank; a rusted iron pan propped against its handle. The island was obviously where Todd had been looking, panning the scree. Speake remembered though what his friend had said about having found the gold close to where he had a privy, and this he soon discovered behind the makeshift tent, behind a large fallen boulder at the foot of the rock face. A short, fractured metallic stripe, fringed by white crystals of quartz, ran across the surface of the rock, the golden tone of the seam scoring the dull grey stone. Around it there was a lighter, lichen-free area where a sheet of rock had split away through the effects of rain and frost. The displaced stone, which would have held the seam concealed for eons, lay on the ground below, shattered into pieces. Speake called out to Dortmund. When he arrived beside him the young man stood for several moments with his hands on his hips looking at the seam of gold, then started to hoot loudly into the air.

"And they said there was no more gold," he said, as he turned to Speake, a broad grin furrowing the sides of his face, and then added without any further discussion, "I believe there is work for us to do." He turned quickly back to the seam, pulling a knife from the inside pocket of his coat, its blade sheathed in a wrap of leather, its blade ground almost as thin as a needle. Speake was struck by how prepared the young man was; the knife, its overly honed blade, was the ideal tool for the task in hand. As there was only sufficient space for one to work at the seam itself, while Dortmund set about prising out the gold in the rock face, Speake started to search for whatever had fallen to the ground. Every now and then, as the wind changed, he would catch the pungent smell wafting across from the freshly dampened latrine.

Little more than half an hour had passed before Dortmund stepped back and announced he had retrieved all he could of the embedded seam. As he spoke, his eyes continued to scan the rock, searching for other veins. Speake's own search had become fruitless too; at first, he had found a number of pieces without much effort, but he had not unearthed anything for several minutes, even with the shard of stone he had been using as a makeshift trowel. From the scant knowledge of prospecting he had garnered, he knew that if there was more gold buried deeper in the rock, it would require more time and heavier tools than they had to retrieve it.

"We ought to start back down anyway, before this gets worse," Speake said, turning the palm of his hand up to gauge the deteriorating state of the weather. They were by now engulfed in a fine drizzle. Miniscule water droplets gathered and glittered on their clothing, and gleamed like diminutive pearls on Dortmund's hair. His face was still glowing with the excitement of their discovery. Speake had felt an initial surge of exhilaration too – to have found gold. Now he had some understanding of what lured so many to search for it, even in the face of hardship and repeated disappointment. The reasons for his being there, however, the provenance of the gold they had found, had quickly dispelled his elation.

"How much do you think we have found?" Dortmund asked.

"I've no idea, but it must be several hundred dollars. We'll share it equally. I would never have found it without your help."

"No! I do not want it. You may take it all!" the young man almost shouted, his exultation displaced by surliness.

"In heaven's name, why not? Think what you could do with it. It can't be easy living here on your own."

"There is enough here to satisfy my needs. The land and forest are generous enough if you understand them, and as you have seen, I have my bow to give me meat when I need it." Speake had been surprised when he had met Dortmund that morning to see the bow and a quiver of arrows slung across his shoulder. He had not seen him armed in that way before. The ensemble was patently hand-made, the bow a bent ash stave strung with animal gut, the arrows tipped with shaped shards of bone, and with unmatched feather fletches. On the climb to Todd's claim Dortmund had quickly unshouldered the bow and pinioned a rabbit as it sat on the path ahead considering their approach for too long. The bow had been powerful and the arrow true despite their makeshift appearance.

"I have no use for gold, for money," he continued. "It only brings bad luck," he added, barely loud enough for Speake to hear. Speake could tell that the young man's thoughts had gone back to the accident in his family's mine, the search for this precious substance which had put them there, had exposed them to the dangers subterranean workers faced. He could understand his thinking, illogical as it was; the desperate searching for an explanation, however unlikely and superstitious the discovered reason might be.

"I know you have your reasons. I'll not try to persuade you," he said. "But if you change your mind, the money will still be there." Dortmund looked at him and shook his head slowly then started to gather his things together.

"You know that I saw him, don't you?" Dortmund said unexpectedly as they were walking back down towards the town. They had been descending in silence for some time, the sullen echoes of their last exchange still reverberating between them. Dortmund had a small tote bag slung over his shoulder, next to his bow and quiver. He had found it inside Todd's shelter. Inside it was the gold, and the few items of Todd's belongings they had considered worth keeping.

"The day with Todd, when he was killed, I saw it," he continued, nervously readjusting the bag on his shoulder.

After his initial surprise, Speake was glad the young man had finally admitted what he had seen. He knew it would make no difference now; if he said anything after such an elapsed period of time, people would say he was only making it up as repayment of some grudge, or for some other self-seeking motive. It made a difference to Speake however, relieving him of his lingering doubts about whether Todd's death had indeed been the outcome of a deliberate act. He nodded to Dortmund, to encourage him.

"I saw Sullivan hit the horse. He let go of the reins and struck it with his hand. It was obvious his intention was to kill you, not Mister Todd. But it was not an accident. Of that, I am sure."

"Thank you. But why didn't you say at the time? You saw him kill a man and believed it was deliberate, yet you said nothing. Was it a question of loyalty?" Dortmund brushed his dampened hair from his face. The rain was now falling freely, and their progress had been hesitant, slowed by the precarious state of the ground.

"No. I simply thought it would serve no purpose. A man was alive, and then he was dead," he said, his voice tightening. "That is how it is here, is it not? My father was alive, and then he was dead. My uncle and grandfather the same. No reason is to be found in any of it. The only difference was that a man I knew was the cause of that one death, not some unknowable power, and that I saw it happen."

"You could have made sure the man was punished for his crime. Surely that would have meant something." Dortmund looked at him, his face now hardened in defiance.

"Yes, I could have done that," he said. "Sullivan might have been punished, but your friend would still be dead, and what difference would any of it have made, for me? My life would most likely have been made worse."

Speake closed his eyes momentarily and turned his head away as he struggled with his own conflicting emotions. He knew he should feel resentment at the young man's failure to reveal the facts of the crime at the time, his self-motivated justification for silence. If he had told what he had seen, the sheriff might have been inclined to believe what Speake claimed about the incident. Because Dortmund had lied, Sullivan was still free, his felony unpunished. But he also understood the young man's explanation. It had probably felt to him that he had no choice; that he had become subject to an overwhelming feeling of impotence. Nothing he could have said or done would have made a difference. Speake recognised that feeling, had felt it keenly in Chicago as he watched his father die. Sometimes it did appear the world was set up such that the choices had already been made for you. There was nothing you could do other than act in a fixed, almost predetermined way.

He lifted his head and glanced across at Dortmund, saw himself reflected, the sadness and desperation set deep in the young man's eyes. He realised then how neither of them had really stood a chance. Not in the face of the devastating events that had confronted them. Not in this hard world where it could suddenly be required of a young man to relinquish all vestiges of youth and be grown up and strong.

18

The Old Sleuth
Library

The life Speake had experienced in Chicago had been one of middle-class gentility. Beyond his daily studies in the rarefied halls of the University, his social routine had consisted largely of visits to restaurants and tea-houses, theatres, galleries, concert-halls, picnics on the lake shore in the summer months, soirées and genteel garden parties held at the houses of colleagues and friends. The world of working men, of hard-drinking men and their needs was not one he had ever experienced. In Chicago there had been a clear divide – on one side, the genteel suburbs along the lakeshore and around the University, on the other, the stockyards that brought the city its wealth, around the yards, a hinterland of tenement slums and shanties where the people who laboured in the yards lived. These were parts of the city where people of

Speake's class never went, other than as tourists to see the great machine of the stockyards in operation, turning living animals into the meat they ate at the expensive restaurants they frequented. There were parts of the city where people like Speake would never dare to go, for fear of both their safety and their reputations. It had therefore required several visits, and the palliative distractions of Lucy and her conversation before he had eventually become accustomed to being in the saloon.

The first few occasions he had been here - having understood the necessity to acquaint himself with the workings of so central a part of the town - he had found himself unable to relax, had been too aware of the tensions which seemed always present. The isolated situation of a large number of men, most without wives or family to temper their drives; the competition to find gold, the ever-present sexual spur of Sullivan's ladies, the combined additional frictions of gambling and alcohol, all seemed to him to keep the saloon's clientele in a constant state of agitation. On almost every occasion he had been here, certainly during the first few weeks, at least one argument or physical fight had broken out.

During daylight hours though, the saloon was quieter, most of the men off toiling at their workings, or going about the general commerce of the town, Sullivan's ladies sleeping, their working day mirroring that of everyone else. Often Speake would come here to write his stories, to linger in the warmth over a cup of coffee as he wrote, but he had come today with the intention of finding Lucy. There was something he wanted to ask her - a question aroused during his recent trip into the mountains with Dortmund. As he pushed open the door, he saw her sitting with Belinda at the table in the small alcove at the far end of the bar where the girls gathered to gossip and complain about the world when things were quiet. Lucy was engrossed in filing her fingernails, while Belinda flicked casually through the pages of a penny magazine, not pausing to read as she skimmed through it.

Speake was familiar with the type of thing they liked to read. They were not dissimilar to the *Penny Dreadfuls* that had been popular back in England, and were equally as hyperbolic. The narratives they told always involved a detective story, a murder or mystery to be solved; a dashing, resourceful sleuth to uncover the solution, a beautiful yet vulnerable young woman to be protected, and won; and of course, a dastardly villain to be eventually bested. They had grandiose titles like *'The New York Detective Library'*, and *'Secret Service; The Young and Old King Brady, Detectives'*. The women kept a box of them behind the bar; dime novels or story-papers they called them. From the dun shade of the paper, the brightly coloured cover, it looked as though Belinda was reading a copy of a series called *'The Old Sleuth Library'*.

Speake had read a few titles from their thumb-worn collection, when he had been bored or had nothing else to do. Some he had even found entertaining, though mostly he had found the content of the stories unbelievable. The repeated claim that they were all - thousands in total in all of the numerous publications - based on true events did little to convince him of their credibility. This country could not be as unremittingly lawless as the stories portrayed; at least

Speake had not thought it could until he had come to this place called Hope.

When Belinda saw him approaching, she raised her hand, and a gentle smile crossed her lips. They had hardly spoken to each other since the day he had gone to her room to read Jack Bunney's letter. He had thought a great deal about what she had said that day - her bland depiction of her life, her reasons for being here, for doing what she did. Her words still seemed empty to him, an inadequate explanation for what he thought must be a colourful, if unconventional life. He had wanted to talk to her again, to see if he could unearth the real motivations and feelings that lay beneath her phlegmatic exterior. Since that day, however, the brief glimpse of herself she had let show, she had retreated into her more usual remoteness.

Distracted from her manicure by Belinda's reaction, Lucy looked up, and seeing him, she also smiled. It was a smile much like the one Belinda had given him; no different from the welcoming faces she and the other girls displayed to the world all day long, to all the men, to any potential customer. Speake was unable to read anything into it.

"I'll leave you two to it," Belinda said, standing and throwing the magazine onto the table. As she passed him, she laid her hand against Speake's arm. "You don't need me around as chaperone."

Speake sat down in the vacated chair and started to flick through the pages of the story-paper while Lucy remained occupied in her manicure. She seemed indifferent to his presence, neither pleased to see him, nor eager to start a conversation. With her head bent forward over her hands, from where Speake was sitting the wide sweep of her cheek-bones was even more pronounced, making her look almost feline. He was disappointed that he was unable to see the brilliant blue of her eyes.

"It feels like you've been avoiding me," he eventually said, placing the magazine back on the table. Lucy glanced up, then immediately returned to her manicure. He realised then just how little he understood her. There was nothing in the moulding of her face, her mouth, her eyes, to give him any indication of what she might be thinking.

"No. Not really. I just thought... you know, after what happened, you might need some time."

"It would have helped having someone to talk to. A friend."

"I know. I wanted to, but..." She hesitated, and her eyes flicked up again, and locked briefly on his. "But that's not all you want is it, Thomas..., friendship? I'm not sure I can give you what you want."

"You seemed quite excited about the possibility on the afternoon of the party. Was I mistaken?"

"For a time, I did get a little carried away with the idea. But, nice as the prospect was, I assumed you were only flirting with me. I know now you weren't, and it's still a tempting proposition, but you shouldn't get your hopes too high. I'm not what you think I am."

"I know what you do. It's fine with me." She laughed, and then sat looking at the table, shaking her head in disbelief.

"Oh, it's fine with you, is it? Well, I wish it was fine with me! But that wasn't what I meant. Listen...! They all think I'm a timid little thing, that I wouldn't harm a fly. You do too, and that's fine. It suits me to let you all go on believing that.

Truth is, if I really was how you all thought, I would never have made it even as far as this. You wouldn't want to know some of what I've done, not even for a good story in your newspaper."

Speake could imagine that what she said was true. A woman could not be in the position she had found herself in and survive for long if she was not in possession of some inner strengths. Equally importantly, she could not have allowed herself to be constrained by the usual feminine inhibitions and reservations. The strictures his mother saw as a social necessity would not have helped Lucy in any way. He was curious, but decided he did not really want to know the details of the things she had alluded to.

"I had an interesting conversation with Dortmund the other day," he said, deciding instead to ask about the thing that had been his reason for wanting to find her. It related to something Dortmund had said to him as they continued their descent from Todd's claim.

"He asked if I was married, or there was anyone important in my life. He seemed quite put out when I told him I held some affection for you." Speake smiled to himself as he recalled the first thing the young man had said after he had told him he was neither married nor engaged.

"You do not like women then?" Dortmund had asked. Speake had laughed at his impertinence, and had pushed him playfully to one side.

"Of course, I do. To be honest, there might be someone. Here, in Hope," For some time he had been nursing the urge to tell somebody about his growing feelings and confusions.

Dortmund had slowed and turned back to face him, and had then come to a halt.

"You mean Miss Harrigan, from the saloon?" His voice had wavered, and a blush of colour had spread across his face.

"Is it that obvious?" Speake had asked. At the time he had attributed Dortmund's reaction to nothing more than his age - an embarrassment caused by incomprehension. He had however been surprised at the young man's reaction. He had sounded more forlorn than pleased, as Speake had expected he would be on hearing of his infatuation.

"Who else could it be?" Dortmund had replied flatly. Speake had laughed again, picturing the options - the matronly storekeepers, the rugged prospector's wives, their untamed teenage daughters, the other, more world-hardened women at the saloon.

"No, that's true. And you? Is there no-one...?" Speake had started to ask in return.

"No! There is no-one," Dortmund had interjected sharply, a ring of petulance in his voice. Then he had dropped the bag containing the gold and Todd's things at Speake's feet, and had hurried off along another path that ran off at a tangent, leading away from the town. Speake had decided it would be best to just let him go, but the incident had continued to trouble him. At first, he could think of no reason why the young man should have behaved in such a way, beyond his original conjectures. Then it had come to him: Dortmund's reactions had been driven by jealousy.

"Do you have any idea why he should have reacted that way. Has he ever indicated he might have feelings towards you?" he asked Lucy now, lowering his head to one side until his cheek was almost laid against the cigarette-seared table top, to try to draw her attention. Her eyes flashed across at him through a fringe of hair before they returned again to what her hands were doing.

"How should I know what's eating him?" she said, addressing the table more than him. "Why would he have feelings for me? I hardly know him, other than I see him hanging around Brogan. He's just a kid. We don't have any reason to talk."

"He might have become infatuated at a distance. On New Year's Eve you mentioned a boy involved in some way with you and Sullivan. It wasn't Dortmund?" She looked up slowly, and this time held his gaze.

"What would make you think such a thing?"

"I'm just curious. You said it had something to do with your miscarriage."

"You and that curiosity! I said you should forget it. It wasn't important." Her guardedness struck Speake as unnecessary; none of what he had already learned about her had affected the way he thought about her. What more could she tell him that might offend him or dissuade him from his affections?

"Listen, if you must know...," she said after several seconds of silence had passed. Speake had not known what else he should say, whether he had the right to enquire any further. "There was a young man, passed through here last spring. Put simply, I fell for him. Brogan wasn't too happy, and it became ugly for a while until the guy decided it would be best if he were to leave." As she spoke, she tapped the point of the nail file repeatedly against the top of the table. "I was being stupid. He was young, sweet, but too young, probably seventeen, eighteen at most, though he acted a whole lot older with me.

I guess that's why I called him a boy. It's what Brogan always called him when we were arguing about him."

"But you spoke about it as though he were still here."

"Did I...? Well, maybe that was just wishful thinking. He was cute, and attentive, as most men I get to meet aren't, and something about him set him apart. A bit like you, I suppose. It seems I'm attracted to the ones who are different, who notice me for what I am." She paused again, examining his face, and then she asked in a plaintive voice, "Is that really such a bad way to be?"

Speake shook his head, but said nothing, taking solace in her oblique admission of attraction to him. He did not know whether he should believe her story. It sounded plausible, and he had no reason to doubt her. Something about it, though, did not ring true.

"It was probably his baby I lost," Lucy added, apparently content to take his gesture as answer. "I hadn't been too care-ful. Maybe some part of me wanted it, thought in some way it might offer a way to escape. Some dumb idea, eh?"

"Not if it had worked out that way," Speake said. "You don't see the same possibility with me?" Lucy looked at him, her eyes scanning his face again. He saw the faint glimmer of tears forming along their lower lids.

"I don't know, Thomas. It wouldn't be easy, for either of us. There'd be so much to learn, and even more to forget. So much that's too deep a part of me. Sometimes, when it's late and I'm tired, and I'm wondering how I'll get through another day, then I'm tempted." Her hand moved across the table to brush the back of his hand with her fingertips. He looked at her face, believed he could see the affection - or was it only a need, driven by loneliness and fear? - hiding behind the expressed doubt, the denial of the possibility of any such emotion.

"A couple of times I've even been on the point of coming to the boarding-house to get you." A smile shaped her mouth for a moment, and then as quickly faded. "Other times I know I shouldn't allow myself to think about you, or anyone, in that way, or in any good way at all."

19

The Swedish Boy

"Hadn't expected to see you back. Thought you'd unearthed all the stories there was to find in my little repository. What can I do for you?" Allenby was standing on the porch outside his shack, one hand hooked by the thumb into the top of his trousers, the other holding his pipe close to his mouth. Speake raised his hand in greeting.

"No, I'm afraid it's still stuck under my skin. I was wondering, if it's not too much trouble, whether I might take another look."

"In the barn? Sure, no reason why you shouldn't. I'll go get the key," Allenby said, and immediately turned and went back inside his shack.

Speake was surprised at the old man's accommodating demeanour, especially after the soured atmosphere of their meeting in the store on New Year's Eve. It was a side of him he had not seen before. Something appeared to have changed.

Maybe it was the approach of spring, evident in the slow lengthening of the days, in the green shoots of foliage, the first flowers emerging through the gradually thinning cover of snow. On his way up to the barn at least half a dozen people had voiced the words "Good-day!" to him, rather than the muffled growls or silence he had become more accustomed to. A general sense of wellbeing pervaded the town. Or maybe it had been only his own sense of relief that the change of the season meant that his stay in this place was drawing to an end.

"You're keeping it locked now?" he asked as Allenby came back onto the porch, a small bunch of keys jangling in his hand.

"Times are strange, the town dyin' on its feet. You never know who might come creepin' around." Allenby smiled at him, a smile devoid of sarcasm or spite, and then headed towards the barn. Speake was again surprised to have seen a more avuncular side of the old man's nature leaking out through his pale grey eyes.

"No personal offence intended," Allenby added, glancing back over his shoulder.

"None taken," Speake replied, smiling to himself as Allenby turned away again.

Inside the barn, Speake had to again accustom himself to the subdued light. It all looked much as he had remembered it, apart from the fresh blocks of ice stacked around the walls, the new bodies brought here since New Year's Eve. There were three of them; Ingram Todd's, and two others - the first a fattish man, with a red moustache and goatee beard, who had been Isaac Brown, a mendicant preacher, and the other, his boy Toby, both of whom had died a month previously of influenza. The coffins Speake had seen before all had their lids closed now, and were stacked on top of each other at the rear of the barn. The newly arrived ones were still open, their covers resting at an angle against the wall beside them. Speake gave Allenby an inquisitive glance.

"Runnin' out of space, and there's no need to check on the old ones no more," the old man explained. "It's been a quiet winter all told, other than that little flurry around Christmas. I'll soon have 'em all buried though."

It was now the last week in March and since Christmas there had indeed been but the three deaths in the town. With that, and with no gold being found, there had been little for Speake to write about. The stories he had been sending off for the past few weeks had been mostly about the landscape, the weather, the local fauna and flora, interspersed with a wedding, a dispute over the ownership of a batch of claims, local gossip.

"So, what're you lookin' for now?" Allenby asked.

"The same as before. The Swedish boy. You haven't had any further thoughts?" Allenby looked at him for some time, and at several points Speake had the impression he was about to say something, but eventually the old man only shook his head.

"Is there any way I could...? Speake hesitated. He was aware it was an unusual and indelicate thing he was about to ask. "Could I take a closer look at him?"

"At the boy?"

"Yes; at his body. Underneath his clothes." Allenby gave him a quizzical look.

"You sure have some strange notions. I'm not sure it'd be right. You ain't kin or anythin'. Plus, it'd be difficult now. I'd have to open the casket..., and the boy's clothes would probably be froze solid."

"I understand, but I wanted to see whether there was anything to indicate the bruises could have been inflicted by a human hand." Allenby looked at him again, his watery eyes scanning his face, making some calculation about him.

"How long've you been here?" he eventually asked. It was not the response Speake had expected.

"More than five months. Almost six."

"You seem an honest man. Someone you could trust to do the right thing, unlike most round here." He hesitated, once more examining Speake's face, as though seeking confirmation there of the judgement he had made. "If I told you somethin' would you promise you'd not print it in your paper, leastways, not let on it came from me?"

"That would depend on what you told me."

"Well, let's just say it might save you the need to take a look at the boy."

Speake looked away, toward the coffin holding the body of Ingram Todd, wrestling with the sense of frustration that had welled up in him. First Dortmund, now Allenby. Both had known something; both had elected not to tell the things they knew. If the old man had spoken up those months ago, Sullivan might have been punished for his crimes, and Todd would be alive and gone from here, enjoying the rewards of his discovery.

"You know something?" he said, when he turned back to face Allenby. He knew there was no point in letting his frustration show. Some change had come about in Allenby; he did not want to risk pushing him back into his more customary defensive ways.

"Yes," the old man said, his eyes now locked on Speake's. "I wasn't quite honest with you before, nor with anyone. That day, when he was found, you know I said I'd seen the boy? Well, he wasn't the only one I saw."

"Sullivan?" Speake asked, anticipating what Allenby was about to reveal. Allenby nodded. Another wave of frustration, now closer to anger, washed through Speake. "Did you see what happened?" he controlled himself enough to ask.

"No, only him up there with the boy. I recognised it was Brogan by his horse. Had it tethered to a tree close by. They spoke for a while, then the boy went off up the track, out of sight. Brogan hung around, looked like he took a leak, then after ten minutes or so, headed up on foot in the same direction, came back down about half an hour later. The boy I didn't see again until they found him. I'd kept tellin' myself I must have just missed him leavin'. Not that any of it necessarily means anythin'. It could still have been an accident."

"How did you manage to see this?"

"I was out front, choppin' wood. There's a real good view of the path they were on from there. It's not much more than a coupla hundred yards across to the other side."

Speake remembered standing outside the barn the day he had first come here, looking back down to the town, his eyes following the line of the path which wound up along the other side of the valley into the mountains. The valley here was narrow and steep-sided, more like a gorge. The ice barn and the shack behind it where Allenby lived had been built on a flattened plateau of soil and debris. An almost sheer wall of rock climbed behind it. You could not get much higher on this side of the valley than the shack and the patch of ground behind the barn that served as the town's graveyard, or beyond that to the small rock-enclosed lake fed by a tumbling waterfall where Allenby cut his ice. Still, he wondered whether he would have been able to identify someone over such a distance; whether the old man's eyesight could be that much better. The horse, though, he conceded, would have been easy enough to recognise. The boy too, by his size.

"Why didn't you say anything before?"

"I guess I'm like most round here, wary of strangers. I didn't trust you till I knew what sort of man you were. And you've seen how Sullivan is, what he gets away with it. I figured he'd just come up with some smart explanation no matter what I said."

"And now? Why tell me when there's nothing either of us can do to prove it? As you said, he'll get someone to say he was with them, to show you were mistaken."

Allenby extracted the pipe from the crook of his mouth and began to tap its bowl against the cupped palm of his hand. "I just think it's gone on too long," he said thoughtfully, still looking down at the pipe. "Somebody has to stop him, else where's it goin' to end? The boy, Bunney, your friend Todd. It'll be you next, maybe me, most likely."

"You still believe Sullivan killed Bunney?" Speake said, trying to ignore this blunt reminder of his own vulnerability. For the most part he had kept out of Sullivan's way since New Year's Eve. He had not gone to the party in the saloon, had spent it in a near state of shock, alone in his room at

the boarding house. Sullivan though, he knew, would not have relinquished his animosity so easily. Speake had also spent much less time with Lucy of late, minimising at least one of the causes of friction between him and the man. His recent conversation with her had shown he had little reason to expect their friendship would ever become more intimate. But was it likely that Sullivan would try to kill him over what amounted to little more than a difference of opinion, a conflicting set of moral values?

"You know well enough what I think," Allenby said, as he pushed the stem of the pipe back into the side of his mouth then wiped the displaced spittle from his hand along the leg of his trousers. "Who else would have wanted him dead?"

"Anyone here Bunney owed money to. A drifter, maybe the one they suspected. Even Belinda Curtis. She has as plausible a motive as any; if Sullivan was blamed for it, she would be free. The same would be true of any of the women at the saloon."

This final thought surprised Speake, though he realised it was not beyond credibility. If anything, Lucy had even more reason for wanting to be free of Sullivan than Belinda. Unlike her, she had been given little choice in her career, her situation. By her own admission, Belinda was here of her own volition, and had few complaints about Sullivan as master. He pushed the uncomfortable thought away, reassuring himself that Lucy was not the type to kill an innocent man just to further her own ends.

"Yeah, but Bunney and Belinda were pretty close," Allenby said. "She's a tough woman, but I don't think she'd have gone that far. I still think it was Sullivan. I pushed him about the boy too, New Year's Eve, at the party. Thought he might be in the mood for confessin'. I was a bit worse for wear, so can't be too certain how exactly he answered. Let's just say I don't recall him bein' offended. I suppose he thought I already knew."

"But why would he do something so obvious? Even though almost everybody believes it was him." Allenby made a noise half way between a laugh and a cough.

"He had nothing to lose then, did he? He knew he'd get away with it. Always has. He no longer cares what folks think. There's none here's gonna stand up to him. You do know killin' Todd wasn't what he intended? It was you he was after." He glanced across at Speake, gauging the effect of what he had said. Speake stared back at him, nodding his head gently, not daring to respond.

For some reason this admission affected him more than had Dortmund's similar confirmation. Maybe Allenby's words carried more weight for him than those of someone of Dortmund's more credulous years. He had always assumed, had known in his heart that the horse's charge had been directed at him, but hearing Allenby confirm it as fact had brought back the memory of that terrible moment in a way the younger man's account had not. He could almost hear again the wet, cracking sound of the contact of the horse's hooves against Todd's skull, the short, plaintive cry that had escaped his friend's lips as he had been bludgeoned from consciousness.

"I'm real sorry about your friend. He was a likeable sort, what I knew of him," Allenby said. "But I do remember Brogan tellin' me that much, that same night. As if he thought none of us knew it." He laughed unexpectedly and shook his head.

"I pulled a gun on him then. He just laughed at me. I suppose I should have tried to kill him."

"Why didn't you?" Speake asked, relieved to have a distraction from his unquiet memories. Allenby thought about this, his eyes flicking erratically around the walls of the barn.

"Lack of mettle... And a touch of loyalty, I suppose," he finally said, still not looking at Speake. "Me and him go back a long way, thirty years and more. It's no simple matter to kill someone you've known that long. And, like I said, I was pretty drunk. Probably would have missed him with my little pea-shooter, even if I'd tried."

"You might have got lucky."

"Maybe," Allenby chuckled wetly, and then a more concerned expression settled across his features. "I have to say, though, I'm surprised you've the guts to still be here. I'd rather take my chances out there with the wolves than stay here with a man like him as enemy." The old man's concern sounded genuine, and hearing his words, Speake realised how it might have been wiser if he had found a way to have left Hope some time ago. Was he really that brave, or merely foolish? What presumption had led him to think he could better a man like Brogan Sullivan? Somehow, though, it had not felt like a conscious decision, only a compulsion to do what he believed was right.

"You never know, maybe somebody'll do us all a favour," Allenby continued. "I quite fancy dyin' with my boots off, lookin' out over the valley. Unless, of course, you were thinkin' of... Got a little pop-gun back in the shack I could let you have. No-one'd blame you."

"Thank you, but I wouldn't have any idea how to use it."

"Just point the damn thing and shoot. Don't stop to think."

"As you did, you mean?" Allenby laughed, and again Speake saw the more amenable side of his nature leaking out from wherever it was habitually locked away.

"Fair point," Allenby said, still chuckling quietly. "I damn near shot myself tryin' to get it out my pocket, and then these old man's fingers would barely fit round the trigger."

"Come now, you're not that old."

"Old enough to have known better," Allenby said ruefully. "I pulled a gun on him. He had every right to shoot me. Man must've been in a good mood, with all the celebrations."

20

An Unorthodox Education

"Hey! Boy! I need a word." Roused from his thoughts by the sound of the voice, Dortmund looked up and saw Brogan Sullivan coming towards him from the other side of the street. He noticed the sense of purpose in the man's stride, the set of his body.

Despite the insistence in the command, Dortmund was almost glad of the distraction. Recollection of Speake telling him of his feelings for Lucy Harrigan on their return from Ingram Todd's claim had been darkening his mood. On one side he was jealous, fearful of losing her to an older, more eligible man. Set against this was the question of what he himself had to offer; whether the vision he had for his life, and how Lucy must see hers, could ever conjoin. The world at large was not a place for him; this much he knew. Here in the wilderness, living a simple life, was where he belonged. He could not expect her to forsake any dreams she might hold, just to be with him.

As Sullivan drew closer, Dortmund saw that the look on the man's face echoed the tone of his voice, his walk. It was a demeanour he was becoming familiar with. It had not been like this before winter had set in. Then Sullivan had been a different kind of man. Of late, though, the more amenable side of his nature had become more difficult to discover. Now, mostly, he was aggressive – not only with him, but with everyone. He had no patience, and what had been expressed previously only as disdain or sarcasm, now slid over too easily into anger, spilling out and quickly taking on physical form. He had even started a fight in the saloon a few weeks back; an argument about nothing, not even about money, or cards or the women. It had taken three men to pull him away.

"Tonight, her room. Be there at eight." Sullivan said abruptly when he had drawn close. Dortmund understood exactly what the instruction meant, and that he had no choice but to comply. That was the other thing with Sullivan now - there was no room for negotiation.

"Like before? We are starting again?"

"You have a problem with that?" Sullivan asked, almost casually.

"Well, I..." Dortmund hesitated, uncertain whether he should voice his reservations. Sullivan lowered his head to one side then turned his face to look up at him.

"Well, do you?" he said, more sharply, and then his left hand grabbed the collar of Dortmund's jacket and pulled him closer. As he drew him in, his right hand came up and struck him across the side of the face.

"You sure about that, boy?" he hissed, his mouth pressed close against Dortmund's ear. "It wouldn't be wise to be mistaken." Dortmund turned away his head, from the words, from Sullivan's hot breath against his skin. The blow had surprised him more than hurt. Still, it had made his eyes water, and he could taste blood. He examined the inside of his mouth with his tongue, chasing along the line where his inner cheek had been split, forced against his teeth by the blow.

"No...! I mean, yes," he managed to say, his head still turned away, his tongue still exploring the wound. "I meant only, I thought it was over."

"Well, it isn't." Sullivan pushed him away, releasing his grip on his collar. Dortmund stood up straight, readjusting his clothes, then spat a wad of bloodied spittle away to one side.

"Have you told her yet?" he asked. He knew it was dangerous to continue to question Sullivan's command, but he needed to know what Lucy's response had been, to gauge how she might behave that evening. He thought it unlikely she would have said anything about what had taken place recently between them.

"No, not yet," Sullivan said, reaching across and making a final, almost gentle readjustment to the collar of Dortmund's jacket. "She'll do as I say. I don't know why you're complaining. You'll get paid for it, same as before."

"It's not the money. You know I don't need..." His voice trailed off. There was no need to remind Sullivan how his motivations for having previously agreed to this had changed.

"What, you don't enjoy it? You're worried about the right or wrong of it?" There was an arch smile wrapped across Sullivan's lips, countering the tone of concern.

"No! Not that. I just..."

"In which case, there's nothing more to discuss, is there?" Dortmund saw the tension rising again in Sullivan's neck and upper body, and decided it would be best to let the matter drop.

"Be there at eight!" Sullivan said, nodding to himself in recognition of Dortmund's silent acquiescence before turning away.

While the other inhabitants of Hope had been at best indifferent to his situation, too occupied with their own lives and losses, Brogan Sullivan had been good to him, Josh Allenby too, in the first awful days after the accident. On several occasions Allenby had sat with him up at the ice barn, when it had been most painful, having them near enough to touch, yet not being able to say the things he had been denied the opportunity to say. The quiet, reassuring things Allenby had said, his calm presence had really helped.

It had been very different with Brogan; a stranger relationship than he could ever have imagined having with any man. Other than Lucy, no-one in the town knew anything of it - the history the two of them shared going back before his father had died. Some would have said, had they known, that Brogan had been more than good to him, giving him access to a thing he could not otherwise have had; others, that he was a pervert, and that the things he had made him do with the girl were wrong. Despite his recent denial, he still did not know about the right or wrong of it. All he knew was that it had been a pleasurable, if unorthodox education, once he had grown accustomed to the unnatural circumstances, the things that had happened those nights in her room above the saloon.

It was still not clear to him why he had agreed to it; nor could he understand the pleasure the man had got merely from watching. If he had been older and stronger, braver perhaps, he might have struck Brogan down just for asking. Perhaps, if it hadn't been for the money, the gold he had received as payment, he might have found the courage to say no. Always, though, he had insisted on being paid in gold.

He recalled the nights he had sneaked out to the workings to place the tiny nuggets around his family's claim, placing them where he hoped the men would unearth them and not be suspicious of not having discovered them before. He remembered how he had felt like a *kobold*, a German mine sprite, whenever he stole up to the workings, unsure whether it was a good or deceitful thing he was doing. If they failed to find the gold, if it got lost among the leachings, he had figured he could always go back to Brogan and the girl for more. Usually though one of them had found the traces, and on those nights when they had come home, their bodies bent and tired and dusty, you could see how inside they were bursting with pride and exhilaration. It wasn't much - what he had thought of then as nuggets had been little more than mites of gold-dust - but it had helped to keep them all fed, and his father believing he had made the right choice in dragging his family across an ocean and a continent to live little better than animals in this god-forgotten place.

He had been barely fifteen years old when it had started. It had made him feel he was making a contribution; it had made him feel like a man. That was the only reason, other than curiosity, and his juvenile lack of strength and courage, why he had agreed to take part in Sullivan's twisted games. But in the light of what eventually happened - the terrible deaths of the adult men in his family - his feelings about it now were shaped more by doubt and guilt. He could not escape from thinking that the products of those evenings with Rosie and Sullivan had served only to keep alive in his father and uncle their dreams of finding gold. Would they have remained, exposed themselves to danger for so long if they had found nothing? From the paucity of what they had brought home, beyond his meagre contributions, their mine had been barren. Perhaps his grandfather's stories had held some element of truth. Perhaps some actual *kobold* had laid the seeds for such a terrible end. But no; it had been him - a well-intentioned, if mistaken youth - not some impish creature with malign intent. Without his contributions would his father and uncle have left this place, given up their dreams of discovered wealth in favour of a more certain living in some American city, resuming their trade as printers and makers of books? Would they all still be alive? That, he would never know.

One night, after he and Lucy had performed for Brogan, while Brogan had gone down to his office to get the gold, he had asked Lucy if she could see a reason why a man like him should want such a thing.

"I think he just needs to torture himself watching something he can't have." He had not understood what she meant.

"Haven't you noticed? He isn't interested in women, other than the one, and whatever his reasons, he can't seem to muster up the courage to take her." Once she had said it, he had realised he had never seen Brogan go with a woman. He was charming to them, saying things which from the outside looked like flirtation, as though he was a genuine lady's man, but from what he had seen, Brogan had never taken the process to its natural end. He had asked Lucy if she knew who the woman was.

"Of course. She's right here in this town. Haven't you seen the way he looks at her?" He had realised then who the woman was, and later, on the day she had killed herself and burned down her husband's store, it had been plain something had died inside Sullivan too. After the fire he and Lucy had not had to perform for him again.

"Why doesn't he just take her, like he does everything else?" he had asked.

"Maybe he's afraid he won't be able to do it…, if you know what I mean." They had both laughed at the thought, especially in a man like Brogan. "Why else do you think he gets you to do it? Why not just take me himself? I'm not that hideous, am I?"

"No…of course not… In fact…" She had hung on his words, a half-smile shaping her face, her eyes focused on his mouth. "In fact, to me, you are beautiful," he had finally blurted out. They had heard Brogan returning then, before she could tell him whether she was pleased or not that he saw her that way.

Then had come the first of the nights when the life he had

slowly become accustomed to - living in this wilderness town to satisfy some misplaced dream of his father, the nights with Lucy and Brogan, the secretive trips to the mine - had started to collapse. Lucy had complained she was feeling unwell, but an unusually urgent Brogan had refused to listen, had insisted they should put on their show. He, the boy he still was, had been too afraid, too uncertain of where his loyalties ought to lay to argue with him or to speak up in the girl's defence.

"Just do it! Do as I damn well say!" Brogan had insisted. "You can't cry off just because you don't feel like it." Dortmund had never seen Brogan like this before. He had always been polite, almost embarrassingly so, trying to keep them both sweet during these improper transactions.

"You're a whore! That's what I pay you for! It's not as though it's a hardship, for either of you. It looks to me like you both enjoy it. Something going on between you, is there?"

"No! Of course not!" Lucy had protested. Her eyes had flashed across at Dortmund then, leaving him perplexed for days debating what such a look had meant. Complicity - a belated recognition of what he had said about the way he saw her: or only frustration at having to argue this out with Brogan while he remained silent? But he had known that nothing he could have said would have helped her, would only have made the situation worse.

"I really am in pain, Brogan. Here, inside," she had tried to protest again, cupping her lower abdomen with the flattened palm of her hand. "I really don't feel well."

"Stop whining, woman! It's not that time, is it?" Lucy had shaken her head.

"Then do as I say. Now!" Brogan had shouted at her, his

reddened face pushed close to hers, his voice thickened by anger. He had made to hit her, and she had started to cry. He had not thought Brogan would hit her. From what he had seen, for all his callousness and arrogance, he had never shown himself to be that type of man. Now, though, his expectations of him had changed.

He wondered still what he would have done if Brogan had hit her. He would have felt obligated by their shared acts to try to defend her, but the reality was he had been little more than a child. And then, during the act, when she had started to bleed, sitting astride his hips, the blood coming in a thick, warm flow over his chest and stomach, he had panicked, just as a child would, even though until that moment he had been going earnestly, and to all appearances effectively through the motions of being a man.

At first, he had thought it was something he had done; that he had been too eager in his efforts to please her, to appease Brogan's anger. There had been so much blood they had to burn his underclothes and the things she was wearing. They were covered in it, and some, he guessed, of the remains of what there had been of the child. It had been freezing in the yard at the back of the saloon, him naked in the cold night air, and Brogan, in only his long-johns, had almost hit him, out of frustration, and – as he now realised – from the compulsion of his own fear. The girl could have died, and all of the town would have asked questions about what had been going on in her room.

He remembered the way the moon had hung, staring down at them like an accusing eye from behind the two gnarled pine trees that clung to the rim of the high wall of rock at the back of the yard. It was there that the Pearce girl had died, her own clothes also soaked in blood. Lucy had been more fortunate. Hers had been an act of nature, not of choice. And she had survived.

During the weeks that had passed since the death of Emilie Henderson he and Lucy had barely spoken. Whenever they passed in the street she would act as though she had not seen him, or she would nervously strike up a conversation with anyone who happened to be at hand. She was a grown woman, a prostitute, without any reason to acknowledge or speak to the orphaned son of an impecunious and married prospector; of a man of propriety who had had no need of any contact with a whore. Dortmund's own reaction had been very different; every time he saw her, his heart had leapt in his chest, and colour had risen to his face. Always he had been too scared to speak.

For a long time, he had been unable to decide if what he felt for her was a genuine emotion, an adolescent infatuation, love even, or simply a longing for the satisfaction of a baser human need. All he knew was that the cessation of their unions had left him feeling empty. He had been surprised too to discover he was jealous of Speake. He acknowledged that the man had every right to hold such feelings, and whatever Speake might think or say, it would be of no consequence if she did not reciprocate. Still, knowledge of a rival for her affections had not sat easy with him.

Neither did he know what Lucy felt for him. Her reactions when she saw him could have arisen from embarrassment, or disdain, or could equally have been self-protection - a denial of emotions that she knew, given their situation, would always remain beyond the possibility of expression. Then, just a week previously, she had come to the cabin he was building out in the woods, and with hardly a word of explanation passing between them, they had made love slowly and tenderly.

"Just for you and me," she had said, as she laid her naked body against his. It had felt so different, with no one watching or directing their motions, or deriving their own perverse satisfaction from their actions.

When they were done, she had tried to leave, but he had pulled her back, and they had coupled again, laughing and giggling all the way through it like children. When they had finally finished, she had jumped from the bed before he could prevent her, and had dressed quickly, and coming to him where he lay on the bed watching her, had kissed him gently on the forehead.

"This was just the once. I wanted you to know," she had said with tears in her eyes. He had tried to protest, to tell her everything he felt about her, but she had stilled his words with a finger laid against his lips.

"You know this can't happen again. Not here. Not with Brogan around. Maybe, one day," and then she had left without saying another word.

21

Wilderness

"Are you proud of your handiwork? Is this what you call making an honest living?" Sullivan had marched up to Speake where he was sitting alone at a table in a quiet corner of the saloon. As he spoke, he slapped Speake against the shoulder with the folded newspaper he was carrying, and then threw it into his lap. Speake retrieved it, refolded the pages that had blown open, and placed it on the table. He did not need to read it; he knew what had put Sullivan into his present state. It was the piece Speake had written about the death of Ingram Todd. From the moment he had wired it off, he had harboured doubts about the wisdom of the insinuations he had made. He had been hoping a copy of the edition of the paper that carried the piece would not arrive in Hope until after he had left.

"Those whores have more integrity than you." Sullivan flung his arm out behind him in the direction of where

Belinda and Lucy and a couple of the other women were standing, anxiously watching the confrontation.

"Just how much grave money did you get from that claim? I bet you weren't hollering about murder at the assay office counting up his gold."

Speake decided it would be best to say nothing, to give Sullivan's anger time to exhaust itself. He picked up his cup, hoping his hand would not shake too visibly, and took a sip. Sullivan stood watching him, flexing the fingers of his right hand. As Speake was raising the cup a second time Sullivan's hand lashed out. The ends of his fingers caught the cup and knocked it from Speake's grasp only inches from his mouth. The cup flew away and smashed against the wall.

"Come on you coward!" Sullivan bellowed; fists clenched at his sides. "Stand up, and let's put an end to this now." Speake wiped the remnants of coffee from his mouth and inspected his fingers to see if he was bleeding. There was only coffee. He could feel grains of it still on his lips, and one side of his upper lip thickening where the cup had grazed against it as it flew from his hand.

"I'm not going to fight you. It wouldn't prove anything," he said, remaining seated. He knew that if he stood up Sullivan would put him on the floor before he could rise fully to his feet. He looked up and stared back at Sullivan's darkened face. He was scared, more scared than he could remember ever having been; fearful of how much pain might be inflicted on him, if he would even survive.

"I couldn't give a dime what it proves. Stand up, damn you! I just want the satisfaction of making you bleed." Speake did not move, even more convinced that to remain seated was the wisest option. After a few moments Sullivan stepped back and called out to the group of women who had now moved away into a huddle around their private table in the alcove at the end of the bar.

"Lucy! Get yourself over here," he shouted across the room. Lucy hesitated and shuffled closer to the bar, her hand reaching out to take hold of the brass rail that ran along its length. The fear in her eyes was perceptible even from across the saloon. Belinda moved closer to her and ran her palm reassuringly up and down Lucy's bare upper arm.

"Go on, girl. You don't want to make him any madder than he is," Speake heard her say in a quiet, consoling voice as she pushed Lucy gently forward by the shoulders.

"Come here, you dumb bitch," Sullivan shouted again. "I thought it was your leg that was crocked, not your brain." Lucy looked back once more towards the other women. Belinda nodded to reassure her, and she walked hesitantly towards Sullivan.

"There's no need to get personal, Brogan. I was just scared, that's all. I don't like it when you get like this. I heard you well enough," she said as she drew near. She sounded pathetic, but Speake detected a hint of steel in her eyes, behind the half-formed tears.

"Then move faster, damn you. Come here!" He reached across the remaining distance between them, grabbed her by the wrist and pulled her roughly towards the table. "There's a man here wants to talk to you," he said, spinning her around and twisting her arm up behind her back.

"Let go of me Brogan. That hurts!" she cried.

"Good! Now shut up!" Speake's immediate reaction was

to stand, to try to protect her, but he knew Sullivan still had a physical advantage over him, even encumbered as he was. Standing up only to get immediately knocked down would do nothing to help her. The only thing he could do was to try to calm Sullivan and deflect his anger away from her.

"This is between you and me, Sullivan. You don't have to take it out on her. I apologise if the piece offended you. I was upset at Todd's death and was still shaken by it. I can write another piece, say everything has been resolved."

"What do I care about your stories? What hurt can they do me a thousand miles away? I've stopped better, more determined men than you; men armed with guns and knives, not ink and paper, and it's only the pointlessness of your stories has kept you alive. Your clever words mean nothing here. They're just sounds, lost on the wind to the forests and mountains. So, you see, I find the matter in hand much more pressing." Sullivan flashed an inane grin at Speake, and then pushed Lucy roughly towards him. The top of her body lurched forward as the front of her legs came up against the edge of the table. She grunted softly at the impact.

"Well, you want this piece of trash or not?" Sullivan barked, pulling her back upright.

"Stop it! There's no need to hurt her. You make it sound as though she's yours to give away."

"And who's to say she's not? You?" He paused, giving Speake a chance to answer. There was nothing he could say, at least nothing he had not already said, none of which had made any difference, other than to bring about the death of Ingram Todd.

"I thought not. Now listen. If you think she's entitled

to her freedom, I'll make you a deal. You can have her, in exchange for what's left of Todd's gold. I'm going to have too many women here soon anyway. But once you have her, what do you plan to do with her? Take her back to Chicago, to England? Marry her, introduce her to your family; make a respectable woman of her? Or keep her hidden away in some rented attic so none of your fancy upright friends can see her, and fuck her twice a week and pay her ten dollars for her time to keep her happy? Maybe rent her out to those friends from time to time if you find yourself short?"

"I'm not Jack Bunney. I'm not going to bargain with you over someone else's freedom. You don't own her."

"Oh, but I do. Those are the rules, the game we play out here. I have control of her, as you can see." He pushed Lucy forward against the edge of the table again. "Therefore, in every practical sense I do own her." Speake saw the flash of steel again, the frustrated anger burning in Lucy's eyes.

"But *she* didn't have any choice in it. It's not a game for her. The same was true for Rosalind Pearce. What gives you the right?" Sullivan looked around, grinning broadly. He still held Lucy's arm twisted behind her back. Her tears were more genuine now. Sullivan nodded in various directions at the people in the saloon, all now openly watching the altercation, and at others passing by outside.

"They do," he said. "All the people who live here; all of them who knew what was happening and did nothing to stop it, or voiced the slightest hint of disapproval. The law, these upright citizens, their self-righteous indifference; they were all prepared to go along with the game, found it entertaining. *They* give me the right."

"And that makes it acceptable?"

Sullivan let out a short, brittle laugh. "Did I say that? There was something I wanted, and I didn't see anything or anyone to stop me." He gave Speake a hard stare. "I still don't. Can you see any way to change it?"

Speake did not know what to say. The only way he could see was to fight Sullivan and - do what? Kill him, or more likely, be killed? The alternative would be to agree to the transaction the man had proposed. He did not want to buy Lucy, to make her his possession, even if it would be no more than a token gesture made solely to release her from Sullivan's tyranny. To do so, he felt, would be to lower himself to the same level as Sullivan and Bunney, but before he was forced to give an answer, a man's gravelled voice broke into their discussion.

"Leave 'em be, Brogan. Or I'll do it this time." It was Allenby. He was standing about ten feet behind Sullivan, pointing a small twin-barrelled gun at his back. Speake assumed it was the peashooter the old man had offered him up at the barn. Sullivan released Lucy's arm and groaned in exasperation then turned to face Allenby.

"Not again, Josh."

"I might just do it this time, so don't push me. I'm not drunk neither, so *you* just remember that. I know exactly where that hard, shrivelled heart of yours is beatin', and my aim's good enough when I'm sober. So, step away now. Leave 'em be."

"You'll regret this, you know that?" Sullivan's voice was flat; he almost sounded bored.

Allenby nodded. "Probably," he said. "But I'm past carin'. Someone's got to try and stop you."

"Put the gun away, Josh. You won't use it, not on an unarmed man, not with all these good people watching. You wouldn't stick your neck in a noose because of me."

"No? Well, maybe I don't need to. I could just tell what I know about you and the Swedish boy." He glanced across at Speake, a tentative look, as though inviting him to corroborate his insinuation. "D'you think they'd just stand by and let you carry on about your business if they knew?"

Speake looked at Sullivan's face. He was curious to see how he would react to being confronted in such a way. If what Allenby had told him about Sullivan and the boy was true, then he had said all that needed to be said. The mere mention of the boy would be enough to start people speculating about the cause of his death again. It had been the only thing Speake had seen which had moved the people here to express what he considered the normal human trait of compassion. Despite the explanation Allenby had given back then, suspicions remained, with Sullivan's name being mentioned in most speculations about what had really happened. Now, Allenby had provided those suspicions with something tangible to focus on. Sullivan rolled his tongue around the inside of his mouth as though he was going to spit, and then a sneer twisted one side of his face.

"I've no idea what you're talking about. But go ahead! Tell them what you like, but you *will* regret this," he said to

Allenby, jabbing a finger at him. "And you will too," he added, turning back to Speake, then he leaned across to Lucy, taking hold of her roughly by the upper arm, and whispered in her ear. Surprise and then anger swept across her face, and she turned her head, first to glance at him and then at his hand holding her arm. Standing back from her, Sullivan tugged at the lapels of his jacket pulling it tight across his back, and then looked in turn at Lucy, then Allenby and finally at Speake.

"You will all regret it," he said, and walked away towards the stairs that led up to his rooms above the saloon.

After he was gone, Speake finally stood and went over to Lucy. As he drew close, he reached out to touch her shoulder to console her. At his touch her body stiffened, but she relaxed as soon as she realised it was him. She turned to face him, took a step forward, and allowed her head to fall against his chest. She started to sob, her arms hanging passively at her side. Speake felt ill at ease; other than his mother and aunts when he was a child, he had never held a woman close before. He coughed nervously, then put his arm around her shoulders and clasped her tighter to his chest. He leaned his head down, nestling his cheek against the top of her head, savouring the rising smell of her scent.

"It's alright. It's over now," he mouthed, aware of the untruth inherent in his words.

"Thank you, for coming to our rescue," he said to Allenby over Lucy's shoulder. "I don't know how it would have ended otherwise."

"You could have given him the money," Allenby said, smiling, then shook his head. "But think nothin' of it. It felt good to be actin' for once." A more anxious look came to his face. "Guess I'll be havin' to pay for it soon enough."

"You think he'll try to hurt you?"

"Damn near certain! Kill me, most likely. But you, you should get away from here while you can. Me, I've nowhere else to go, and not much of a life left worth savin'." Lucy raised her head from Speake's chest. Light tracks of tears trailed across her cheeks. Speake lowered his arms and she moved a half step away from him.

"He's right," she said, brushing her cheeks with the heels of her hands. "Sullivan will kill you both. Me too, if he feels he has no further use for me. You have to leave."

"If I go, will you come with me?"

"No. I'm sorry. I can't," she said, placing a hand gently on each of his forearms. "I have to try to sort this out." Speake was surprised at her bravery, that she still believed she could influence Sullivan.

"What can *you* do against someone like him?" he asked. Lucy shook her head and pursed her lips.

"I've no idea, but I have to try."

Speake turned away from her and looked out through the window. What she and Allenby had said was true; Sullivan would feel he had no option but to kill him, Allenby too. He had lost too much face in front of his clients, his employees. Word of the encounter, of his being faced down by Allenby, would spread quickly through the town.

Outside, to the west, the sky was darkening; in less than thirty minutes it would be nightfall, too late in the day to leave, and anyway, where could he go? He could set off on foot into the unknown darkness, but he would probably not survive the night. Even if the wolves didn't get him, the following day, on horseback, Sullivan would catch up with him as soon as it was light. There was only the one track leading in and out of the town, steeply sloping rocks and forest rising on either side. The first staging station, from his recollection of his journey into Hope, was close to sixty miles away. He would not be hard to find.

He was stuck here, in a situation largely of his own making. He could have kept to the narrower remit of his original purpose for being here, made sure he stayed on the right side of a man like Brogan Sullivan, allowed the death of the Swedish boy to pass as the accident it might well have been. After all his delving he still had no proof it was anything other than that. It was his own curiosity and pride that had led him into this situation rather than any genuine sense of rectitude. Now there was nowhere left for him to go. The best he could hope for was that Sullivan would be distracted by some other aggravation.

In the morning, if he survived the night, if Sullivan was not waiting for him, he would try to buy a horse with the money from Todd's claim. Failing that - he had no idea what price a fully saddled and harnessed horse would be, especially if by then he had a price on his head - he would try to hitch a ride with someone who was heading out of Hope, if there were any brave or foolhardy enough to help him. People were starting to leave in greater numbers, now that the worst of the winter was over. It would make no difference to Speake who they were, how far they were going, in which direction they were heading.

22

The Way the World Was Set

Lucy sat staring at her reflection in the mirror. The face that stared back at her was one she barely recognised. The woman in the mirror looked so much older than she thought herself to be; the painted lips held taut, as though resisting even the possibility of amusement, the lines of worry drawn tight around the too heavily made-up eyes. There was a stubborn set to the eyes themselves - iced pools of ultramarine amidst the smeared shadows of her tear-washed mascara - that made her feel uncomfortable, experience a sense of loss; the alertness and vitality they had once held hardened now to resignation. Only the depth of the colour in them still held true.

She had been sitting there for half an hour or more, intermittently crying, struggling to imagine what she could do or say later to dissuade Brogan. In less than an hour he and the boy would be here. While she had sat, seeking answers in the reflected world of the mirror, her thoughts had fluctuated only between the opposing poles of full confession and blank refusal. Neither option had seemed to offer a safe resolution, and as hard as she had tried, she had found nothing else that would. Killing Brogan - putting an end to him and trusting the consequences to justice, or at least to the better part of human nature - had been the only alternative she could see, and that, she knew, was just another extreme, leading to a different kind of entrapment.

"Dear God! What did I do to deserve this?" she asked her reflection, as she brushed away the latest flow of tears with the top joints of her fingers, her motions drawing more trails of mascara across the upper curves of her cheeks. If anything, the possibility of an end to the situation she and the boy now found themselves in, one that would provide them both with a satisfactory way out, was receding further from her grasp.

Sullivan had become so urgent in everything, so irascible of late. In the past, his fits of choler, infrequent as they were, had always been directed at the other girls, never at her. Something in her, it seemed, had invoked the protective side of his nature. Or had it been only pity - a question of pride that would not allow even such a dissolute man to vent his vexations on a partial cripple - a false inhibition displaced of late by some greater necessity? Now he had become un-predictable; she felt as vulnerable to his rancour as were the other girls, unsure of what physical form his anger might take. The argument in the saloon had given her some indi-cation of how much his attitude to her had changed, and how violent he was becoming.

"We'll forget about this for now," he had said, after Allenby had interrupted his argument with Speake, when he had leaned over and whispered to her, his face hidden from the others behind the folds of her hair.

"I'll be coming to see you tonight, at eight," he had added before he pulled away. "The boy will be with me." While he was saying this, he had pinched the looser flesh at the back of her upper arm between his thumb and forefinger, also out of sight. It had been all she could do to not cry out and to hold back the tears.

It had been simple enough, what Brogan had said; easy enough to understand. It was her purpose to be available to serve the needs of men. Still, it had upset her. It had been several months since Brogan had last summoned her and Dortmund. She had thought that was over; she did not want to return to a situation where she would now find herself torn between conflicting needs.

The truth was, she had missed the boy, the brief, infrequent moments of desire they had shared under Brogan's salacious gaze. She had missed his innocence, the earnestness with which he had set about his task, trying to please her, to mollify Brogan, battling against his own callow need for release. Often, in moments alone, when the reality of her situation would come creeping in like the cold air from outside, insinuating itself through the cracks in the door and window frames, chilling her to the bone, she had found herself recalling the warmth and softness of his skin, the tautness of his young muscles beneath - an unknown landscape for her to discover.

Then there had been the smell of him. There was always

something of the outdoors about him, the empty, electric smell of the frozen air that clung to him. Every time she savoured it on his skin, she had felt her own depleted resources being replenished. It had provided relief from the sickly echoes of cheap scent and stale sweat and alcohol and tobacco smoke - the too familiar odours of the place that lingered always around her own body.

She remembered the night he had told her he found her beautiful. The difficulty had started then. Until then, the nights with him and Brogan had been just one more imposition she had no choice other than to endure, the boy just one more man whose needs she was required to satisfy. It had made no difference that Brogan was the one paying. But once the boy had made his confession, she had become increasingly aware of the tenderness in his touch, the intensity in his eyes as he moved inside her, a look she had always thought had been shaped by fear or embarrassment, or simply from concentration.

Those were the things she had gone looking for, the tenderness and intensity, which she had yearned to savour one more time, that day she had gone to find him at his shack out in the woods. She had not been disappointed. They had made love as she had never experienced it - as something fulfilling, not empty, or devoid of any context or meaning beyond money and necessity - but it had left her even more confused. Never before had she felt so needed. It had been difficult to leave him, to tell him this would never happen again.

She had known, though, that there could be no future in it, only transitory consolation to be taken in its memory, and behind those reminiscences, the looming shadow of frustration and disappointment. Brogan would never allow it. He would never set her free, certainly not out of compassion or decency, and the boy was unlikely ever to have the means to negotiate any contract that would satisfy Sullivan. And now she was being instructed to make love to him again - to service him, as she had always previously considered it - not for her own fulfilment, nor for his, but for Brogan's unfathomable, embittered gratification. She still could not understand why Brogan required it, why he had not taken the Henderson woman as his own while he could.

And then there was the Englishman Speake; offering her the possibility of an entirely different resolution, a man of words and thoughts appealing to a part of her that remained equally unnourished. She had been among the brightest in her class during the few years she had had the freedom to attend school, before her parents had died; before she had been forced by circumstances, by men, to become what she was now. Her quietness here, her reservation, which they all took as indication of a lack of imagination, or worse, was simply a defence. Her intelligence, her interest in literature - she had wanted to become a teacher, of English, of books - had no place here. She had pushed it away, denying a part of herself that had always given her consolation. The closest she came to it now was the box of dime novels the other girls all loved to read. She had found it easier to pretend than to try to persuade them to an interest in some higher art.

Speake, an educated, sensitive man; how passionate could such a man be? He was always so inward, so intense. The one thing she did know was that she needed passion - a self-knowledge confirmed by the stolen hour with Dortmund.

She craved it, as reward for all the years she had spent dispensing gratification of that hunger in others. To know what it felt like to receive. Not just the once, and not furtively; for a lifetime, or at least until she grew old and was past the point of feeling any need for such things.

But what did she have to offer a man like Speake? Her own dark past, the things she had done, most often in self-preservation, but sometimes too, simply from spite - the deep well of resentment inside her boiling over into a need for revenge against the injustices done to her, to others like her, that had eventually overwhelmed her, leading her to acts for which she knew she would never be able to forgive herself. Would Speake be able to forgive her if he knew? That, she doubted, despite the understanding of the needful imperatives of her past he claimed to hold.

And what about the boy; what would he think of her if he knew? She suspected that of the two, he would prove more forgiving. From what she knew of him he drew his own conclusions, taking his measure of right and wrong from what he saw around him, from the disinterested laws of Nature, not from some acquired and inflexible set of rules to live by - written by men, of course - which took no account of circumstances, of relative needs and injustices.

She knew she couldn't fight those rules - the way the world was set against her, against all women. Not on her own. Would Speake, or Dortmund, either of them, be strong enough to help her resist it? She had tried once on her own, when that resentment had overwhelmed her, had even succeeded momentarily in her goal, taking a knife to an overzealous customer, leaving her mark on him - a token of resistance for him to consider for the rest of his life. It had felt good, for that instant, to seize control, to believe she had some power to wield, but it had made no real difference. The reality of her world, the pages of the weighty book of man-given rules had closed in around her again. Once the man was gone, you could not even see the minute tear she had made in its fabric.

Her thoughts drifted back to the night Rosie Pearce had died. The sight of her standing in her doorway, bloodied and wounded, her face pale and confused had shocked her. Until that moment she had not realised the true extent of the hopelessness of Rosie's, of her own situation. As she had hurried to fetch the doctor through the falling flakes of snow, the old resentments had mounted inside her.

Had they no shame, no sense of compunction, these men who used them in any way they chose? What was it, what arcane right, she had wondered, that gave them their assumed sense of entitlement? From what she had seen, none of them deserved or had earned it, and she had seen many men in her time. Where were they when the dues were to be paid? Nowhere to be found! It was always the likes of her, of Rosie, who ended up repairing the damage, paying the emotional and physical cost of their decisions, of their unsettled debts of dishonour.

At least she could console herself that Jack Bunney had paid for his crime. But it had not been enough; death had been too easy an escape for him. To have allowed him to linger forever as he was - a drunken bum, the butt of jokes and insults - would have been a far sweeter punishment. When looked at from Bunney's point of view, she could almost grudgingly concede that his had been a crime of the moment, at worst, an ill-conceived question of personal survival. There could be no such excuse for Sullivan. His many crimes had been wilful and on-going; they still were. He had kept Rosie prisoner; there was no better word to describe it. Only death had released her. It was this realisation that had shocked her.

She was a prisoner too, just as Rosie had been, her own sentence indeterminate and on-going. Would death be the only escape for her too? Here she was still, her twin in the mirror her only confidant and refuge, still subject to Sullivan's arrogant assumptions, still waiting for someone to exact the required price on him for his actions. For someone to set her free.

She looked at her watch; it was almost half past seven. Brogan and the boy would soon be here. She looked again at the near stranger facing her in the mirror, and took a cloth and began to wipe the tear damaged make-up from her face. The fingers of her free hand combed intermittently through her hair, trying to give it some semblance of order, as she continued to wrestle with the possibilities of what to do and say when they arrived. Would she be able to conduct herself in such a way as to allay Brogan's probable doubts? Or would she somehow find the strength, the courage to do what was required of her; to try again to tear a hole, however small it might be, in that stifling fabric.

23

The Turn of a Card

Dortmund watched nervously, wondering what Lucy would say as she paced back and forth along the space between the foot of her bed and the window. Each time she turned, as she came back towards them, she trailed her fingers along the rail of the brass bedstead. In her free hand she held a cigarette pinched between forefinger and thumb, the lit end shaded within the cup of her palm.

"Why, Brogan? You've let it pass for weeks, months. I thought we were done. Why start again now?" she asked, coming to a halt at the near end of the bed, facing them both. "You know it won't change anything. She's gone."

Beyond his concerns about what would happen, as he watched Lucy moving around the bed, Dortmund felt a familiar thrill returning. Despite the reluctance he shared with her at having to again indulge Sullivan's demands, the new uncertainty of his unpredictable humour, he was excited. He had missed these moments with her, the shared intimacy, despite the contrary elements that had worked always against any true intimacy between them - the forced circumstances, another man watching, taking his own vicarious, unfathomable pleasure; the mercenary nature of the transaction.

He had missed the feel of her skin, the soft lines and folds of her body. The smell of her too - the perfumes she wore, the milky smell of her naked skin, the rising scent of her sex. He missed the sensations those contacts had aroused in him. Her recent visit to his cabin, their first and only private lovemaking, had re-awakened his desire. To go back to how it had been, Sullivan watching and controlling, did not feel right anymore, not that it ever had.

"You trying to tell me something you think I don't know?" Sullivan asked Lucy in a mocking tone.

"No! I just meant, there must be a reason why you're asking us to..."

"And if there is, what would a whore need to know of it?" Sullivan interrupted. "Stick to your job and hold your ideas to yourself. You can think and say what you like behind my back, but while I'm paying..." He left the sentence unfinished, allowing the look he gave her to convince her.

"I don't know, Brogan, she said, slowly tamping out the cigarette in a small glass dish amidst the feminine paraphernalia of her dressing cabinet. "It just doesn't..." She looked across at Dortmund, her eyes searching his face. Did she hope he could explain the situation to Sullivan more clearly? He could only stare back at her; he could no more risk admitting his feelings than could she. Sullivan turned to face him, then back to Lucy.

"Oh, I see! There's something going on between you two, right? Love is it? You've developed feelings for each other?" He spun around suddenly and grabbed Dortmund by the lapel of his jacket, then pulled him forward so their bodies were no more than a few inches apart. He had sounded amused by the notion. His eyes, close in front of Dortmund's, held a different emotion.

"Let me tell you something about love, boy. It won't get you anything but hurt. Not even when you imagine it's for free."

"Leave him be, Brogan. It's my fault. It's me who has developed feelings." Lucy had drawn close to Sullivan and had laid a hand against the inside of his elbow, trying to turn him away. "He was so sweet and gentle, and I guess I needed that, to feel someone might think I was special. I shouldn't have, but I told him, after I thought we'd stopped. That's why I was stalling. It just wouldn't feel right now, him knowing... Come on, Brogan. Take it out on me if you have to. He's just a kid."

Dortmund felt momentarily hurt by hearing himself described in this way, after the things they had done together in this room, her recent visit to his cabin. Then he realised she had said it to protect him. It was a realisation he found equally discomforting; that she thought he needed a woman to protect him when he should have been the one defending her. Before he could say anything to assert himself, to draw the man's attention from her, Sullivan pushed him roughly away. As he stumbled back, he heard a sound, like something snapping, as Sullivan span round and slapped Lucy on the side of the head with his open hand. She stumbled to one side, her body following the arc of the blow. As she staggered,

Sullivan stepped forward, halting her fall with a hand grasping her upper arm, and threw a short punch into her midriff with the other hand. Lucy exhaled sharply and crumpled to the floor.

"Damn you, bitch. I don't pay you to go falling in love."

"Damn yourself...! Go rot...in hell," Lucy managed to say between raking gulps of breath.

Dortmund's whole body was shaking. He could feel the fabric of his trousers moving against his legs. The moment had arrived he had feared might one day come. He could not allow Sullivan to hurt Lucy without trying to prevent it. Pushing away his fear, the concerns he had always had about the physical advantage and experience of the older man, he strode towards Sullivan.

"Leave her, Brogan. It is enough. You will kill her," he said, his hand grasping at the material of Sullivan's jacket at his shoulder, trying to pull him around. Sullivan turned, and with a single push sent Dortmund hurtling back across the room.

"You want some too, whelp?" he heard Sullivan say as he fell backwards onto the floor. Sullivan turned back and threw another punch at the prostrate figure of Lucy, deliberating over his target before delivering the blow.

Still seated on the floor, Dortmund reached behind him. During the exchange earlier with Sullivan he had understood this evening might turn out differently. He pulled out the knife he had slipped into his belt, wrapped in a length of buckskin.

"I mean it, Brogan. Leave her," he said, standing up, unwinding the leather from the blade. "You cannot keep making people do what they do not want to do. She... We do not want to do this anymore."

His hand was trembling; he could barely maintain his grip on the knife. It was his father's hunting knife. The blade had been honed so often it was now little more than a stiletto, about five inches in length. He closed his fingers tighter around the horn handle to try to still the shaking in his arm.

Sullivan turned to face him. There were flecks of blood on his cheeks and forehead. As his hand came up to brush his hair from his eyes, Dortmund saw blood on his knuckles too. He could hear Lucy sobbing where she lay on the floor. Sullivan walked slowly towards him, smiling and shaking his head.

"So, you've finally decided to be a hero. All these months of getting it for free, being paid for it, you've finally decided to see how it feels to be a man. Claiming it as your own now, are you? What *is* going on around here, you and Speake both worrying after the same piece of meat?" He glanced back in the direction of Lucy. "Personally, I don't see the attraction. Damaged goods as far as I can see."

Dortmund held the knife out in front of him trying to keep the blade still. He did not know the correct way to hold it as a weapon. His fingers and thumb were wrapped around the handle in a tight fist. It did not feel comfortable; he had to force his hand down at the wrist to keep the blade level, and there seemed no way to easily adjust the angle to strike at a moving target. He had never really been in a fight before, just a few scraps with other boys when he was younger - boys being boys, trying to prove something to each other, to themselves. A few grazes, given and received, a bloodied nose once, but never anything with serious intent or consequences. Now it seemed he might be fighting for his life.

Sullivan was standing about three feet in front of him, the knifepoint no more than a foot from his belly. He had his hands on his hips and was studying Dortmund's face. "And?" he said, amusement still playing across his face.

Dortmund did not see the blow coming. He only felt its impact, high on his forehead, delivered by the driven heel of Sullivan's hand. His head snapped back, and he collapsed to the ground. Made senseless momentarily, his grasp slackened on the knife. It fell from his hand and stuck point first into the wooden floor. Sullivan recovered the distance between them, picking up the knife in mid-stride. Bending down, he drove the blade through the muscle above Dortmund's left collarbone, pinning him to the door of the tall cabinet he had fallen against.

"Does that hurt, boy?" Sullivan croaked; his voice thick with anger. Dortmund could not reply. He could feel Sullivan's heated breath against the side of his face, but his other senses were still numbed by the blow.

"I said, does that hurt?" Sullivan hissed again, then pushed the hilt of the knife upwards through a quarter-circle. Dortmund groaned as he felt the edge of the blade tearing muscle.

"No!" he spat out, finding defiance from he knew not where.

"No, you say?" Sullivan said, jerking the knife out of his shoulder. With its pinion removed, Dortmund's body slipped closer to the floor. He no longer had the strength to support himself. His left fist had clenched into a tightened ball.

Sullivan was still kneeling in front of him. Dortmund could see a balding spot on the top of his head, found it odd that he had never before noticed it, this sign of fallibility.

"We'll just have to try a little harder then, won't we?" Sullivan said, driving the blade again through Dortmund's shoulder.

"So? Tell me now. Does *that* hurt?"

Dortmund nodded his head slowly, all defiance gone, pursing his lips tightly around his teeth to keep from screaming and the tears from forming as pain danced around his neck and shoulder. There was a final, searing flash as Sullivan pulled out the blade and stood up. He threw the knife to the floor behind him. Again, its point stuck into the wooden floor.

"You ought to get that shoulder seen to boy, before you bleed to death."

The tears had now broken over Dortmund's face. He tried to stand, but the shadow of the burning steel slicing through his flesh when he moved kept him pinned to the floor. His head ached from the first blow Sullivan had struck, and his arms would not obey his commands to push his body up from the floor. He looked down at the blood flooding the material of his shirt. He had thought the wounds were only to the muscle, that nothing vital inside had been punctured. Could it be true what Sullivan had said; he could bleed to death from such injuries?

"Why, Brogan? They will punish you for this," he managed to say. He was surprised at how feeble, how distant his voice sounded.

"And if I say I heard a commotion, and when I came up, I found you attacking her, trying to rape her. She looks pretty beat up to me, and the rape part shouldn't be hard to fix. Anyway, how could they tell with a whore? I'd tell them you pulled a knife when I tried to stop you, and unfortunately you got hurt in the struggle. They'd not question my side of it, and I've a suspicion the bitch will never tell."

While Sullivan had been speaking, Dortmund had caught glimpses of Lucy, first struggling to her feet, supporting herself against the bedstead, then moving unsteadily towards them. Blood was seeping from her lip, and another thread ran down the side of her face from a cut high on her forehead. At one point, when his eyes had remained focused on her for more than a few seconds, she had shaken her head, raising her fingers to her mouth. Then she had seemed to stumble. At first, he had thought she had fallen, weakened by Sullivan's blows, but she quickly stood again, his knife in her hand. He allowed his eyes to close, to avoid giving any indication to Sullivan of what she was doing.

"Don't try to understand me, boy," Sullivan said, kicking the sole of his boot to reclaim his attention with the jolt of pain this sent flashing through Dortmund's shoulder. "There's nothing to understand other than what I am. How are you making out down there? You're starting to look a little..."

Sullivan let out a sharp yelp of pain. His body jerked back to one side, his hand clutching wildly behind his shoulder. Dortmund raised his head. Lucy was hanging from Sullivan's back, her legs swinging out in erratic arcs as he writhed and turned. She had driven the knife high into his shoulder and was holding on desperately to its handle as Sullivan tried to remove it.

"Die, you bastard! Just die!" Lucy screamed. She had managed to loop her free arm around his neck, to support the weight of her body, and her heels were locked around the front of his thighs. She too was pulling at the handle of the knife, trying to retrieve it to strike again.

"You're going to pay for this, bitch!" Sullivan shouted, as he turned his shoulders forcefully from side to side, trying to dislodge her. Dortmund felt helpless; he could do no more than lay where he was, his body beyond conscious control. As he watched, the frantic dance between them slowed, until, exhausted, Lucy finally let go of the knife. She slid down his back and slumped to her knees on the floor. With her hand no longer around its hilt, Sullivan pulled the knife free. He leaned over her, his face inches from her face, his eyes locked on hers, and placed the point of the blade against her cheek.

"You'd better be careful, girlie," he said. "You could get hurt." Lucy laughed, a flat, bitter laugh, then pulled back her head, gathering saliva in her mouth, and spat into his face before he could pull away.

"You just don't want to make it better, do you?" he said, wiping away the spittle. Lucy shook her head, an expression of regret shaping her features.

"Oh, it would have been so sweet, to make you pay for what you did to Rosie," Dortmund heard her say through his dulled senses. Her words had been barely more than a hoarse whisper. They sounded so incongruous to him, coming from her, and uttered with such violence and hatred. He thought he heard Sullivan laugh.

"It was just the turn of a card! What else could I do? Bunney could have stopped it any time he chose." There was only a hint of protest in his words.

"Yes, you could say that, to absolve yourself. But like I said that night, someone will make you pay. Remember?"

"I remember. But as *I* said, if *you* remember, it won't be you. Listen girlie, you stay here and be nice to your boyfriend while he's still breathing. I have something I need to do. I'll be back to deal with you later."

Dortmund felt so tired he could barely keep his eyes open. The pain though had largely ceased. He could not really feel anything anymore, his senses reduced to what he could see and hear. As he struggled to stay awake an image formed in his mind of the final moments of his father, of the three men drowning, huddled together in the mine. He wished that his father, all of them, were still here, so he could tell them he loved them. To apologise for what he had done, for all it had led to. The last thing he saw before he lapsed into unconsciousness, his vision disintegrating into a cloud of swirling motes of dust, was Sullivan pushing Lucy almost gently to the floor, then heading towards the door, and once he was gone, Lucy, turning and crawling towards him, mouthing the words "I'm sorry", her face framed by thick strands of blood-wetted hair, her cheeks threaded by mingling streams of tears and blood.

24

The Ice Barn

There was a sharp knock on his door. Speake was in bed, huddled under the covers fully clothed. He sat up with a start, his heart pounding. Despite his fears that Sullivan might come looking for him he had almost drifted off into sleep, exhausted by all that had happened that day, the anxious hours of waiting that followed.

He had been half awake, half dreaming. In the dream he had been walking on a frozen lake; the surface of the ice had started to crack and tilt beneath his feet as he moved further from the shore. The buildings rising along the shoreline were twisted and tilted like broken, branchless tree trunks. With every step he had taken he had feared the ice would break and he would be pitched into the water. He had known the water of the lake was deep; that once beneath the surface the ice would quickly close above him.

"Who is it?" he said tentatively, shaking his head to clear

it. If it was Sullivan, there was little he could do. He had no weapon to defend himself other than a chamber pot and the rickety chair. He reached for his pocket-watch on the table beside the bed. In the poor light he thought the watch showed about a quarter to nine.

"Mr Speake! There's a visitor for you," his landlady's voice said from behind the door. "You know we don't allow female guests in the rooms." Speake let out a shallow sigh of relief. "She's from the saloon. Should I tell her to go?" The woman's voice sounded dismissive, even through the door.

"No. I'll be down in a minute."

He wondered who could want to see him at this time of night. Lucy, maybe, he thought, his heartbeat quickening again at the possibility. He sat up, swinging his legs from under the covers and pushed his feet into his boots without tying the laces. His back ached from laying curled up on the cot; it was the only way he could fit into its too-short length. He straightened his clothes, and tried as best he could to slick down his pillow-twisted hair in the pale reflection of the mirror. As he went down the stairs, he could see the lower half of a woman's body pacing round the room. From the way she moved he could tell it was not Lucy.

"Belinda, what brings you...," he started to say as soon as he realised who his visitor was.

"There's been a fight. At the saloon," she interrupted him. She looked upset; her eyes filled with panic. Her hair was wild, as though she too had just come from her bed. She had only a shawl draped around her shoulders to protect her bare arms against the cold.

"It's Brogan! He's near killed Dortmund, and beaten up on Lucy."

"My god! How is she? Is she alright?"

"She's shaken up, cuts and bruises, but she'll survive. Dortmund's been stabbed and knocked a bit from his senses, but he's young so he should recover. Sullivan's gone off, saying he's going to kill Allenby."

"How did it happen?"

"Nobody knows. It probably just carried over from this afternoon. From the little Lucy was able to tell he just started in on them. Maybe he thought there's something going on between them." Her conjecture struck Speake as odd, given the conversation he had had with Lucy only a couple of days previously. Other than the defensive reaction of Dortmund to his inquiry he had seen no indication that might have led anyone to suspect such a cause for Sullivan's violence.

"And is there?" he asked.

Belinda looked at him. Her eyes were cold, her expression one of exasperation. "I don't think that really matters now, do you?"

"No, of course not," he agreed. "So, what can we do?"

"Best stay out of the way, I'd suggest." She shook her head. "I'm sorry. I don't dislike the old man, but who's really going to miss him? I don't want him to suffer, and the way Brogan is acting he could take his time up there getting his satisfaction. It's you I'm more worried about. As he set off, he shouted out, in the middle of the street, that when he was done he was coming to finish off his business with you. I'm surprised you didn't hear it."

"No, I was..." He realised he did not need to offer any

explanation. Everyone in the town would know what was going on.

"What can I do? I can't just hide here while Allenby is murdered." Belinda managed to raise a brief smile through her obvious agitation.

"So, you're going to stop him, are you, big, tough city boy?" Speake shook his head.

"I don't think I'd know how."

"Would this help?" Belinda put her hand into the pocket of her skirt. She pulled out a gun and held it out in front of her.

"I don't know. I'm not sure I'd be able to use it."

"Take it. It can't hurt to have it. You never know what you might find out about yourself. People make surprising choices when they've no other options. No-one would blame you."

He reached out and took the proffered gun. The metal felt cold in his hand, and he was surprised at how heavy it was. He had never held a gun before, let alone fired one. He weighed it in the palm of his hand. It disturbed him how comfortable, how natural it felt to hold such a thing, the power it contained. It had looked unwieldy in Belinda's small hands.

"You have any idea how to use it?" Speake looked up at her. There was no need to give an answer.

"Here, let me show you," she said and moved closer, cupping her hands around his hand holding the gun. Close up, the smell of her scent took him back to the day in her room, more than three months before, when she had shown him Jack Bunney's letter. It was the evidence contained in the letter, he realised, that had truly set his argument with Sullivan in motion, had brought them all to this situation.

"It seems Brogan might be hurt," Belinda said quietly

beside him, as she showed him how to prime and hold and point the gun. "One of them managed to cut him or something. He was leaving a trail of blood."

The cold light of a full moon fell on the broken track which led up to the barn, making everything seem closer, bringing the world into sharp relief. The ageing banks of snow that still remained had been moulded by the wind and thaw into organic, almost animal shapes that seemed to watch and follow his movements as he passed. Although much less intense than the light of day, the moonlight made everything seem more solid, more real.

He had been climbing fast, hoping he would get to the barn before Sullivan had a chance to wreak whatever revenge he had in mind for Allenby. His heart was pounding wildly, from the exertions of the climb, and from anticipation of what might await him. He felt for the gun in his pocket for reassurance; its cold touch only brought into sharper focus the danger he would be facing. Ahead, he noticed a few dark spots on the surface of a large boulder, glistening in the moonlight. He dabbed at one of them with the tip of his finger. It was wet. He raised his fingers to his nose, recognised the tang of iron, then smeared the blood away across his fingertips.

As he approached the barn, his knees bent and his back arched low, trying to make himself as inconspicuous as he could in the revealing moonlight, he saw the pale glow of a lamp burning behind one of the windows of Allenby's shack. As he drew closer, however, he saw that the door of the barn was open. There was light falling from the doorway, and he could hear snatches of Sullivan's voice coming from inside.

"…think it would make any difference…?"

"…could burn it all down with you…"

Coming to the door, Speake pressed against the side of the barn and peered in through the narrow gap between the door and frame. Two kerosene lamps placed on the floor dimly illuminated the interior. The blocks of ice stacked against the walls reflected their yellow light, lending the space an unearthly glow.

Allenby was slumped in a rail-back chair, his body half turned towards the door. His hands were tied behind his back, and the lower half of his face was darkened with blood. His nose looked as though it had been broken. Sullivan was pacing back and forth in a close arc in front of him. As he moved, his twin shadows thrown by the light of the lamps loomed and danced around the walls. Speake noticed he was favouring the right side of his body. There was blood drying on his hand, and dark stains on the cuff of his shirt protruding from the sleeve of his overcoat.

"So, old man, what *am* I going to do with you?" Sullivan said, coming to a halt with his back to the door, placing his left hand on Allenby's shoulder. "Strip you naked, leave you here to freeze? I doubt that'd work though, you're such a tough old goat."

"Do what you like. Makes no difference to me," Allenby mumbled, his face lowered to his chest.

"Oh, I will Josh. You've been the bane of my life for… How many years is it now? Thirty? I should have shot you back in Chicago."

"Maybe you should've. At least then I'd have been spared

seeing what your indifference did to Emilie. That's what killed her," Allenby mumbled again, his head lifting and turning to challenge Sullivan. Sullivan laughed and leaned down with his face a few inches from Allenby's.

"Maybe she was just sick of your ugly face always trotting behind her. Maybe she couldn't see any other way to get away from you."

Speake gathered his courage and tightened his grip on the gun. There was no point in having come here if all it would accomplish was to be witness to Allenby's torture and execution. His heart was pounding, and his breathing had reduced to almost nothing. Despite the cold, the palms of his hands were damp with sweat; the grip of the pistol felt slippery in his hand. He took a deep breath, pulled the door open sharply and took a single step inside.

"That's enough, Sullivan," he said. "Let him go." He had tried to shout, to give some conviction to his voice, but his words had sounded weak, almost apologetic. Sullivan turned, and immediately started to laugh.

"That's just perfect," he said. "Now I don't have to come back down to get you. Come on in. Josh and I were discussing old times."

"Untie him," Speake said, moving further into the barn. His arm was shaking. Even with the gun held at arm's length, his elbow locked straight, the hand holding the weapon supported by the other hand, it was difficult to keep it aimed where he wanted, at Sullivan's heart.

"Are you really going to use that? Allenby's tried twice, and look where it's got him. Eh, old friend?" He reached across and pushed against Allenby's nose with his thumb, the top joints of his finger hooked behind his jaw. Allenby groaned loudly, twisting his head away.

"You think you can do better than old Josh?"

"Leave him!" Speake said, managing to raise the tone and level of his voice.

"Use it, man. Shoot him, God damn it!" Allenby barked. He looked up and glared at Speake, his eyes burning in the darkness of his face, and then he said more softly. "You know he'll not leave you be."

"He has a point," Sullivan said, a mischievous smile on his face, as he glanced back and forth between them." I'll make it easy. They say it's easier to shoot a man in the back so you can't see what he's feeling. Never tried it myself. The jolt of understanding in their faces, the recognition of the power you have over them is…gratifying."

As he finished talking, he turned away and walked casually towards the blocks of ice stacked at the rear of the barn. There were tools - saws, axes, hooks and crowbars - scattered on top of the ice. Coming to a halt, he took hold of the heavy chain hanging from the hoist beam that ran along the length of the barn, supporting his weight. Speake heard him groan quietly. It was some consolation to know the wound to his arm was not inconsiderable, and he began to hope Sullivan would collapse from loss of blood, relieving him of the need to use the gun.

"How's it going back there? Finger stuck on the trigger?" Sullivan asked, and then his free hand rose rapidly to the pile of tools. He spun around, his arm moving through the air in Speake's direction. Speake saw something spinning towards him. He ducked to avoid it. The iron hook clattered against the door behind him and fell to the floor.

As he stood up, turning rapidly to face Sullivan, he heard a rumbling sound, the screech of metal on metal. The chain with its heavy pulley was coming towards him, its loose end flicking through the air like the tail of an angry cat. He tried to jump away, but the end of the chain caught him high on the forehead. He staggered to one side, and went down on one knee. He could feel blood running down the side of his face, pooling around the corner of his eye. Before he could regain his composure, the weight of Sullivan's body slammed against him.

The force of the impact knocked him over, and the gun flew from his hand. As he fell back, his arm struck against the side of Ingram Todd's coffin. The coffin rocked forward as he grabbed at it to halt his fall. He glanced up at the frozen face inside. The cold had contracted the features of Todd's face, pulling his lips back in a ghastly rictus.

Without thinking, he thrust his arm behind the casket and levered it from the wall. The arms of Todd's corpse had been bound against his sides; the rigid body fell forward in a straight arc. Its hard weight struck Sullivan's back as he tried to turn away. Without the weight of the body inside it, the casket rocked on its base and fell back against the wall. Sullivan cursed loudly as he toppled sideways and ended up on the ground, half sitting up, his torso supported by one arm beneath him, the stiffened corpse settled in the hook of his hip and waist, its ghoulish face turned towards him.

"Jesus Christ! You'll pay for this!" Sullivan cursed again as he scrambled to crawl free, pushing desperately at the corpse with his hands and feet, a horrified expression on his face. Before Speake could locate and recover the gun, Sullivan was rising again, still cursing, Todd's body beside him face down on the floor. Speake pushed himself away, scuttling back across the ground towards the wall of the barn. He could taste blood in his mouth, from the wound to his head, or from some other unregistered injury when Sullivan had charged against him.

Sullivan was coming at him again, half crawling, half trying to stand. Panic gripped Speake, extinguishing the temporary sense of relief he had felt. As he pushed himself back closer to the wall, his hand fell on something cold and hard. He glanced down. It was the iron hook Sullivan had thrown. It was no more than a piece of iron rod, about eighteen inches long, shaped at one end to form an elliptical handle, and bent square on at the other into a sharply pointed hook.

Sullivan was now standing. His dark eyes glared in the reflected lamplight as he leaned down to grab Speake, his hands reaching for his throat. Speake could feel the cold wetness of blood on his skin as he tried to fend his hands away. He grasped the sharpened end of the hook and swung it round as hard as he could. The edge of the iron handle caught Sullivan a glancing blow high on the side of his head. He staggered and sank to his knees, a hand clasped to his temple. After a few moments he raised his face. There was a look of surprise in his eyes as he pulled his hand away and inspected the blood on his fingers.

"Shit, boy!" he said. "You're really starting to annoy me!"

"I thought that happened a long time ago," Speake said, struggling to his feet, and readjusting the hook in his hand to get a firmer grip. Sullivan was kneeling in front of him. His head, with its balding patch the size of a silver dollar on its crown, hung down only a few feet from Speake. He raised the iron tool above his shoulder and took a step forward, as Allenby shouted, "Kill him, you fool! Kill him!"

Speake's mind was a riot of confusion and doubt. He could hit him; incapacitate him further. Break his arm or collarbone at least. Or he could kill him, bring an end to his callousness and spite; cave in the skull, crush the soft mass of brain within. He blinked several times, to drive such violent images from his thoughts. Could he kill a man? He still thought not. Not even in the heat of a fight. Not even this man, who was trying to kill him, with all the things he had done. To resort to that, he decided, would make him no better than Sullivan.

"Why do you hate them so much?" he asked instead. If he was going to die he wanted to have some understanding of what motivated Sullivan. A quizzical look slid across Sullivan's face. "The women," Speake added in explanation. Sullivan let out a low cough of amusement.

"It's not a matter of hate, boy; it's indifference. I've never allowed myself to be distracted by who they are, what they might think or feel." He let out a short, vicious laugh. "Beyond oneself, no-one else matters. Did you not learn that from all those clever books you've read?" He wiped the blood from his hand onto his sleeve, then began to crawl around on the ground as though looking for something. Speake thought he must have been disoriented by the blow, and was trying to crawl away, but when Sullivan stood again and turned to face him, he held Belinda's gun in his hand.

"Let's just put an end to this here and now," Sullivan said.

He was swaying slightly, the gun held in the hand of his damaged arm, his other hand nursing the swelling rising on the side of his head. He raised the muzzle of the pistol, pointing it unsteadily at Speake.

A deafening explosion reverberated around the barn. Speake felt the force of the bullet tug sharply at his clothing, a flash of pain sear through his side just above the point of his hip. The side of his body jerked, his leg lifting momentarily from the floor in reaction to the impact. Something inside of him reacted too. He flipped the hook over in his hand, took a couple of rapid steps forward and swung it at Sullivan's head. The sharpened point sunk into his temple. He could feel the cracking of Sullivan's skull transmitted through the iron. He had expected there would be a spray of blood, but there was nothing, only Sullivan coming to an abrupt halt, the gun dropping from his hand.

Speake had the impression of the eye on the side of Sullivan's head where the hook had entered darkening and bulging slightly in its socket. A glutinous trail of blood trickled from his nose across his upper lip. When he saw Sullivan's eyes glaze over he let go of the iron hook. He watched as it wavered in time to the dying man's pulse, its movements gradually lessening. A series of brief shudders passed through Sullivan's body, then his eyes went blank, and his body crumpled to the ground.

Speake stood, his heart pounding, barely able to breathe. He was waiting for Sullivan to get up again, not daring to believe it had ended. After a few moments had passed and the body had not moved, he looked across at Allenby, an expression of anguish carved across his face. Allenby let out a sound that could have been a groan or a laugh of relief, and shook his head.

"You sure took your time about it," he said. "Why the hell didn't you just shoot him?"

Speake did not answer. Having killed Sullivan anyway, there was no explanation he could offer.

Part 4

Spring

25

A Tainted Gift

Speake was surprised to see Allenby in the hallway when he answered the knock at his door the evening before he was due to leave. The old man looked well, and to have recovered from his ordeal. They had spoken to each other briefly the day after the fight, but he had hardly seen him since, other than walking along the street on the few occasions Allenby had come down into the town. His nose looked reasonably straight again. He had fixed it himself in a mirror that night, when they returned to his shack. Speake had not been able to watch as he pushed the bone and gristle back to where he thought they belonged, his eyes welling with tears of pain.

"Are you alright?" Speake had asked in the barn, once the fight was over, as he went over to untie Allenby. Apart from the bloodied mess of his nose, his top lip had been split. A blackened tooth had lain on the floor beside the chair.

"I'll live, thanks to you," Allenby had said, lifting his hand

and cautiously running his fingertips over his face. "What about you?"

It was only then that Speake had taken stock of the damage to his own body. There had been much blood, though some of it, he had reassured himself, would have been from Sullivan's wounds. His clothes on the side he had been shot had felt cold and heavy. Undoing his coat and jacket, their linings sodden with blood, then the lower buttons on his shirt, similarly blood weighted and darkened, he had finally eased the fabric of his undershirt away from where it had started to adhere to the wound. A furrow of white flesh had shown where skin and fatty tissues had been stripped away, blood seeping from it in small globules.

"It's only a flesh wound," he had said bravely. "But you should probably get stitches in your lip."

"Go into town…? No. It'll wait," Allenby had replied. "I can patch that up for you, and you can bunk here till mornin'."

Speake had wanted to see Lucy, to let her know he was alive, that Sullivan could no longer harm her, but had not had the strength or resolve to make the journey back into town, or to offer explanations. Everyone would have been waiting, curious as to the outcome, fully anticipating it would be Sullivan who returned, that being the only answer they would need. The charge of the fight no longer coursing through his body, he had felt deflated, beaten almost. He had nodded agreement to Allenby's offer.

The old man looked uncomfortable, almost bashful, once Speake had invited him into his room. He kept his eyes lowered to the ground, the comforting pipe noticeably absent from his mouth or hand. They had to stand only a few feet apart in the narrow space between the bed and the wall; the room was so small. The low light of the oil lamp heightened the bands of bruising that still discoloured the softer tissues beneath Allenby's eyes.

"I wanted to give you somethin'," he eventually said. "A token of... You know... It's about the only decent thing I have. Made it myself, long ago, when I was a different kind of man. Here, I want you to have this."

He handed Speake a small, flat object wrapped in blue and white gingham cloth. Speake unwrapped it; inside was a wooden picture frame, its edges inlaid in a geometric pattern crafted from different veneers. In one of the bottom corners Allenby had created the image of a tiny mouse.

"This is beautiful. I can't take this. I only did..."

"Take it. I've no need of it no more. It's served its purpose, probably longer than it should've."

"Thank you," was all Speake was able to say. He was touched by the gesture, that Allenby should have given him something so personal. The palpable sadness of the man, the sense of loss that pervaded his being, left Speake not knowing what else to say.

"What will you do now?" he asked, after they had stood in silence for some time.

"Stay here, as long as there's folks as need me. Then I suppose I'll grow old savourin' my victory. Then I'll die, like everybody else."

"Your victory?" Speake asked cautiously, some sense alerted. It seemed an odd way to describe what had happened. He remembered then something the old man had said that night, about having finally beaten Sullivan, as they had been leaving the barn.

"Yes. Over Brogan. I beat him in the end…, no small thanks to you."

"You make it sound as though it was a competition."

"Well, it was, for me. Always had been, goin' back to Chicago. He always got whatever he wanted. Or more often, just that he didn't want nobody else to have. Seems like I spent half my life tryin' to find some way to best him."

It dawned on Speake then, the thing he had been missing, the detail he had always suspected he had overlooked. He finally had the answer to the mystery he had believed was there. When he thought back, he realised that in different ways, often too subtle to have registered, it had always been about Allenby. The deaths, the articles he had sent back to Chicago, his pursuit of that frequently questioned mystery; Allenby had played a central part in all of them. The life of the town had revolved around him as much as it had around Sullivan.

"It was you, wasn't it?" he said, feeling surprisingly untouched by the realisation. "You killed the boy." Allenby's eyes flicked away from his and drifted steadily around the room, his tongue visibly searching the inside of his mouth, seeking the consolation of the absent pipe.

"No, I… I wouldn't say I killed him as such," Allenby eventually responded, his eyes re-engaging with Speake's. There was a renewed light of challenge in them, and Speake was reminded of the final look Sullivan had given him out on the street on New Year's Eve. It struck him how alike in nature, at heart, Allenby and Sullivan had been.

"But yes, I was there. And yes, you could say my bein' there was…instrumental," Allenby continued. "But it really was more by way of an accident. And, you know, you could still just let it be. There'd be no point in sayin'. What they know now is what they always wanted to believe."

"So, we just leave it at that, because it's convenient?"

"Why not? Nobody needs to know, and it wouldn't change a damn thing for anyone, other than me if they did. The boy's parents're long gone. How'd you come to realise it?"

"Sullivan's horse. Where you claimed you saw him riding is too steep and rock-strewn, not the place anyone would take a temperamental animal like that. Not even Sullivan. He liked to ride hard and straight." Allenby nodded, though whether in agreement or in appreciation of the deduction Speake was unable to tell.

"Always said you were too smart for us simple folk."

"Maybe you just made a simple mistake. What happened?" Allenby paused before answering, his eyes again scanning the walls of the room.

"I swear I'd never thought it through to turn out like that," he finally said. "I was up there, keepin' an eye out for ice and timber when the boy came along. We spoke for a while, and then I got the crazy idea maybe I could do somethin', make people believe it was Brogan's doin', if I told them I'd seen him up there too. I just set off after the boy, no real plan in my head, just all those years of hatred for Brogan burnin' up inside, pushin' me on."

"When I finally found him, down in some gulley, searchin' for the gold he'd said he hoped to find, I tried to grab hold of him. He was layin' half on the ground, half out on the ice, delving' with his arm in the water. I only wanted to scare him. Jabbered some nonsense about my name bein' Sullivan, that he needed to remember that." He paused, a wry smile crossing his lips as he shook his head.

"I'd put a kerchief over my face so he wouldn't recognise me later, as if it'd make any difference. And then..." He turned his face away, as though trying to avoid the picture that had formed inside his head.

"You know, it would've been alright if Sullivan hadn't showed up. I'd got used to her not wantin' me. It was enough just havin' her here."

"Her...? Who are you talking about?"

"Emilie. Emilie Henderson." Speake did not know how to respond. It was hard to imagine Allenby as an impassioned man, or that he should harbour such feelings for someone so inappropriate, not only in her marital state, but also her refinement that only amplified Allenby's coarseness. That she had been the object of his and Sullivan's contending emotions did however explain the animosity between the two men.

"Henderson's wife? You...?" Allenby nodded, a self-conscious smile on his lips.

"Crazy, eh? Needless to say, the feelin' wasn't mutual. What I couldn't get used to though was seein' her still wantin' Sullivan." He shook his head violently, as though trying to deny the things he knew were true and could never be revoked. "Honest to God, I tried to catch him, tried to pull him from the water... Then he was gone."

"You lied to me, and you used me!" Speake shouted when Allenby finished, his anger finally breaking through the shroud of resignation which had descended over him when he had first realised the truth.

"But the man was a killer. He murdered your friend. Surely you can...," Allenby tried to protest.

"He could have killed me too! It was only by dumb luck I survived. You put my life at risk. For what? Your need for revenge, over a woman who never loved you?" He thrust the wooden picture frame back at Allenby.

"I can't take this. It wouldn't be..." He was unable to say more, his anger strangling his words. Allenby's hand, shaking visibly, rose and took the frame, and then his arm fell back to his side.

"No, I can see how you wouldn't... But it really was an accident. The poor lad wasn't supposed..." Allenby managed to say before his voice finally broke and uncontrollable sobs coursed through his body. Speake had to steel himself against pity. From how Allenby had related it, the death of the boy may have been an unintended outcome, but it had been brought about by Allenby's own choices. As for the killing of Sullivan, Speake saw now how the old man had manipulated him, had first planted and then nurtured the seeds of suspicion, feeding him lies to stoke his resentment and sense of injustice, had even been prepared to put his own life at risk to achieve his desired outcome. There was nothing to pity or forgive.

"So, why didn't you stick to your lie and blame Sullivan?" he asked once Allenby's sobbing had eased. Allenby's head flicked up, and he brushed the tears from his cheeks with the back of his wrist.

"I thought folks'd come to their own conclusions, decide

it was him for themselves, and I knew I couldn't prove it. I'd needed the kid to say. And then the thought of her hating me if she ever discovered..." He paused, looked down at the wooden frame in his hands. "Then one thing kinda led to another," he said slowly. Another flash of comprehension came to Speake.

"You killed Jack Bunney too," he said. It had been Allenby who had first directed suspicion onto the drifter Stone. Again, he felt oddly untouched by this new understanding. A sense of complacency had overtaken him, brought on by the realisation of how mistaken he had been, how he had been used, and how powerless he was to change any of it. Allenby nodded once or twice as his chin again sunk towards his chest.

"I still don't understand why you said nothing."

"Me neither. The two things just sorta happened." He smiled to himself and gave a low chuckle. "Mind you, the idea of it was never far from my head. I'd had a belt made just like Sullivan's, with its big silver buckle, and boots like his. Suppose I had half a thought it'd be, like a disguise, if an opportunity ever did come along. I guess you'd say that made it kinda premeditated. The fact is, it made me feel better, as important as him. Then I saw Bunney layin' there in the alley, and got this notion, seein' as the thing with the boy hadn't worked out as I'd hoped... And with the boy, once it was done, I felt so ashamed I was scared to open my mouth. I thought it would be obvious to everyone I was lyin'."

"So, two innocent people died for nothing, and I killed a man because you persuaded me he was guilty of a murder you had committed. To what end?"

"The one I got, even if it's too late now to make a differ-ence." Allenby answered with barely a hesitation.

"I think you should leave," Speake said, as he squeezed past Allenby to open the door. He was finally in possession of the facts, the all-encompassing story he had been hoping to find. And yet he still did not have any concrete answers. Behind the resolved mystery he had found another, and all the knowledge he felt he had gained of the way the world truly was, and of himself - his own limits, and indeed his capabilities - yielded no guidance as to how to unravel it. What would drive a man to behave in such a way? What passion; what self-serving sense of conviction? Not love, of that he was certain.

Allenby glanced at him quickly, a look of confusion on his face. His head flicked twice in a gesture that Speake was unable to tell if it was in acceptance or denial, and then he turned and started to shuffle uneasily from the room.

"Sometimes he comes lookin' for me, you know," he said, pausing and turning back in the doorway. His voice had soft-ened, and he looked almost embarrassed. "The boy, that is. Him..., and Jack too sometimes. Especially in the night-time. Especially when it's cold. Both of 'em lookin' at me more confused than angry. The three of us up there in that shack, none of us really knowin' the reason why. Some ghosts never die, you know. Some ghosts never grow old!"

A Bloody Encounter:
May Bring a New Order

Hope, March 27th 1900

Following a dispute, which took place in the late hours of March 25th, initiating in a private room above the Broken-O saloon, Mr Brogan Sullivan, proprietor of that establishment came to a violent and bloody end.

Another participant in the dispute, a Master Thomas Dortmund, was also injured during the fracas, apparently the consequence of a needless argument that had been proving for some time, which had arisen over Mr Dortmund's relationship with Miss Lucy Harrigan, an employee in Sullivan's saloon. This, according to the statement Miss Harrigan has made, in which she has also told of having herself attempted during the initial incident to kill Sullivan, in her own defence, and in a valiant, yet unrewarded attempt to protect the young man.

Many here report Sullivan as having acted erratically and with uncharacteristic aggression of late, and but weeks ago he was involved in an incident which resulted in the death of an innocent young man, Mr. Ingram Todd. Few, therefore, are inclined to doubt Miss Harrigan's story. There had also been an argument, one witnessed by many, between herself and Sullivan earlier that day, which may have further contributed to the incident.

The wounds to her own person, and those inflicted on the body of the young man also serve to corroborate her story of what transpired.

Miss Harrigan, it appears, had been entertaining the young man, a close friend, in her private room when Sullivan forced his way in and started to make improper demands of the young couple. An altercation ensued, in which Miss Harrigan was struck violently several times about the head and body. Mr. Dortmund, as would most finding themselves in such a situation, rushed to her assistance, but was himself then set upon by Sullivan, who in the meantime had armed himself with a knife. With this, he delivered two wounds, both debilitating, but neither fatal, to the body of the young man.

Having recovered somewhat from her own beating in this interval, Miss Harrigan was able to retrieve the knife, which it seems Sullivan had arrogantly discarded while he had gloated over the agonies of the injured young man. This she tried to use to attack Sullivan, but was able only to stab him once in the shoulder before he fled.

Sullivan, apparently still fired up in a fit of temper, next made his way to the abode of Mr Joshua Allenby, town undertaker, with the loudly broadcast intent of killing him. Mr Allenby had earlier in the day intervened in the argument between Sullivan and Miss Harrigan, apparently thus incurring Sullivan's ire. A further incident then took place inside Mr. Allenby's ice barn, of which the full details are still unclear, but which resulted ultimately in the death of Sullivan, and in Mr Allenby's happy escape from a violent end.

A third party is known to have been involved, an acquaintance of Mr Allenby, as yet unnamed, who on hearing of the situation had come to his aid. Mr Sullivan suffered several minor injuries but succumbed finally to a single wound to his head, delivered apparently by one of the iron implements used in handling the ice stored in Mr Allenby's barn. It has been rumoured that it was the said acquaintance who delivered the fatal blow, although this has not been confirmed by those involved.

"Let's hope this brings a new sense of order to the town. Sullivan more or less ran the place, mostly according to his own law," Mr Allenby said the day following his fortunate escape. "There were some as tried to stand up to him, but our efforts mostly came to no good end."

Miss Harrigan and Mr Dortmund are

both recovering from their injuries, and find themselves the object of much gossip and attention.

The saloon is now in the ownership of Miss Belinda Curtis, previously also an employee of Sullivan. This by virtue of a document she has submitted to the sheriff, claiming an agreement had been drawn up between herself and Sullivan but a few months previously. No-one has come forward to contest the document, dubious as its authenticity might be.   TES

26

Spring

The warmth in the early morning sun pinched gently at his face. Speake was standing at the end of the main thorough-fare through the town, at the upper end of the lagoon. A few thin, greying islands of ice still floated on the surface of the water. He looked around at the tree-filled valley, at this desolate place called Hope scarring its heart, the wild and certain mountains beyond. Snow still covered the crowns and slopes of the mountains above the tree line, but down here in the sheltered valley, in the sunlight, you could tell by the feel of the air that spring had arrived. At the depot up the road the stagecoach was being readied, the horses fed, watered and harnessed. Within the hour the coach would be setting off on its journey East. Speake would be among its passengers; the time had come for him to leave.

The world seemed to him particularly beautiful today. The sounds of melt-water running down from the valley slopes came to him, chattering across stones and boulders, and somewhere in the distance, feint and steady, the intermittent rattle of a woodpecker. Closer to him, the shrill and chatter of avian mating calls punctuated the air. Even the town looked gay. Work was nearing completion on the rebuilding of Henderson's store; its new weather-boarding a glowing cream between its still smoke-greyed neighbours, a freshly gilt-painted sign spanned above its windows and doors. Pots of flowers adorned the stoops of many of the houses, and faded red, blue and white bunting, residues of the New Year celebrations hung still across the front of the saloon. The town was having to adjust to the saloon's new owner, the changes she had made in the way it was run, the services it provided, but Speake expected Belinda would do well in her newly elevated position, at least for as long as this place called Hope survived.

Standing by the placid lake, it was hard to believe that winter had finally passed, and that he had survived. He felt so much older, no longer the ingenuous young man he had been but a half-year gone. While the ghosts that had brought him here had for the large part receded - his experiences having shown him that, as concrete as such things might feel, there was no real substance to their imagined agency - the echoes of their keening still lingered in the deepest recesses of his thoughts. His credo now was that all a man could do was make peace with himself, or with God or the Devil - if such entities existed. He had seen no evidence during the months he had been here to encourage him to believe in the existence of either. Whatever happened, whatever shape an individual life might take, it was simply a question of blind, disinterested fortune, like the random turn of a card. There was no hidden reason or purpose. A man simply had to decide for himself - answering to his own conscience, and not in blind obedience to a God, or to some acquired set of beliefs - whether a thing was in itself bad or good.

There were of course those who understood yet chose to embrace the wrong in what they were doing. Brogan Sullivan had known the consequences of his actions, yet he had appeared to have felt neither guilt nor remorse. He had been a predator; he had used and controlled those who did not have the strength or courage to resist him, disposed of those who were no longer of use, or who stood in his way. Did that make him evil? Speake did not know. Like God, like the Devil, he did not know whether such things as good and evil existed, not in any absolute sense. Who knew, maybe Sullivan had wrestled with ghosts of his own - ancient fears and phantasms rendered inert through the enactment of his illicit acts?

And what judgement should he make of himself; had he behaved any better? He too had killed a man, and he could not escape his culpability in the death of Gillam Todd. If he had not pressed Sullivan, Todd would in all probability still be alive. The only consolation he could take was that he had made good use of the gold from Todd's claim. It had not been a fortune, around eight hundred dollars, less the small amount he had used since to make his own life here more tolerable. Eventually, though, he had persuaded Lucy to take what remained. At least then, he had told her, to assuage the last of her doubts about accepting it, if she used it to get away and build a new life for herself then Todd's death would have been of some avail.

He had said his goodbyes to her earlier on the veranda outside the saloon, the place where he had first seen her the day he had arrived. He had asked her again to come with him, to be his wife. As they had talked, however, he had come to the realisation - given the knowledge they had of each other, of the things each had done - that it was an impossible thing he was asking, both of her and of himself. Such knowledge would have stayed with them always, an enduring reminder of all that had happened. The shadow of guilt, the gnawing spectre of regret; even if such things should haunt only their own individual hearts and never be voiced openly, they would remain interred at the root of their relationship, eventually driving them apart.

"Thank you, Thomas," she had said. "But whatever we may have done in common, I'm really not like you, and even if no-one else ever knows about my past, you will." She had paused and looked up into his face. He had seen the doubt in her eyes, how difficult it was for her to deny him, the chance of a different life being offered.

"I don't think I could live with that, the constant fear that at heart you were ashamed of me," she had finally said, echoing his own doubts.

"No, I would be proud of you, always. What right would I have to judge you?" he had asked, fully understanding that his willingness to forgive was entirely subjective; it could do little to heal the damage and shame she herself felt. Who was he to judge her? He had taken the life of a man outside the sanction of the law. Any rationalisation he might make about saving the lives of others did nothing to alter the fact of it. Sullivan had been a killer, a sociopath, a man who had probably deserved to die. Speake had encountered no difficulty in making that particular judgement, but as much as he tried to persuade himself that his being Sullivan's executioner was not a question of right or wrong but merely one of blind Fate, he was only slowly coming to terms with what he had done.

The morning after the fight there had been a thick layer of hoar frost on the ground, the thinned disc of the sun sliding up behind the shroud of mist that overnight had filled the lower reaches of the valley. His body, all of his joints had ached. He had rolled gingerly from the cot where he had slept surprisingly soundly, having fallen asleep almost the moment he had laid down. The broken sounds of Allenby's snoring had still rattled out every few seconds from the old man's room at the rear of the shack. Pulling on his coat, he had gone to the door, opened it as quietly as he could, and stepped outside.

Sullivan's body had still been lying on the floor of the barn, the various marks of blood congealing to black. The hook protruding from the side of his head had reminded Speake of the key on the clockwork soldier he had owned as a boy. The soldier had been one of his favourite toys, until the clockwork inside had broken.

It was foolish, he knew, but he had half-expected the body to no longer be there. Sullivan had seemed so enduring, immortal almost. It would not have surprised him to have discovered him, gun in hand, waiting calmly in the rail-back chair for Speake to return.

"It was self-defence, Thomas. He would have killed you,"

Lucy had said, breaking his dark reverie. "But not me. Sure, he would have knocked me around some, tried to keep me quiet through fear so I…" Her voice had trailed off, and she had shaken her head in an attempt to drive away the memory.

He had looked down into her face. The scar on her forehead from Sullivan's ring was now no more than a lightened, depressed crescent of skin, the bruising on her cheek faded to a lozenge of pale yellow ringed with feint patches of blues and greens. What she said was true; their lives, their experiences in most other respects were worlds apart. He could have no real comprehension of the parts of herself she would have had to close off, the courage and strength she would have had to muster every day simply to survive the life the arrogance and callousness of men like Bunney and Sullivan had determined for her. Any claimed empathy he might express could be no more than speculation, an entirely masculine projection of a for him unknowable reality.

His heart still felt weighed down by the decision they had arrived at together, but he knew it was the correct one to have made. She had smiled up at him, an uncertain, self-conscious smile. He had still thought she was beautiful, had still found it hard to believe the startling, almost inhuman depth of blue in her eyes. He had raised his hand, to touch her once more, but she had stopped him.

"No, Thomas. The money is more than I deserve. The chance to start again, that's all I ask. Please don't make it difficult."

Speake had also said his equally saddening farewell to Dortmund the previous afternoon. The young man had been making his way back to his cabin in the mountains, Lucy and

Belinda having failed to persuade him to stay to recuperate in the room they had prepared for him at the saloon. He had maintained he was well enough, even though his wounds were far from healed and caused him to walk with his upper body skewed and his arms held protectively to his side.

"I can manage on my own," he had replied when Speake expressed concern at the wisdom of returning to the mountains alone. "I cannot stand more of those women fussing constantly over me," he had added in a lowered voice.

"What will you do now?" Speake had asked.

"I will stay here and live a peaceful life. Soon there will be no one else left, and I will have this place to myself."

"Won't you be lonely?"

"I will have company enough. The trees, the birds and animals. And other men will come."

"And Lucy? There was something between the two of you, yes?" he had asked, feeling genuine concern for the feelings of the young man, despite his own past ambitions in respect of her.

"I cannot ask her to stay. She has spent too long having to do things at the bidding of a man. With Todd's gold she can be more than she has ever been allowed to be, or if she were to stay here with me. I do not want to leave. I have to let her go."

"Is the world so awful?"

"For me, it is. I do not want to live amidst the greed and selfishness I have seen. I do not understand the way it uses and destroys without putting anything back. Here I understand how things must be. Everything in nature has a reason, and that reason is never bad. You may say it can be vicious and violent, but it is never evil. In nature, the killing of one creature is always to give life to another. You can rarely say that of the world of men, other than within their own justification."

Speake was struck again by the wisdom of the young man, far in advance of his years, and of his limited experience of how the world operated. But Hope had been an effective classroom, a microcosm of many of the world's ills. It had led Speake to similar judgements, though his were shaped more by cynicism and personal regret. Dortmund's words were full of optimism, for the life he wanted to live at least, even knowing it would be devoid of luxury and human companionship.

"Some people are good," was all he could say, echoing the feeble argument he had offered to Gillam Todd as consolation.

"This is true, but most do not understand the consequences of what they do. As superior as men may feel, we are but stewards, of this planet, of everything on it. It has not been put here simply for us to use and destroy."

"You sound as though you believe there is no hope," Speake said forlornly. He had expected a sad though far less melancholic parting. Dortmund turned away from the town towards the lake, the encircling walls of forest and mountains. Speake turned with him, to take in the view across the lake, hoping to carry an image of its current beauty with him as antidote to the terrible things he had experienced here. The surface of the lake flowed with the motions of the gentle breeze, like oil, slow and viscous. As they looked out a heron flew in, chasing its reflection above the lake's mirrored surface, then came to a stuttering, almost weightless landfall on the opposite shore.

"Only in places such as this, maybe," Dortmund finally said. "These people here, can they not see the beauty, the value of this? In days to come men will pay the price for what they do now. This will be gone. They will regret it, and yet they will not understand."

27

Dust

He had been dead for more than three days when they found the body. Nobody in the town had missed him. Nobody had realised he was dead. There were only two people there who cared whether he lived or died, or who knew much about him, who he was, what he had been. Both of them, for their own different reasons, had long wished him dead.

It was said by some in the town, those who did not know him, that back in the gold-rush days he had been the town's carpenter and undertaker; a respected and prosperous man. Of late though there had not been much call for a carpenter, not since most of the prospectors had left. Most of the men who were here now were loggers. They already knew about trees, timber, the forest. What carpentry needed to be done, they made it themselves, and the work they did required more robust skills than the ones he had presumably once possessed. His was the first death in the town since a man called Brogan

Sullivan had been killed in a big fight that rumour said had involved near half the town. That had been more than four years past; that was how long it had been since anyone had gone up to the ice-barn to ask the old man to make a casket, or for anything else.

Nobody had known even if he was still willing, or had the strength or skill any more to make anything in wood. After Sullivan was buried he had simply withdrawn from the life of the town, a town that was itself dwindling almost to nothing. All that had remained for their imaginations to work on were the ghosts of old man Allenby's past, the rumours about him, drifting around the outer edges of the town, haunting its memories and dreams.

"You think it's true he kept only the women froze, so he could carry on usin' them, if you know what I mean, let all the men just rot?" one of the men said with a dry laugh. These were the sort of things the loggers said about Allenby, the idea of him nurtured in their minds by rumour and indifference, the reactions that mention of his name usually provoked.

During the early winter of the previous year, before the men returned to their homes in the city, there had been smoke coming from his chimney, and in the spring when they returned he had been seen regularly, chopping fire-wood or tending his vegetable patch, or sitting in an old rocking-chair of an evening on his porch, sucking on his unlit pipe and chattering away like a five-year-old to his mongrel dog. The past few weeks it had been noticed he had taken to walking with a stick and had started to move slowly, and the expectation - the spiteful conjecture - was that he would not make it through the next winter. It was only the troubled, endless barking of the dog that had alerted them to the possibility their idle speculations had been fulfilled.

The shack beside the barn where he had lived was a shambles, and the ice barn itself had not been used since the town had been reduced to little more than a hamlet, numbering during the winter months less than a dozen souls. Neither of the buildings had fared well through the combined effects of neglect and the climate they had up there. The winters had been uncommonly hard the past couple of years, and the ensuing thaws had sprung much of the outside cladding from the walls of the barn, and a good part of the shingles on the roof had split, or had been blown away, or had rotted to dust. The iron hooks, the heavy chains and pulleys which had once been used to manoeuvre the blocks of ice, the saws to cut it, which hung still on the inside walls of the barn, were covered in rust and thick encrustations of green and orange lichens.

It had been eerie and strangely cold in the deserted barn with the wind creeping in through the broken walls and roof, and with the metal implements groaning and grating against each other in the wind. As they stood there thinking of what this place once had been, the sound of the wind had seemed to some of the men like the lingering voices of all the dead souls who had lain there frozen throughout those winters, waiting for the thaw of spring. None of them had wanted to stay in the barn for too long, or be in there alone.

When they discovered the body, they also found a couple of finished pine boxes in the barn, their planks greying and twisting, so they laid out the body of the old man in one of them, nailed a makeshift lid on it, and buried him in a shallow

hole in the graveyard he had set up at the back of the ice barn. One of them mumbled a brief prayer, a few insincere words about him, and then they marked the spot with two pieces of wood roped together to form a cross and hammered into the ground. On the cross-piece of this sparse memorial, they painted in thick black paint: J. ALLENBY ??-1904. None of them had known how old he was, when he had been born.

At first they had been reluctant to go inside the shack. The old man's dog had stood guard at the door, growling and slavering. The beast was emaciated and shaking, and was so weak it could barely stand, but no matter how much they coaxed or threatened it would not let them pass. When they called out for Allenby, there had been no reply. No-one had wanted to take hold of or get too near to the dog; its coat was covered in mange, and its bared teeth were black with rot and dripping with foaming saliva.

"Looks like the brute's gone crazy," one of the men said. "If it bit ya you'd be dead inside the week."

"Poor thing's too weak to ever 'mount to much anymore. Might as well put it out of its misery," someone else said, and so they brought up a gun from the town and shot it. Even in the enfeebled state it was in it took three shells to stop its growling. Then, still, there was the ghost of the old man, the twisted memories of him, of his ghoulish occupation, making them pause before they entered.

Inside, the shack was a mess. It stank of shit and old dust and decay. There were old newspapers, and piles of rotting vegetables and coils of blackened dog-mess all over the floor, and the air was black and noisy with flies. In the back room they found the body of Allenby lying on his side on the floor behind a small wooden table. There was an overturned rail-backed chair on the floor behind him. His body, locked stiff, with his hands straight down at his sides, echoed the shape of the chair, as though he was still sitting in it. There were greying teeth marks on the back and in the palm of his lower hand; it looked as though the dog had pulled him from the chair. He must have died while sitting at the table, the men decided after some discussion, and had sat there, becoming rigid, until the dog had tried to rouse him.

"Perhaps the dog wasn't mad after all," one man said. "Perhaps it was just tryin' to help its master. Maybe we oughtn't to 've shot it." The men murmured amongst themselves for a while, feeling sorry about the dog, and then began to search the shack.

"Hey! It was just a scrawny mutt. It was already half-dead," one of them said as they separated, trying to ease his own conscience, and to reassure the others.

On the table where he had been sitting, they found an old ledger bound in red leather. It was Allenby's manifest, his record of all the deaths that had taken place in the town - of the bodies that had passed through his hands, the caskets he had made for them, the trimmings he had added. Those who read it thought some of the later entries were a touch strange, and his observations about the people he was burying too personal. In them, Allenby had taken to adding asides, passing comment or judgement on the events, and on the character of the other inhabitants of the town, on the roles they might have played in bringing him his reluctant trade. The earlier entries had stated only names and dates and causes of death, details of height and weight, and the type of casket he had made; how much he had been paid for his trouble.

"Looks like the old man was the one who'd gone crazy," one of them said, laughing, when he had read the last few pages.

"You can see him gettin' more and more mad. Seems to have thought there was somethin' goin' on in the town," another of them said.

"Yeah," the first man replied. "Seems to've all started around the time of the death of that Pearce girl, whoever she was." Several of the men pulled down the corners of their mouths and shrugged to show they had no idea who she might have been.

"They called her Rosie," the oldest one among them said. His name was Henderson. He owned the only surviving store in town. He was one of the two there who remembered. The other, the blond German, had not said a word, but then he never said much of anything to anyone, and kept pretty much to himself. Some of them wondered if he was quite right in the head, but others said he had been that way only since the men-folk in his family had all been killed in an accident up at the old workings. They were in the manifest, recorded as items number thirty-five to thirty-seven. Henderson remembered though - remembered Allenby, the things that had gone on in the town, all the deaths recorded in the latter part of the manifest. One in particular he remembered only too well, though he had never uttered a word, had never let show his feelings about it to anyone.

"Rosalind Pearce was her name. A pretty little thing," he said quietly. "And so young. An unfortunate child who made some bad choices and found herself here in Hope, where she had no place to be."

"You knew her then?"

Henderson nodded, his lower lip jutting out. "Knew of her. We all did. She was... She wasn't here long. She worked for Brogan Sullivan up at the saloon, became his property in a manner of speaking, through no fault or choice of her own. Brogan won her in a game of cards, and we all just stood back and let it happen. Can you believe that? She deserved much better than she got."

"Say, the other woman in there, the one who set fire to herself, the one named Henderson, she wasn't your wife?" someone else asked him. "Is it true, the things he...?"

"Hold your stupid big mouth," a stern voice growled at him. But Henderson said, "It's alright. It's all in the past," and nodded again, and lowered his head to hide his face, and the other men were all silent for a while.

The only other possessions they found in the shack, apart from Allenby's bed, and his table and chair, and his rocking-chair out on the porch, were his pipe, a tin coffee pot and mug, a couple of chipped enamelled plates, and some rusted and dented pans and cutlery. One of the men found a small picture frame discarded on the floor. The frame contained no picture and had parted at its corners. Much of the veneer that had once decorated its surface had sprung, and as he picked it up, dried and cracked flakes fell from it like confetti. The man turned it once in his hand and threw it back onto the floor. On the table beside the ledger were two pens and a dried-out inkwell, and a gold tooth. Henderson said he thought the tooth had been Brogan Sullivan's; it had been almost a trademark of his, and the men all shuddered, and then started to laugh at the odd ways of the man they were about to bury. In a cupboard at the back of the scullery they found a moth-eaten, tan-coloured suit with a black velvet collar, a pair of expensive snake-skin boots, and a studded belt with a large silver buckle moulded in the shape of a bull's head.

"Don't quite seem fitting apparel for an undertaker," someone said, and they all turned back to look at the body on the floor, at the sweat-stained undershirt, the worn corduroy trousers it was wearing. The soles of the sturdy workman's boots turned towards them were worn through and patched up inside with wood shavings and cardboard, and the toecaps were scuffed and furred.

"Yeah, we had a good idea he was odd. But this... It sure leaves a lot of questions. But if they weren't his, who the hell did they belong to?"

"I might be wrong," the man called Henderson said. "But it's much like one of the suits Brogan Sullivan used to wear. Maybe they brought it up here for Josh to bury him in and he thought it too good to let rot in the ground. Maybe he kept it, and buried Sullivan naked or in some old rags, just to spite him. There was quite a story going on between them back then. Not a lot of love lost either way."

The other men all nodded, and murmured solemnly, conceding to Henderson's experience, his personal knowledge of a time and circumstances none of them had known. Apart from Henderson, they had all been sent to this place called Hope by a logging concern based in Seattle, to reap a greener harvest from the land now the gold was gone. The German boy too had stayed on after the prospectors had left. He had wanted to stay in Hope, they all knew, to tend the graves of his family, to make sure someone remembered. And because, in ways none of them could figure, he had "gone native", as they called it, living in a cabin he had built away from the town, higher up in the mountains near the old workings, wearing clothes and boots and moccasins he made from animal hides, eating berries and grains he gleaned from the wild, game and fish he caught from the tracks and rivers in hand-made traps, or shot with a bow and arrow.

It was all he needed, he said. Living from the land, with the land. He knew the ways of the seasons, what provender each would offer. Still, the loggers found him strange, if personable enough, what little of their lives intersected with his during the months they were in the forest, culling it, reducing it to moribund lumber, to inanimate produce for the world – the false human world, as Dortmund saw it – to consume. They knew he resented their presence there each summer, what they were doing to the forest. But the thing they really could not figure was his choosing to be out here alone. It seemed to them so empty, to offer so little reward or pleasure. They could not wait to get back to the city, to spend the money they had earned, stuck out here for weeks on end with nothing to do but cut down trees, split logs; to eat and sleep, play cards in the dead hours between felling, and to argue amongst themselves, mostly about nothing in particular; to dream of the comforts and distractions the city had to offer, hundreds of miles from this wilderness nowhere. They were simply doing their jobs, they persuaded themselves, when those dead hours opened up their thoughts to doubt and questions; doing what they could to survive in the world - be it false or not - the world they knew as home.

"Yeah, that sure looks like what it is," Henderson said, stepping forward and peering closer into the cupboard. "Does seem a bit of a lean cut for Brogan though. He was a thick-set man. This looks like it would have fitted Josh a whole lot better, but maybe I'm just remembering them both wrong." He reached out to touch the suit. At the last moment his hand withdrew.

"Anyway, Brogan had collars like those on all his suits, and the buckle..." He laughed softly to himself and shook his head. "That old buckle was well-nigh famous, even back in Chicago, when we were all young and none of us knew much better."

"You knew him back then?" someone inquired.

"Yeah! He and I, and poor ol' Josh too, we travelled a long way together. Each in our different ways, though it feels like it was always me who led the way. All of us left there in '71, headed out West, after the fire. Wasn't much left there for any of us. Or so we thought." He smiled ruefully to himself and scratched his head as though remembering some of that journeying, or was thinking of the life he could have rebuilt if he had stayed in Chicago.

"And those boots? I ain't never seen boots fine as them before," the youngest of the loggers said.

"Yeah, I guess Brogan'd have been wearing them too, or something pretty much like 'em," Henderson laughed again. "Brogan always liked to look his best for the ladies."

As none of them knew any other of Brogan Sullivan and his ways, the things that had happened back then, they declared the matter closed. Henderson had known the man, had seen him buried; they had no cause to doubt him. He didn't seem, from what they had got to know of him, to be the type of man to say such things simply from spite. He was a good man, if a little dull and prone to imposing a suffocating order on all and everything he did. Allenby, they agreed, must have kept the suit when Sullivan had been brought up to the barn for burying. None of them thought it a strange thing to have done, other than it being a dead man's suit, and not all of them would have wanted to wear it. It was said to bring bad luck, wearing a dead person's clothes.

The only other clothes, the only other things they found in the shack, were two spare shirts, and two collars and studs, and the things Allenby was wearing. Once they had finished searching and had found nothing of use, and nothing which would indicate his death had been other than from natural causes, and once they had straightened him out as best they could and put him in his makeshift box to carry him to the graveyard behind the barn, and had elected Henderson the new owner of the gold tooth and the silver buckle, if he wanted them - for nostalgia's sake, and because he was the closest thing to living family the man had - they took away the leather-bound ledger and set fire to the shack and everything else it contained.

Epilogue

Chicago, April 1905

"Thomas. I believe it is time." He could barely hear his mother's voice; it had diminished to a strained dry whisper. Lying in her bed, surrounded by folds of pillows and mufflers, Speake thought she looked beautiful. There was a calotype image of her on the mantelshelf in the drawing room; it had been taken by Henry Fox Talbot on the lawns of Lacock Abbey, around forty years previously. In the photograph, she was wearing a broad-striped skirt and a tight-fitting tweed jacket. A ladies' top hat was perched at a jaunty angle on her head, and she was shielding herself beneath the shade of a parasol. She had been twenty-three or twenty-four years old when it was taken; she had never been able to remember which.

Looking at her now, aged and dying, the flesh of her face turned to soft mouldings of translucent wax through which her veins ran like ravelled threads, he could discern the contours of the attractive young woman's face in the photograph still vibrant beneath the sallow skin. It did not seem believable to him that she would soon be dead.

"Are you certain?" he asked her, leaning closer. Her eyes closed briefly, and she allowed her head to sink and rise in a shallow nod, and then her face pinched tight against another surge of pain.

"Yes. There's no reason for me to stay. Other than for you," she whispered, once the pain had passed. "I'm sorry, Thomas. You'll be fine without me." A shade of a smile moved on her lips.

Speake gently squeezed the fragile, long-boned hand he had been holding for most of the afternoon. He held her hand for a few moments more, feeling the weak pulse gently moving her fingers, and then he got up from his chair and crossed to the mahogany console table that stood below the window. Outside it was snowing. Hopefully the last snow of winter, he thought, the last cold streams of air pouring down from the frozen north. Three days ago, when Lucy's letter had arrived, the envelope bearing only his name and that of the newspaper, it had been almost like summer; the temperature of the air had risen to over sixty degrees. He still had the letter in his jacket pocket.

Through the window, he could see glimpses of the lake between the tall buildings that were being constructed all along its shore - the Gold Coast people were calling it - their outlines softened by falling snow. The wind caught the snow and swirled it into organic shapes that drifted and swirled past the window. He was reminded of the snow-angel Dortmund had made in Hope, and of those he had himself made in Bath as a boy, the winter it had snowed, some twenty years ago.

When it had arrived, the letter had unsettled him - such memories, and many more, had come flooding back to him. Many had been good, like those of the angels, but some had been of the dreadful things that had happened, taking him back to a set of circumstances he had thought to have put behind him. It had been five years since he had left Hope, since he had killed Brogan Sullivan. So much in him had changed since he had first set out to write stories about life in a remote mining township, and to escape the memories of his dying father. Now, though, he was glad Lucy had sent the letter; had felt the need, the wish to tell him how her once broken life had been transformed.

Several months after leaving the township, she had written, she had given birth to a baby girl, a child blessed with an angelic smile and a peaceful disposition. She had named the child Hope, in bold defiance of her own experiences. Regardless of all it had been, she had said, it was the place that had finally set her free. When she had left, she had gone to Boston, had met and married a man there, a teacher of piano and violin, a liberal-minded, peaceful man who had accepted Hope and loved the child as his own. Where they were living she did not say, only that it was on a smallholding close to the edge of a town, and there they grew their own food and raised their own animals, and that she was employed part-time as a teacher at the local school. Her husband sounded like a good man, and her letter had given Speake the impression she was happy in the new life she had found.

He smiled to himself at the image that came to him, which she had described in her letter, of Lucy and her daughter, the child's face intent within its thick halo of golden hair, learning to play the piano together. German Polkas, it seemed, were the child's favourite tunes.

During one of their quiet hours together in Hope, Speake had told Lucy of the death of his father, how the guilt he had felt at being unable to help him escape his suffering, his father's damning reaction, had been the thing which had really brought him to Hope. Her response had offered him some consolation.

"You did what you thought was right. Honesty of error - you can't expect anything more of yourself than that." Her words had helped him greatly in quieting the ghosts, and in questioning the need even for their existence. The memory of that conversation would give him the strength to do what he was about to do. He hoped his actions now would go some way to redress the failures of the past.

He opened the single drawer in the console table and took out the phial. When his mother's illness had been first diagnosed, he had made the necessary enquiries, had collected the preparation more than two months ago. He had wanted to be certain it would be ready to hand if, and whenever the need might arise. Unlike with his father's illness, this time he had no doubts. As Dortmund had said that final afternoon in Hope - everything in Nature has a reason, and the one thing we can change is the way we think and act. Pain, death, loss were the inevitable consequences of the human condition; what remained within our control was the way we chose to respond. He and his mother had discussed it - a long, distraught conversation in which he had learned that she too had struggled with feelings of guilt and helplessness while watching her husband's agonised passing. She did not want that for herself, she said; she did not want to undergo such denial of her dignity in her final days, nor the pain. He held the bottle up to the snow-filtered light of the window. The liquid inside the phial was the colour of gold. He unscrewed the cap and raised the opened neck to his nose. It smelled faintly of alcohol.

"Will it be painful?" his mother asked as he turned back to face her. He smiled and slowly shook his head.

"No. I was told it will be like falling asleep. No more pain. I promise."

Tomorrow he would need to start making arrangements for taking her body back to England. His mother had told him she did not want to be buried here, in what was for her still a largely alien and unwelcoming land. The visits from her supposed friends had diminished in frequency as her illness progressed, reduced finally to delivered messages of apology and goodwill. She had no family here, other than himself, and the interred remains of her husband. It would be an uneasy journey for him to make, leaving behind the friends he had made, his good position with the newspaper, returning alone to the family home, no doubt in need of much repair and refurbishment, his mother's body stowed below in the hold, and worst of all, leaving his father's grave to go unvisited and untended. He would miss too the burgeoning energy of this teeming city, the placid expanse of the lake, its seething, cracking surface in the deep of winter; this apartment where he had come to feel comfortable, and the quite evenings spent enclosed by its warm wood panelling, reading beside his mother, playing cards with her; but he realised then that he too would not be coming back.

There was nothing to keep him here either. There would be new friends, a home, a new career, maybe even love, or at least deep companionship to be discovered in England. Spring was approaching, the world was renewing itself; it was time too for him to start anew.

The time of waiting, the dark winter he had been travelling through would soon be coming to an end. The memories that had lain stored away in some frozen part of his being could finally be buried; the ghosts of memory laid to rest.

Ian Pateman is a retired Civil Engineer, and occasional collector of early twentieth century European glass and ceramics. He has been writing novel-length, historically situated fiction for a number of years.

His first novel, *The Third Heaven*, a first-person narrative of personal and artistic discovery set against the birth of Humanism in fourteenth century Europe, was published in December 2020.

In earlier manifestations, *The Ice Barn* has been runner-up in the inaugural First Novel competition run by Long Barn Books in association with The Guardian newspaper, and has been short-listed in the To Hell With Prizes Prize.